The Ghost in Love

Also by Jonathan Carroll

The Land of Laughs
Voice of Our Shadow
Bones of the Moon
Sleeping in Flame
A Child Across the Sky
Black Cocktail
Outside the Dog Museum
After Silence
From the Teeth of Angels
The Panic Hand
Kissing the Beehive
The Marriage of Sticks
The Wooden Sea
White Apples
Glass Soup

The Ghost in Love

Jonathan Carroll

TOR®

A Tom Doherty Associates Book
New York

THE GHOST IN LOVE

Copyright © 2008 by Jonathan Carroll

A Tor Book
Published by Tom Doherty Associates, LLC
175 Fifth Avenue
New York, NY 10010

www.tor-forge.com

Tor® is a registered trademark of Tom Doherty Associates, LLC.

Library of Congress Cataloging-in-Publication Data

Carroll, Jonathan, 1949–
    The ghost in love / Jonathan Carroll.—1st Tor ed.
        p. cm.
    ISBN 978-0-7653-2305-7
    1. Future life—Fiction.   I. Title.
    PS3553.A7646G58 2009
    813'.54—dc22

                                          2009028227

First Edition: October 2008

First Tor Trade Paperback Edition: October 2009

Printed in the United States of America

0 9 8 7 6 5 4 3 2 1

With hand on heart, a deep bow to
Richard Parks and Joe del Tufo

The Ghost in Love

One

The ghost was in love with a woman named German Landis. Just hearing that arresting, peculiar name would have made the ghost's heart flutter if it had had one. She was coming over in less than an hour, so it was hurrying now to make everything ready. The ghost was a very good cook, sometimes a great one. If it'd spent more time at it or had more interest in the subject, it would have been exceptional.

From its large bed in a corner of the kitchen a mixed-breed, black-and-oatmeal-colored dog watched with great interest as the ghost prepared the meal. This mutt was the only reason that German Landis was coming here today. His name was Pilot, after a poem the woman loved about a Seeing Eye dog.

Suddenly sensing something, the ghost stopped what it was doing and eyeballed the dog. Peevishly, it demanded *"What?"*

Pilot shook his head. "Nothing. I was only watching you work."

"Liar. That is not the only thing. I know what you were thinking: that I'm an idiot to be doing this."

Embarrassed, the dog turned away and began furiously biting one of its rear paws.

"Don't do that. Look at me. You think I'm nuts, don't you?"

Pilot said nothing and kept biting his foot.

"*Don't* you?"

"Yes, I think you're nuts, but I also think it's very sweet. I only wish she could see what you're doing for her."

Resigned, the ghost shrugged and sighed. "It helps when I cook. When my mind is focused, I don't get so frustrated."

"I understand."

"No, you do not. How could you? You're only a dog."

The dog rolled his eyes. "Idiot."

"*Quadruped.*"

They had a cordial relationship. Like Icelandic or Finnish, "Dog" is spoken by very few. Only dogs and dead people understand the language. When Pilot wanted to talk, he either had to get in a quick chat with whatever canine he happened to meet on the street when he was taken out for a walk three times a day, or he spoke with this ghost—who, by attrition, knew more about Pilot now than any dog had ever known. There aren't that many human ghosts in the land of the living, so this one was equally happy for the dog's company.

Pilot asked, "I keep meaning to ask: Where did you get your name?"

The cook purposely ignored the dog's question and continued preparing the meal. When it needed an ingredient, it closed its eyes and held out an open hand. A moment later the thing materialized in the middle of its palm: a jungle-green lime, a small pile of red cayenne pepper, or particularly rare saffron from Sri Lanka. Pilot watched, absorbed, never tiring of this amazing feat.

"What if you imagined an elephant? Would it appear in your hand too?"

Dicing onions now almost faster than the eye could see, the ghost grinned. "If I had a big enough hand, yes."

"And all you'd have to do to make that elephant appear is imagine it?"

"Oh, no, it's much more complicated than that. When a person dies, then they're taught the real structure of things. Not only how they look or feel, but the essence of what they really *are*. Once you have that understanding, it's easy to make things."

Pilot considered this and said, "Then, why don't you just re-create *her*? That way, you wouldn't have to fret about her so much anymore. You'd have your own version of her right here."

The ghost looked at the dog as if he had just farted loudly. "You'll understand how dumb that suggestion is after you die."

Fifteen blocks away, a woman was walking down the street carrying a large letter *D*. If you were to see this image in a magazine or television advertisement, you'd smile and think, That's a catchy picture. The woman was pleasant looking but not memorable. Her best features were her sloe eyes, which were sexy, full of humor, and intelligent. Otherwise she had even features that fit well together, although her nose was a little small for her face. She was aware of that and often self-consciously touched her nose when she knew she was being observed. What people remembered most about her was not the nose but how very tall she was: an almost six-foot-tall woman holding a big blue letter *D*. The only things she had in her pockets now were one key, a bunch of dog treats, and a small toy Formula One racing car. Her father had given her the toy fifteen years ago as a good luck charm when she left home for college. She genuinely believed it had some kind of good juju. Treasuring it, she had always kept the small object close by. But she was about to give it away to someone she both loved and disliked. Because he really needed any help he could get now to change the way his life was going. She knew he didn't believe in "powers" or talismans, so she planned on hiding it somewhere in his apartment when he wasn't looking. Hopefully just the toy's aura near him would help.

She wore jeans, a gray sweatshirt with ST. OLAF COLLEGE written in yellow letters across the chest, and scuffed brown hiking boots. The boots made her taller. Funnily enough, her height never bothered her: the nose, yes, and sometimes her name. The name and the nose, but never the height, because everyone on both sides of her family was tall. She grew up in the midst of a bunch of blond human trees. Midwesterners, Minnesotans, they ate huge meals three times a day. The men wore size thirteen or fourteen shoes and the women's feet weren't much smaller. All of the children in the family had unusual names. Her parents loved to read, especially the Bible, classic German literature, and Swedish folktales, which was where they had harvested the names for their children. Her brother was Enos, she was German, and her sister was named Pernilla. As soon as it was legally possible, Enos changed his name to Guy and would answer to nothing else. He joined a punk band called Kidney Failure, all of which left his parents speechless and disheartened.

German Landis was a schoolteacher who taught art to twelve- and thirteen-year-olds. The letter *D* she carried now was part of an upcoming assignment for them. Because she was both genial and enthusiastic, she was a first-rate teacher. Kids liked Ms. Landis because she clearly liked them. They felt that affection the moment they entered her classroom every day. Colleagues were always commenting about how much laughter came out of German's classroom. Her enthusiasm for the students' creations was genuine. On one wall of her apartment was a large bulletin board covered with Polaroid photographs that she'd taken over the years of her kids' work. She often spent evenings looking through art books. The next day she would plop one or more of these books down on the desk in front of a student and point to specific illustrations she thought they should see. Some days the class wouldn't work at all. They would go to the city museum for a show she thought they should see. Or a film that had significance to what they were doing. Sometimes they would just sit around talking about what mattered to them. German always thought of these days as intermissions, and almost as important as the workdays. When grilled by the students about her life, German talked about growing up in cold Minnesota, her love of auto racing, her dog, Pilot, and her not-so-long-ago boyfriend, Ben. But the students now knew not to ask questions about ex-boyfriend Ben.

She fell in love easily but walked away just as easily from a relationship when it went bad. Some men—and there had been many of them—thought this showed she was coldhearted, but they were wrong. German Landis simply didn't understand people who moped. Life was too interesting to choose suffering. Although she got a big kick out of him, she thought her brother, Guy, was goofy for spending his life writing songs only about things that either stank or sucked. In response, he drew a picture of what her gravestone would look like if he designed it: a big yellow smiley face on it and the words I LIKE BEING DEAD!

Little did either of them know that she *would* like it when her time came to die, years later. German Landis would move into death as she'd moved into new schools, relationships, or phases of her life: full speed ahead, hopes ahoy, heart filled like a sail with reasonable optimism and a belief that the gods were fundamentally benevolent, no matter where she was.

Shifting the heavy metal letter from one hand to the other,

she grimaced thinking what was about to happen. Whenever German went to Ben's place these days to pick up Pilot, there was almost always trouble. They'd argue about big things and small. Sometimes there were valid reasons for these disagreements; usually they occurred only because these two people were in the same room together. Yet, even after all the weird and bad things he had done and said, in the first few seconds whenever they met now, she welled up with a powerful longing to kiss him and touch him and hold both his hands tightly as she'd done so many glad times before.

They had had it—they'd *found* it, found each other, and it had worked like no other relationship she had ever experienced. But now it was broken and reduced to this: sharing a dog and worrying that every time they spoke to each other there would be some kind of clash. One night at the end, right before she moved out of his apartment, German sat naked in the living room holding her talisman toy car tightly in her lap. Eyes closed, she whispered again and again, "Please change this. Make it get better. *Please.*"

They had been so much in love, equally and passionately. Like a spider web that you walk into, it is not so easy to get all the tendrils of real love off after you have passed through it.

Early in their relationship, they had seen the Cary Grant film *The Awful Truth*, about a couple that splits up but, by sharing custody of their dog, reconcile because of their abiding love. Neither German nor Ben liked the movie. But now it stuck on the walls of both their heads like a glowing Post-it note because some of the story had come to pass for them.

They had contact now only because of the dog. Both regarded Pilot as their adopted child and friend. Ben had given it to German on their third date. He had gone to the town animal shelter and asked to see whatever dog had been there the longest. He had to repeat that request three times before the attendants believed him. The whole thing was German's idea. It was the first of many of her ideas that effortlessly touched Benjamin Gould in the middle of his soul. Several days earlier, she'd said she was going to buy a dog that no one wanted. She was going to the dog pound soon and, sight unseen, buy whichever dog had lived there longer than any of the others.

"But what if it's a skeez?" Ben asked half-seriously. "What if it's got a terrible personality and dread diseases?"

She giggled. "I'll take it to a veterinarian. Skeez and disease are okay. I just want to give it some kind of nice life before it dies."

"And if it's ferocious? What if you get a biter?" Ben asked these questions but was joking. He was already a convert.

At the animal shelter they took him to see a dog they'd named Methuselah because it had lived there so long. Methuselah did not lift its head from the floor when the stranger stopped in front of its cage and peered in. Ben saw nothing but entry-level dog. If it had any extras, he sure didn't see them. There was not one thing special about this animal. No soulful sensitive eyes. No puppy's adorable, rollicking enthusiasm. It did no tricks. If it had a shtick, cute wasn't part of it. All the employees at the shelter could say about this uninteresting mixed breed was that it was housebroken, quiet, and never caused trouble. No wonder any prospective owners had rejected it. Every single sign indicated this bland mutt was nothing but a dud.

Although he had little money, Ben Gould bought Methuselah the dud. The dog had to be coaxed from its cage and out onto the street again for literally the first time in months. It did not look at all happy. Ben had no way of knowing that he'd bought a skeptic and a fatalist that didn't believe anything good came of anything good. At the time of its adoption, Methuselah was past middle age. It had lived a difficult life but not a bad one. It had had three previous owners, all of them forgettable. On occasion it had been kicked and beaten. Once it had been struck a glancing blow by a passing truck. It survived, limping for weeks afterward, but it survived. When picked up by the dogcatcher, it was relieved more than anything else. At the time it had been living on the street for three months. From past experience it did not trust human beings, but it was hungry and cold and knew they were able to remedy that. What the dog did not know was that if it was taken to the wrong kind of animal shelter, it would be killed after a short time.

But it was lucky. In fact this dog's great turn of life luck began the day it entered this particular haven. The place was funded entirely by a rich childless couple who loved animals above everything else in the world and visited it frequently. As a result, none of the stray animals brought there was ever euthanized. The cages were always spotlessly clean and warm. There was ample food and even rawhide chew bones, which Methuselah found disgusting and ignored.

It ate and slept and watched for the next three months—a great career move, because it was missing a miserably cold and snowy winter outside. It did not know what this place was, but so long as it was fed and left in peace, then it was an adequate home. One of the joys of being a dog is that they have no concept of the word "future." Everything is right now, and if right now happens to be a warm floor and a full stomach, then life is good.

• • •

Who was this man pulling on its leash? Where were they going? They had walked many blocks through blinding, blowing snow. Methuselah was old enough that the bitter cold pierced his bones and joints. Back home in the warmth of the animal shelter, the dog could go outside whenever he wanted but rarely did in mean weather like this.

"We're almost there," the man said sympathetically. But dogs do not understand human language, so this meant nothing to the now wretched animal. All he knew was that he was cold and lost, and life had just turned hard again after that pleasant respite in the shelter.

They were two blocks from German Landis's building when it happened. After looking both ways, Ben stepped off the sidewalk into the street. Slipping on the snow, he lost his balance. Arms windmilling, he began to fall backward. Startled by this sudden wild movement, Methuselah leapt away and jerked hard on the leash. The man tried to stop his fall while at the same time keeping the dog from bolting out into the street and being hit by a car. As a result of his body going in so many directions at once, Ben fell much harder than he might have if he'd just gone down from the slip. The back of his head hit the stone curb hard with a loud, thick thud, bounced, and then hit it again just as hard.

He must have blacked out then, because the next thing he knew, he was on his back looking up into the concerned faces of four people, including a policeman who held the dog's leash.

"He opened his eyes!"

"He's okay."

"Don't touch him, though. Don't move him till the ambulance gets here."

Across the street, the ghost stood in the snow watching this, utterly confounded. A moment later it fizzled and flickered like a sick television set and disappeared. Methuselah was the only one to see it, but ghosts are nothing new to dogs so the animal didn't react. He only hunkered down into himself and shivered some more.

• • •

The Angel of Death looked at the ghost of Benjamin Gould and shook his head. "What more can I tell you? They've gotten very clever."

They were at a table in a crummy turnpike restaurant near Wallingford, Connecticut. The Angel of Death was nothing special to look at: it had manifested itself today as a plate of someone's finished meal of bacon and eggs. Egg yolk was smeared across the white plate. Inside this smear were scattered bread crumbs.

It was midnight and the restaurant was almost empty. The waitress stood outside sharing a cigarette with the cook. She was in no hurry to clear the table. Having found the Angel of Death here, the ghost of Benjamin Gould had manifested itself as a fat black fly now sitting in the egg yolk.

The plate said, "When Gould hit his head on the curb, he was *supposed* to die. You know the routine: cracked skull, intercranial bleeding, and death. But it didn't happen.

"To oversimplify, think of it as a massive virus that had infected our computer system. Afterwards, a whole bunch of similar glitches popped up across the grid and we knew we were under attack. Our tech guys are working on it. They'll figure it out."

Unsatisfied by this explanation, the ghost/fly paced back and forth across the drying egg yolk, its little black spindly legs getting yellow and gooey. "How can *Heaven* get a virus in its computer system? I thought you were omniscient."

"So did we until this happened. Those guys in Hell are getting cleverer all the time. There's no doubt about that. Don't worry, we'll work it out. For now, though, the problem is you, my friend."

Hearing this, the fly stopped pacing and looked down at the plate. "What do you mean?"

"There's nothing we can do about you until we fix this glitch. You've got to stay here till then."

"And do *what*?" the fly dared to ask huffily.

"Well, doing what you're doing, for one. You can continue being a fly for a while and then maybe change into a person or a civet maybe . . . Changing identities can be lots of fun. And there's other pleasant things to do on earth: learn to smoke, try on different kinds of cologne, watch Carole Lombard films . . ."

"Who's Carole Lombard?"

"Never mind," the plate said and then mumbled, "She's reason enough for you to stay here."

The fly remained silent and unmoved.

The plate tried to change the subject. "Did you know that Ben Gould went to school in this town? That's why I'm here now: to do some checking up on his history."

But the fly wouldn't be sidetracked. "How long will this take? Just how long will I have to stay here?"

"In all honesty, I don't know. It could be awhile. Because once we find the computer virus, then we're going to have to run a check of the whole system." The plate said this lightly, knowing full well that it was on spongy ground here.

" 'Awhile' meaning how long—a year? A century?"

"No, no, not that long. The human body is built to physically last only seventy or eighty years, ninety at the most. There are exceptions, but not many. I would say Benjamin Gould will live no more than another fifty or so. But if you don't mind some advice, I would suggest that, while waiting, you go and stay with him. With the right kind of guidance, he could skip having to live a few lifetimes and move several steps up the ladder."

"I am not a teacher, I'm a ghost—*his* ghost. That's my job. Read the job description."

The Angel of Death considered this and decided it was time to get to the point. "All right, then, here's the deal. They've decided—"

"*Who's* decided?"

If the plate could have made a face it would have pursed its lips in exasperation. "You know very well who I'm talking about—don't play dumb. *They've* decided that because it might take a while to sort out this virus problem and you're stuck here through no fault of your own, they're offering you a chance to try something untested just to see if such a thing works: if you can somehow get through to Benjamin Gould and help make him a better person while he's alive, then you won't have to come back to earth and haunt things after he dies. We know how much you hate fieldwork, so if you succeed here, you can stay in the office and work there in the future.

"We don't know how much longer he'll live, because he was scheduled to die from the fall that day. Now the matter of his fate is anyone's guess. That means there's no telling whether you have a lot of time to work on him or only a little."

The ghost was genuinely surprised by this offer and paused to let the intriguing proposal sink in. It was just about to ask, "If I don't come back here to haunt him, what will I do instead in the office?" But the waitress came to the table, saw the fly in the egg yolk, and whacked it dead with an old newspaper.

·   ·   ·

Somewhere in everyone's inner city is a cemetery of old loves. For the lucky contented few who like where they are in their lives and who they're with, it is a mostly forgotten place. The tombstones there are faded and overturned, the grass uncut; brambles and wildflowers grow everywhere.

For other people, their place is as stately and ordered as a military graveyard. Its many flowers are well watered and tended, the white gravel walks have been carefully raked. All signs indicate that this spot is visited often.

For most of us, though, our cemetery is a hodgepodge. Some sections are neglected or completely ignored. Who cares about these stones or the old loves buried beneath them? Even their names are hard to remember. But other gravestones there *are* important, whether we like to admit it or not. We visit them often—sometimes too often, truth be told. And one can never tell how we'll feel when these visits are over: sometimes lighter, sometimes heavier. It is entirely unpredictable how we'll feel going back home to today.

Ben Gould rarely visited his cemetery. Not because he was particularly happy or content with his life, but because the past had never held much importance for him. If he was unhappy today, what difference did it make if he was happy yesterday? Every moment of life was different. How did looking or living in the past genuinely help him to live in this minute, beyond a few basic survival tricks he'd learned along the way?

In one of the first long discussions they ever had, Ben and German Landis disagreed completely about the significance of the past. She loved it. Loved looking at it from all angles, loved to feel it cross her right now like a thick midday shadow. She loved the past's weight and stature.

"*Stature?* What stature?" Ben asked skeptically, thinking she was joking. The memory of the delicious sandwich you ate for lunch is not going to take away your hunger four hours later.

On the contrary, it will only make the hunger worse. As far as he was concerned, the past is not our friend.

They argued and argued, neither convincing the other that he or she was wrong. It became a joke and eventually a stumbling block in their relationship. Much later, when they were breaking up, German tearfully said, "In six months you'll probably think of me and our relationship about as often as you think of your third-grade teacher."

But on that subject she was 100 percent wrong.

The great irony that held both Ben Gould's life and apartment captive these days was that he lived with not one but two ghosts, because German Landis haunted him too. He went to bed thinking about her and minutes after waking every morning he started thinking about her again. He couldn't stop himself, damn it. It wasn't fair. He had no control over it. Their failed relationship was an insistent mosquito buzzing close around his head. No matter how much waving away he did, it never left or stopped irritating him.

He was at his desk, staring at his hands, when the doorbell rang that morning. He was wearing only underpants and nothing else. He knew it was she. He'd known she was coming but had purposely chosen not to get dressed. In recent meetings with his ex-girlfriend, Ben had grown increasingly remote and sullen, which only made the air between them dense and uncomfortable. Sometimes it got so bad that German thought, Oh, just let him keep the damned dog and forget it. At least that way I won't ever have to see him again. But Pilot was hers; Ben had given him to her as a present. She loved the dog as much as he did. Why surrender only because her idiotic ex made her uneasy for five minutes every few days when she came to get Pilot?

Before the bell rang, Ben had been thinking of the first time they ever made love. They were sitting next to each other on his bed undressing. She wore simple black underwear and didn't seem at all self-conscious about taking her clothes off. When she was down to her bra and panties, she stopped, grinned at him, and said in the sexiest, most deliciously inviting voice he had ever heard, "Wanna see more?"

The ghost heard the doorbell and immediately tensed up. Pilot looked at it and then toward Ben's bedroom. The kitchen table had been sumptuously set with gorgeous food and objects. In the middle of this spread was a full blooming stargazer lily placed inside an elegant faint lavender glass vase from Murano, Italy.

Nothing happened. No sound emanated from inside the bedroom. A minute later the doorbell rang a second time.

"Isn't he going to answer the door?"

Pilot shrugged.

The ghost crossed its arms and then uncrossed them. It made three different faces in the course of eight seconds and, finally unable to stand it anymore, walked out of the kitchen and over to the front door. Ben Gould finally emerged from his bedroom looking both sluggish and confrontational.

The ghost looked at the man in his underpants and glowered. *Again?* He was going to pull this sort of immature, retardo stunt with her again?

Gould rubbed his eyes with the heels of his hands, took a slow deep breath, and opened the front door. The ghost stood two feet behind him, holding a metal spatula in its right hand. It was so jumpy about seeing German that it wiggled the utensil upanddownandupanddown at an incredibly fast speed. Thank God neither person could see this.

"Hello."

"Hey."

Both said their single words in voices as void of emotion as they could muster.

"Is Pilot ready to go?" she asked carefully.

"Sure. Come on in." Ben turned toward the kitchen and she followed. She looked at his nice butt in the wrinkled underpants and closed her eyes in despair. Why was he doing this? Was she supposed to be shocked or embarrassed to see him in his underwear? Had he forgotten that she had seen him naked, oh, several hundred times in their past? German knew what he smelled like clean and what he smelled like sweaty. She knew how he liked to be touched and the most intimate sounds that he made. She knew how he cried and what made him laugh out loud. How he liked his tea and how he absolutely sparkled when, walking down a street together, she put her arm over his shoulder to proudly show the world she was his pal *and* tall lover.

Seeing where the two were going now, the ghost disappeared from its place by the front door and reappeared a second later in the kitchen. When they entered, its arms were tightly pressed against its sides in anticipation.

Everything one could imagine wanting to eat for breakfast was on that table: warm freshly baked scones, strawberry preserves from England, honey from Hawaii, Lavazza coffee (German's favorite brand), a plate laid with long shiny strips of northern Scottish salmon, one more heaped with perfectly prepared eggs Benedict (another love of hers). There were two other egg dishes as well. Mouthwatering fare covered and graced every part of that small round table. It looked like a cover of *Gourmet* magazine. Whenever Ben Gould watched a cooking show on television, the ghost watched, too, and often took notes. Any time German came by to get the dog, the ghost made one of these TV recipes or something else delectable from one of Ben's many cookbooks and had it on the table waiting for her when she arrived.

Of course, German couldn't see any of it. What she saw now was only a bare wooden table with a single spoon off to one side, exactly where Ben had left it the night before after using the spoon to stir sugar into a cup of weak herbal tea. She looked at that spoon a long time now before speaking. It broke her heart.

For those glorious few silent moments, the ghost pretended German Landis was staring in awe because she actually *could* see everything that it had prepared for her, because the ghost knew how much the woman enjoyed breakfast.

Her favorite meal of the day. She loved to buy it, prepare it, and eat it. She loved to shop for fresh croissants and *petit pain au chocolat* at the bakery two doors down from here. Every time she happily closed her eyes so as to concentrate on the heavenly smell of bitter fresh coffee when the owner of the local Italian market ground the beans while she waited. She loved grapefruit juice, ripe figs, bacon and eggs, hash brown potatoes with ketchup. She had grown up eating mammoth Minnesota breakfasts that buoyed anyone over the freezing temperatures and car-high snowdrifts outside. Like her mother, German Landis was a lousy cook but an enthusiastic one, especially when it came to breakfast. She was delighted when people ate as much as she did.

The ghost knew these things because it had sat in this very kitchen many times watching with pleasure and longing while the woman assembled the morning feast. It was one of the traditions German and Ben had established early in their relationship: she made breakfast while he prepared all the other meals.

"Have you been eating?"

"What?" Ben wasn't sure he had heard her right.

"Have you been *eating*?" German repeated more emphatically.

He was thrown off guard by her question. She hadn't said anything so intimate in a long time.

"Yes, I'm fine."

"What?"

"What do you mean, 'What?'?"

German picked up the spoon and turned to Ben. While reaching for it, she put her hand right through the middle of the perfect seven-egg soufflé that the ghost had baked for her. It was a masterpiece. But German didn't see or feel it because ghosts make ghost food that exists only in the ghost world. Although the living sometimes sense that world, they can't occupy that dimension.

"What have you been eating?"

Ben looked at her and shrugged like a guilty child. "Stuff. Good stuff. Healthy things—you know . . ." His voice dribbled off. She knew he was lying. He never cooked anything for himself when he was alone. He ate junk food from circus-colored bags and drank tea.

Pilot got up from his bed and walked slowly over to the woman. He liked the feel of her big hand on his head. Her hands were always warm and loving.

"Hello, Mr. Dog. Are you ready to go?"

Suddenly and with close to a feeling of horror, Ben realized what it would be like in this apartment a few minutes from now when those two were gone and he was here alone with nothing to do. German probably had planned a nice long walk with the dog. When it was over, she would take Pilot to her place where they'd eat lunch together.

Ben had never been to her new apartment but could imagine what it was like. She had used her taste and humor to effortlessly make his home come alive with such things as witty color combinations and her collections of old postcards of magicians, circus performers, and ventriloquists, Matchbox toy Formula One racing cars, and Japanese sumo wrestler dolls on the shelves and windowsills. The rare silver Hetchins bicycle she'd bought for nothing at a local flea market, entirely restored by herself, and now rode everywhere would be placed somewhere prominently because she liked to look at it. That comfortable blue couch she'd bought when they were together and took when she moved out would be the center of her living room. In all likelihood the couch would be covered with large art books both open and closed. That image alone hurt Ben because it was so lovingly familiar to him. Pilot had his place on the couch next to her. The dog would not budge from there unless she did. Her new apartment would have to be light and airy because she insisted on both. German always needed a lot of natural light wherever she lived.

She also liked to open windows even on the coldest days of the year to fill any room she occupied with fresh air. It drove Ben bonkers when they were living together, but now of course he missed that quirk as well as most of her other ones. Too often he remembered how in the middle of winter she would get out of bed in the morning, throw open the window, then run back to bed and wrap herself tightly around him. Then she would whisper in his ear until they both fell asleep again.

The other day, while sitting morosely over another cup of tea at this table and thinking about their time together, Ben had written her a note on a paper napkin from a take-out restaurant. Knowing she would never read it, he wrote what he honestly felt: "I miss you every day of my life and for that alone I will never forgive myself."

"Well! I guess Pilot and I'd better be going."

"All right."

"I'll be back with him tomorrow. Is two o'clock okay?"

"Yes, that'll be fine." He made to say something else but, catching himself, stopped, and walked instead to the other side of the kitchen to retrieve the dog leash hanging on a hook there.

German took the toy car out of her pocket, slipped it into the drawer in the kitchen table, and silently slid the drawer closed again. Ben didn't see a thing.

Unexpectedly a moment came when, handing over the leash, both people let their guards down. They looked at each other with a frank mixture of love, resentment, and yearning that was immense. Both of them turned quickly away.

At the table, the ghost observed all this. When it had sat down, it had pulled the punched soufflé toward its chest with both hands, as if trying to protect the ruined beauty from any further damage.

Now, seeing this dramatic look rocket back and forth between them, the ghost slowly lowered its face into the middle of the soufflé right up to its ears and remained like that while good-byes were said and German left. It was still face-deep in the eggy mess when it heard the front door close.

Ben walked back into the kitchen, sat down across from the ghost, and stared directly at it. The ghost eventually lifted its head from the soufflé and saw that it was being stared at. Although it knew it was invisible, the intensity of the man's gaze was distressing.

Lifting the teaspoon off the table, Ben appeared to weigh it in his hand. In truth, what he was doing was testing to see if any of German's warmth remained in the metal.

Suddenly he flung the spoon with all his might against the far wall. It ricocheted loudly off several places before landing and scuddering across the floor.

The ghost lowered its face back into the soufflé.

Two

The first time the ghost saw German Landis was in a bathroom. Having met with the Angel of Death in Connecticut, the spirit agreed to return to Benjamin Gould's virus-extended life, but only for a thorough look around first. It wanted to scrutinize a number of things before deciding whether or not to accept the angel's extraordinary offer.

The ghost reconvened its ions in Ben's apartment six days after German had moved in there, three months after Gould had fallen down and was supposed to have died after hitting his head on the curb.

When it saw German for the first time, the woman was standing naked in front of a fogged mirror brushing her teeth. Although they were only three feet apart, she could not see the ghost. Its navigation was a bit off and, instead of landing in the living room as planned, it rematerialized standing on top of the lowered green toilet seat in Benjamin Gould's bathroom. Things were so steamy and uncomfortably hot in there that a few disoriented moments passed before the ghost fully realized where it was.

Standing nearby was a tall, athletic-looking woman with no

clothes on and a mouth covered in blue-white foam. She was humming one of her favorite Rodgers and Hammerstein show tunes. The ghost assumed this was German Landis because it had been thoroughly briefed on the life of Benjamin Gould before coming here.

Standing on the toilet seat, the ghost examined this woman: bright clear eyes, small breasts, small hips, small nose, long legs and fingers. It couldn't tell what her mouth looked like because that was hidden in toothpaste foam. An attractive female but no more than that.

Then the ghost casually looked into the part of her brain that knew exactly how much longer her body was destined to live. German Landis had another forty-seven years to go. That is, unless she contracted a fatal disease or was struck down by another kind of computer virus from Hell.

Her most predominant characteristic was that she emanated a powerfully positive aura. Not special, but especially warmhearted and enthusiastic. German Landis *was* an optimist, a romantic, fully at ease in her skin because without reservation she considered life to be her friend.

The ghost, whose name was Ling, took note of all these things without emotion. It could just as well have been staring at a tiger in the zoo or bacteria under a microscope rather than the tall naked woman that first time.

A Chinese farmer invented the idea of ghosts three thousand years ago as a way of explaining to his precocious grandson what happens to people after they die. God thought it was such a novel and useful idea that He told his angels to make the concept real and allow it to flourish within the system. In honor of the inventor, ghosts always have Chinese names and this one was no exception. Ling was called Ling only because that was the next name on the list at the time it was created.

When a ghost first comes to earth, it is imbued with a wide variety of supernatural powers that can terrify the living. Ling had been told that it needed to test these powers immediately on arrival to make sure everything was in working order and to recalibrate whatever wasn't.

Looking around now, it saw the draining bathtub and summoned a sea serpent to fill it. Fortunately for German, the ghost called for the only kind of sea serpent it was acquainted with. That happened to be a *Liopleurodon*, a swimming reptile so huge that only a small part of the tip of its monstrously large tongue squeezed through the drain and completely filled Benjamin Gould's bathtub.

The woman's back was turned so she did not see the terrible tongue emerge in the place where she had been washing herself only minutes before. The ghost recognized its mistake instantly and made the tongue as well as the rest of the sea serpent disappear. Just in time, too, because right after that the bathroom door opened and Ben Gould entered.

"Howdy," he said to her, but his eyes were caught by what was in the draining bathtub. He stared at it instead of his splendidly naked girlfriend. Because the bathwater was the color of sand. Ben's eyes widened but he did not say a word. German and he were so new at living together that he was still embarrassed she might hear the sound when he was peeing in the toilet. Consequently, he wasn't about to ask now why the water in the tub was solidly beige after she'd just bathed there.

"What's up?" She looked over her shoulder at him and said the words around the toothbrush in her mouth.

Ben blinked uneasily several times and, mustering a strange high voice, chirped, "Not a thing!" Then he exited the room fast, closing the door behind him.

The ghost stepped down from the toilet seat and followed

him. Ling walked through the closed bathroom door and into the narrow hall outside. The dog was lying on the floor there, waiting for the woman to reemerge. The two looked at each other. The ghost smiled at the dog and said, "Hiya."

Pilot looked at it but didn't respond to the greeting.

Ling didn't care and walked down the hall.

Pilot had never seen this particular ghost before. Head resting on paws, he mildly wondered what it was doing here. Dogs see ghosts about as often as people see cats. They're there but they're no big deal.

Ling's first thought had been to follow Gould awhile and observe him. But then the ghost changed its mind and chose to have a look around the man's living quarters instead.

Ben worked as a waiter in a restaurant. He was good at his job and genuinely liked the work, but he did not earn much money. That was okay, though, because there was not much he wanted beyond what he already possessed. In that respect he was a contented man.

His apartment was bare, but not the dismal, depressing bare of the impoverished. Rather, it was the home of a person who doesn't care much for belongings. He liked food, he liked books; he owned one nice suit and a decent sound system. His parents had given him several pieces of sturdy nondescript furniture years before that fit just fine into his lifestyle. The well-crafted wooden bookcases in the living room he had built himself. Covering the floor in there was a faded red-and-black Persian carpet that he'd bought for eighteen dollars at a yard sale and then paid fifty dollars to dry-clean.

German liked Ben's apartment because, although sparse, it was obvious her new boyfriend enjoyed and took good care of his few possessions, polishing wood that had never been polished before on a scarred old school desk he'd bought at the Salvation

Army. Or hand mending a large hole in the Persian rug that had been neglected for years. In the center of the living room table were three beautiful large black stones that he'd found in an Italian river. His two pairs of shoes were always polished and lined up by the front door. One peek at the selection of books in his library said that whoever owned them had an inquisitive, wide-ranging mind.

The ghost walked to one of these bookshelves now to check it out. There were an inordinate number of cookbooks, but Ling already knew that Gould loved to cook. His dream had once been to become a great chef. But he was neither talented nor patient enough and in the end had to admit it. He possessed the enthusiasm and dedication necessary but not the creative imagination. A great cook was like a great painter: they saw the world as no one else did. Further, they had the requisite skills and talent to both manifest that vision and share it with others. Ben eventually accepted the fact that he didn't after several wholehearted attempts, including a yearlong stint at cooking schools in Europe. That was why he ultimately became a waiter: if he couldn't make his living cooking exquisite food for others, at least he could always be around it.

"Why are you here, ghost?"

Ling had not heard the dog come into the living room. Turning around, it saw the animal staring from a few feet away.

"Hello. My name is Ling. What's yours?"

"I honestly don't know. I've been called so many different things in my life that I have no idea what my real name is. These days it appears to be Pilot."

"Pilot? All right, then, that's what I'll call you."

Before the dog could respond, Ben Gould walked into the living room and over to the bookshelves. After stroking the dog on the head a few times, he squatted down and ran a finger over the spines of his books until he found what he was searching for: *Serious Pig* by the great food writer John Thorne. Ben wanted to read one of Thorne's essays to German.

When the man had left the room again, Ling asked, "Do you like living here with these people?"

Pilot considered the question before answering. "Yes, I do. It's been a very nice change for me." But the dog got no further than that because a scream suddenly exploded from the bathroom. The door flew open with a wall-denting bang and still-naked German ran out with both hands over her mouth.

"Ben!"

The dog, the ghost, and the man all hurried down the hall to find out what the problem was. When German saw Ben she took one hand away from her mouth and pointed back toward the bathroom. Her eyes were frantic and unfocused.

"In the bathtub. The water's *brown* and there are *fish* in it!"

Ling's shoulders relaxed now because it knew why the woman screamed. Sea serpents have unimaginably filthy mouths and tongues due to the vast array and number of disgusting things they are constantly eating. Dirt takes a holiday in a sea serpent's mouth. That accounted for the brown water. And scores of small fish cling to a serpent's body. Ling assumed that a few of these fish had made their way into Gould's tub after the monster's brief appearance there.

Pilot didn't understand anything the woman said, but her voice was high and screechy. When it came to humans, this was not a good sign. Not good at all. When they used that hysterical tone, it usually meant a dog was either about to be smacked or else ignored way past feeding time.

Ben didn't know what to do. He'd already seen the sandy-brown water in the tub a few minutes before. Ever the gentleman, he'd chosen to remain silent. But now he was being summoned to look at it in German's presence. That meant he was going to have to ask his new girlfriend embarrassing questions he really did not want to ask. In addition, there were now fish in the tub.

Ling was curious to see how Gould would handle this.

The dog walked over to the woman and tentatively leaned against her bare leg to test her mood.

"Ben?"

"Yes?"

"Are you going to go look or not?"

"Yes."

"But you're not moving."

"Oh, yes . . . yes, I am. I was just thinking if I needed to bring anything in there with me. I guess not. I'm going right now." Defeated, he flapped his arms against his thighs and knew there was nothing else to do now but go.

Sure enough, his bathtub was half-filled with water the color of café au lait, and two very small black fish were swimming close enough to the surface to be visible.

German stood pressed against his back. With one hand resting on his shoulder, she, too, peered into the water. Feeling her warm breasts and body against his back, his head filled with sexy images of what he would love to do with her right now instead of staring at dirty water and fish in his bathtub.

All his life, Ben Gould had a thing he did whenever he was in trouble. For a few seconds before having to face facts and figure a way out of a fix, he would fantasize a perfect instance in a perfect world where he did not have to deal with whatever was threatening him.

For example right now, before opening his mouth to comment on the turmoil in his tub, Ben fantasized that instead of being together in the bathroom, he and German were sitting together at the kitchen table. She would still be naked, of course, adding a delightful intimacy to the moment. Laughing merrily, she would say, "The looniest picture just came to me. I was looking into my cup and imagined for a moment that the coffee was water in your bathtub. And there were *fish* swimming in it! Isn't that bizarre? Where did that cuckoo idea come from?"

Ling was closely monitoring Ben's thoughts. It wanted to see how the man was going to handle this matter. At the same time, the ghost knew the whole situation was artificial and unfair. How could you fairly judge a human's ability to reason based on something as preposterous as what had just happened to him?

"No, this is wrong," Ling said out loud, and with a flick of its mind made Gould's fantasy into reality. Ben and German were suddenly sitting across from each other at the kitchen table. She was waiting for his response to her vision. She was naked with her elbows on the table, holding a coffee mug in her hands.

Shocked by the abrupt change from the bathroom to here, Ben grabbed hold of the table with both hands as if to stop himself from falling.

"Ben?"

"Hold it a sec. Just one second." He stood up and without another word hurried out of the kitchen, down the hall, and into the bathroom again. This time the tub was empty. There was no tan water with fish or sea serpents in it. German entered behind him, still holding her coffee cup. She again leaned up against his back.

"Hey, what're you doing?"

"Um. I wanted to see if there were fish in the tub as you said."

"That's sweet of you to look, but it was only a crazy idea I had, Ben."

His mind doing somersaults, his eyes darted everywhere around the bathroom, looking for anything in there that might tell him more about what had just happened.

Its head resting on its bent knees, the ghost sat in the empty tub watching them.

• • •

The theater was in a terrible section of the city. You wouldn't want to go there under any circumstance. Vagrants slept sprawled like the dead in doorways. Dogs howled, whores growled, beggars scowled in the most menacing way. The look in their eyes said, Fork over or I'll get you. One troublemaker got so up in Ling's face that the ghost reached out and touched him gently on the tip of his runny nose. The man fell to his knees, so crushed by searing pain everywhere in his body that he didn't even have the ability to scream.

The inside of the movie theater was much nicer looking than Ling had expected after having just been outside. It was a well-preserved time capsule of the 1950s. A giant, brightly lit refreshments stand smelled of freshly popped popcorn and melted butter. A skinny, pimply kid at the door took your red ticket and, after tearing it in half, gave you back the stub. Comfortable wide velvet seats had so much legroom in front that you could almost stretch your legs all the way out after sitting down.

Standing at the back of the cavernous theater, Ling counted seventeen people in there waiting for the movie to begin. Most of them were men still wearing coats. One fat woman sat way off to the side. She had filled the seat next to her with many plastic bags full of dubious stuff.

The Angel of Death was sitting almost exactly in the middle

of the theater with a brimming bucket of popcorn in his lap and a very large paper cup of orange soda. The angel had materialized on earth today as a middle-aged man. Bald and portly, he wore wire-rim glasses over mild blue nondescript eyes, and was dressed in a green Shetland sweater, an old tweed sport jacket, and green corduroys. The angel looked sort of professorial, but the kind of university professor who teaches something European and difficult to understand, like the historical development of hermeneutics or Foucault. When the angel saw the ghost walking down the aisle, he waved. "Ah, there you are, Ling. Sit down. You're just in time."

The ghost sat down next to the angel. After refusing an offer of the popcorn bucket, it said, "I'm extremely uncomfortable being visible to people. A man outside just came up to me and—"

"I know," the angel said indifferently, tossing a handful of popcorn into his mouth. "Tough. It's important for you to experience what it's like to be human now and then."

"*Why?* I'm a ghost. Knowing what it's like to be human only clouds the issue."

"And that's good! You could use some clouds in your sky. Some clouds, a little rain. Maybe even a snowstorm or two . . ."

Ling had no idea what the Angel of Death was talking about.

The lights in the theater began to dim.

"You are about to see one of Carole Lombard's best films: *Mr. and Mrs. Smith*. It's the only comedy Hitchcock ever directed." The angel took a long drink of soda.

"Who's Hitchcock?"

"Have some popcorn."

"No, thank you."

In the fading light, the angel turned slowly to Ling. For several moments his eyes became enormous, pinwheeling fire everywhere. *"Have some popcorn."*

Ling dutifully took four kernels out of the bucket but only held them in the middle of its palm.

"Eat them."

The ghost put one kernel on the tip of its tongue and left it there. It was salty and buttery and full of edges.

"You don't like popcorn?"

"No, sir."

"Chew it slowly. Listen to the different ways it cracks as your teeth break it down. Taste the flavors. Feel the consistency change as you chew."

The ghost did as it was told but the popcorn tasted only of a bad butter substitute and far too much salt. Ling loved other human food but popcorn was gross.

Up on the screen the movie credits had begun to roll, accompanied by a rousing soundtrack.

The angel said, "I like black-and-white films more than color because they're more artificial. You have to work harder to overcome your disbelief. It's sort of like prayer."

"Do you watch a lot of movies?"

"I have my favorites. Anything with Carole Lombard in it or Veronica Lake, and of course Emmanuelle Béart."

"No men?"

A male voice boomed from behind them, "Will you two pipe down? I'm tryin' to watch the pitcha!"

The angel smiled and wiggled his eyebrows at Ling. He turned around to face the complainer, who was sitting two rows back. "But the film hasn't begun yet," he said in a sociable voice.

The complainer slapped his armrest once with an open hand. "Well, I happen to enjoy watching the credits without people yakking around me. *Capisch?* I didn't pay money to listen to *you* two discuss. Okay?"

Hearing the belligerent tone, Ling was certain that the angel was about to turn this man into a sand flea or a hippo turd.

Instead the angel said, "Okay. You're right," and turned back to face the screen. In a whisper out of the side of his mouth he said to the ghost, "He's got a point. We'll talk more afterwards."

When they left the theater two hours later, it had grown dark and misty. The angel pulled out a foolish-looking wool watch cap and put it on. Then he raised the collar of his sport jacket and looked at the black sky. "What do you feel like eating? Are you in the mood for anything special?"

The ghost shrugged and shook its head. "I'm not familiar with this part of town."

"Come on, I know a good place nearby."

Ling looked dubiously around and found it difficult not to frown. "Isn't this a bad section of town?"

"Trust me."

They began walking and, after some minutes of small talk, Ling could no longer hold back. "I don't understand why you want me to stay here. Gould and the girl are happy together. They're in love. It's a *bore*."

The angel chuckled but said nothing.

Ling continued, encouraged by the other's laugh. "Do you know how dull it is to watch human beings who are in love interact with each other? Kisses and hugs and 'I love you' twenty-three times a day. Who *cares*? I'm so bored that I'm going out of my mind."

"Don't go out of your mind. We need you a while longer. Here we are—this is the spot. Go in here."

The ghost was so frustrated by the subject of Ben Gould's mundane romance that, without thinking, it touched the angel's arm as the other stood holding the restaurant door open. The angel looked at the hand on his arm a long moment and then shook his head No, don't do that. Don't touch me. Immediately, Ling knew it had gone too far and quickly withdrew its hand.

"Go on now—go inside, Ling."

It was a pizzeria. The spicy perfume of tomato sauce, hot olive oil, herbs, and baked garlic embraced them as soon as they entered. It was a small place, basically a take-out joint with six tables thrown in as an afterthought for the rare few who actually wanted to stay and eat their food. At one of those tables Ben Gould and German Landis were eating a pizza that looked about as wide as a car tire. There were so many different toppings on it in so many different colors that it resembled a Jackson Pollock painting.

The Angel of Death pointed to a table as far away from the couple as the small floor space allowed. Even so, they were no more than ten feet apart.

The first thing Ling did after sitting down was to lean across the table and ask sotto voce, "Can they hear us?"

"Of course they can hear us. They're just over there." The angel pointed at the couple. German saw the gesture and smiled in her affable way. The angel smiled back and said to her, "We were just admiring your pizza."

His back to them, Ben turned and glanced over his shoulder at the two people. They looked like an academic couple. It was interesting to see them here. They must be real in-the-know foodies. Although this place was in the rough part of town, it also happened to make the best pizza anywhere. As an added bonus, they also played wonderful Motown music nonstop. In the background now the Detroit Emeralds' classic single "Feel the Need in Me" was on.

German said to the angel, "This pizza is called the *Titanic*. There's so many toppings on it that you sink after eating it."

Ben chuckled and shook his head at the strangers to indicate his girlfriend was joking. "Is this your first time here?"

The angel nodded.

"Then, if you don't mind a recommendation, have something simple like sausage and cheese the first time. They make their own sausage here. It's a kind of chorizo but with an aftertaste of anise, and it makes all the difference. Terrific."

"That sounds good. Thanks very much for the tip," the angel said with a wave conveying both thanks and that the couple didn't need to continue this conversation anymore. The lovebirds could go back to their dinner and each other.

When the angel spoke to Ling again, he switched to Dari, one of the two official languages of Afghanistan. The ghost picked right up on it and they quickly became involved in an intense conversation.

German heard bits and pieces of it and pulled excitedly on Ben's sleeve. "Do you hear that? What language are they speaking?"

"I dunno. I *thought* they looked like teachers. Probably from the foreign language department at the university."

"Yes, but what language is that? Do you know? I've never heard anything like it. Maybe they're spies."

"Do you want me to ask them?" Ben started to get up.

German reached over and yanked him back down into his seat. "If they are spies, they'll shoot you. Forget it." She picked up another heavy slice of pizza and slid the tip into her mouth. Watching her, Ben thought, How could I be happier? How could there be a moment in my life when I am happier than right now? He reached out and touched her elbow. German immediately sensed what he was thinking, dropped the food back into the box, and took his hand in both of hers. "When we're finished here, let's go home and go back to bed for three days. What do you say?"

Ben nodded. "But what about Pilot? He'll need to be walked?"

"We'll switch him to autopilot and let him walk himself."

Ling and the angel heard this and paused to stare at each other. The cook came and took their order, which was for a large pizza the way Ben had suggested and beer.

After the cook left, Ling said, "Will you tell me the truth if I ask a question?"

The angel nodded.

"Do you promise?"

The angel nodded again.

"Do you honestly not know what is going to happen to him now?"

The angel raised his right hand as if swearing to tell the truth in court. "We honestly do not."

"Then why don't you just arrange another death for him?"

"Because we can't. I was telling you the truth before: his fate is out of our hands. Plus, we're fascinated to see what *will* happen to him now. His situation is unprecedented. Look at this." The angel reached into his pocket and pulled out what to the normal human eye looked like a bus ticket. To Ling and the angel, however, it was a history of Benjamin Gould's entire life, second for second, right up till that moment in the pizza place. About a tenth of the way up from the bottom was a thick red line denoting the day and time Ben was supposed to have died. Below it, like an atomic clock recording every fraction of a second that passed, additional notations were registering as Gould lived and thought and dreamed.

The angel slid the ticket to the middle of the table and pointed to the red line. "*That's* where things get interesting. The moment the virus infected our computers and our man over there was sent spinning out on his own. Fantastic. This is very exciting stuff for us. As I said, unprecedented."

"So he's a guinea pig?"

"No, an explorer! A pioneer. Because there's absolutely nothing we can do now to affect his destiny. We can only watch. That's why we want you to be around him all the time, Ling. To keep us in the loop about what's happening and what he's thinking."

Their food arrived. They remained silent while it was placed on the table. When the ghost made to speak again, the angel put up a finger to indicate Not yet—let's eat first.

The ghost rested its chin on its hand and looked across the room at Ben and his girlfriend.

"This pizza really is superb. You have to try some," the angel said while pushing an errant dangle of mozzarella cheese into his mouth.

"Perfect," Ling agreed.

The door to the restaurant opened and a bum shuffled in. About thirty-five, he wore a tattered open trench coat, filthy eight-year-old cargo pants, and a sweater the vibrant orange of fresh fruit. Around his neck hung a hand-lettered sign that said *I am hungry and my heart is broke. Can you help me?*

This man looked like he had been living alone on the dark side of the moon. His nauseating smell alone was enough to send people fleeing.

Upon seeing him, the cook behind the counter yelled, "Hey, you, get the hell out of here or I'm calling the cops!"

The bum ignored the threat and shuffled over to German and Ben's table. His eyes looked like dirty coins. His skin was the color of old books that were once wet. Reaching into one of his many bulging pockets, he took out a brown plastic spool that had once held sewing thread but was now empty. Ever so carefully he placed it on the edge of their table and then stood back, crossed his hands in front of him, and waited. The spool was clearly an offering, a gift with strings attached. I give you this and you give me what I need.

Very coolly, Ben pulled a slice of pizza from their pie and handed it up to the man.

"No, please, don't do that! Now he'll just keep coming back in here!" the cook sputtered, waving the big wooden pizza paddle up and down in his hands in protest.

The bum took the slice and studied it awhile. German watched with fascination but not a bit of discomfort or dismay. She was intrigued to see how both the tramp and her man would act this one out.

Holding the food with two hands and standing still, eyes closed now, the tramp began to eat in slow, deliberate bites. The cook was fuming with frustration behind the counter. He wanted to call the police but didn't want to make a scene. He wanted this smelly creep to leave his place. But now it looked as if the man was going to stay and eat.

Pizza slice cradled in his knobby hands, the bum moved over to the table where the other couple sat. Stopping nearby, he stared at them as he ate. Ling had trouble suppressing a smile. If this human ruin only knew from whom he was about to beg food . . .

But, to Ling's surprise, the angel said in a quiet, sweet voice, "You have to leave now, Mr. Parrish. Take your food and go."

That surprised the bum. On hearing his name pronounced, he squinted distrustfully. He had not been addressed that way for years. And certainly not with a "Mr." affixed to it. The look in his eyes said he recognized the name as something that had once belonged to him but was lost long ago like so much else in his life. He zeroed in on the bald man who was now eating again and watching him.

Perplexed, Parrish took a chomp of pizza and whined loudly through the mouthful of food, "My feet hurt and my heart is broken!" Tomato sauce oozed off his lip and down the front of his sign. He didn't notice.

"Yes, I understand, but you must leave now, Stewart. Go on, there's the door."

Through the dun-colored, forever-swirling mental clouds of his eleven years' living-on-the-street madness, Stewart Parrish was ill at ease when anyone spoke kindly, quietly, or in multiple sentences to him. He was accustomed to a few harsh words, grunts, or most commonly a curse. The bald man's knowing his name and the tender voice disturbed him. Like so much else in Parrish's splintered life, it made no sense. Through cruel experience he had learned always to beware of things that made no sense.

Shoving the rest of the pizza into his mouth, he wiped both oily hands on his coat and then, with surprising speed and grace, whipped out a knife he carried hidden in his breast pocket. He had used it often. Back when he was in prison, Parrish had learned how to hone almost anything to a razor's edge on the concrete floor of his cell. That is what he had done with this treasure. It was the kind of ubiquitous stainless steel bread knife used in school cafeterias, public institutions, and cheap restaurants. However, *this* blade was now sharp enough to cut the air in half.

God creates mankind, but man creates his own individual madness. Because it is so varied and multihued, different from person to person, it's often impossible for angels or ghosts or any being from the other side to keep track of or decipher. More simply put, the Angel of Death had no premonition of what was coming next.

German Landis screamed when the tramp pulled out the knife. The angel heard her scream, glanced up, and instinctively ducked just enough as Parrish stabbed him.

The cook vaulted over the counter. Swinging the wooden paddle with all of his might, he hit Parrish on the back of his head so hard that the bum collapsed as if shot.

Stunned, Ling couldn't believe what had just happened. A mortal had stabbed the Angel of Death and drawn blood? How was it possible? Groaning loudly, the angel tried both to stand and pull the knife out of his shoulder.

"Help me, Ling. Help me up." He groaned again.

On the floor, Parrish began to stir. The cook and Ben Gould leapt on him, pinning him down as best they could. Ben yelled to German to call the police.

Ling stood and grabbed the angel under one of his arms.

"Get me out of here. Out on the street. Now."

Luckily, Parrish began to thrash around violently, taking all of Ben's and the cook's attention and energy just to contain him. German was in the kitchen, looking wildly around for a telephone.

With Ling's assistance the angel staggered out of the restaurant and onto the sidewalk. No cars were about. Looking left and right, he ordered the ghost to help him over to an alley a few feet away. Face contorted, his breathing was ragged. By the time they got there, both of them were covered with blood. If he had been mortal, the angel would already have gone into shock.

"Let me down. Let me down here."

Ling obeyed but kept both hands near the angel just in case.

"Listen to me, Ling. I have to go. This should never have happened. I had no idea—it never should have happened."

The ghost didn't know whether to wait till the angel was finished speaking or interrupt to ask if there was anything more it could do.

"I don't know if I'll be coming back here or if I can help you anymore, Ling. This whole thing is crazy. It never should have happened . . ."

The angel vanished without another word.

Three

German Landis now lived in a dark, clammy dump that she hated and wished she had never seen, much less rented. But when she broke up with Ben and moved out, she'd been frantic to find a place, and this apartment was the only one immediately available in her price range at the time.

German was bad in desperate situations and this awful abode was convincing proof of that. She wasn't aware of it, but almost every time she opened the door to the apartment and switched on the light, she hunched her shoulders and grimaced in preparation for what she was about to see. Once inside, she sometimes walked around singing "Hateful, hateful, hateful" to the walls, the cabinet, and the freestanding cardboard-gray fiberboard closet. Her bright blue couch looked so forlorn and out of place in this dank, depressing dungeon. More than once she had apologized directly to the piece of furniture, promising that she would get them both out of there as soon as she could.

Even the dog seemed to skulk around the apartment, tail and head down whenever he came to visit. But who could blame him?

To compensate in a small way, German bought Pilot the best dog food in the market. When she opened the cans, it smelled so good that she once took a small taste. Not bad. She'd also bought two dog bowls the same color as her couch. They sat next to the refrigerator in her telephone booth–size kitchen. Although their merry blue brightness was a nice attempt, they failed to lift the mood of the apartment even one inch. What on earth *could* in a place like this? She was living in a basement apartment with two small windows and a concrete floor that was always cold. Feeble sunlight leaked into the place almost by accident and never very much, never enough. How could it?

Like some dubious creature in a Kafka short story, German was living now below ground level. She had bought six lamps at IKEA and kept them all switched on all the time whenever she was at home. Her apartment was so unlike Ben's, with its four tall windows facing east and the bright morning light shining in through them, the worn but warm blond parquet floors, and that funny old Persian carpet Pilot liked to lie on. In stark, ugly contrast, her new home was the kind of place where you went to hide or mope or worse. As soon as you felt better, you fled and never returned.

The house itself was adorable, and that's what she had fallen for in the first place. If you stood outside and looked at it only from the street, you thought, Gee, what a charming place to live. The owners were an old lesbian couple named Robyn and Clara who were tightwads with lots of money but resented having to spend any of it. The house was painted a cheerful yellow every few years, and each window aboveground had a flower box. But the paint was the cheapest they could find and all of the flowers were anemic pansies grown from seeds in an envelope you can buy at any nursery for $1.49.

German's apartment, the pièce de résistance of the owners'

stinginess, had for years been used only for storage. Even now it sometimes smelled of damp and mold, at other times of the ghosts of old magazines and soggy cardboard cartons that had lived down there undisturbed for decades. The women resisted throwing anything away, especially if they'd paid good money for it—even if it was years ago.

The only reason they fixed up the basement was because their accountant informed them that if they did the renovation, they could rent the apartment but not pay tax on the income from it because both of them were now over sixty-five. Within days of that revelation, out went the magazines and boxes and in came the tenants, although none of them ever stayed very long.

Both of the old women were quite fond of German Landis, but they made no attempt to make either her apartment or her life there nicer. They also liked Pilot because he was quiet, grave, and well behaved. They didn't even mind it when the dog sat on the small patch of grass in front of German's door, taking the sun. They wished Pilot were a little friendlier and more appreciative when they pet him, but you can't have everything.

On returning from Ben's that morning, German slid the key into the lock and unconsciously began to hunch her shoulders. The telephone in the apartment rang. She almost tripped over the letter *D* because she'd put it down on the ground so that she could work the key.

Waiting patiently nearby, Pilot looked up at her but his expression was blank. All dogs' expressions are blank, but there was something in Pilot's face that usually told her what he was thinking. Or at least she thought so.

German got the door opened, kicked the damned *D* out of her way, and walked quickly in to answer the phone. Pilot followed her. The first thing he did once inside was lift his head and sniff the air to see if any new interesting smells were about. Then the dog walked over to his food bowl to check on its status. Now and then tasty leftovers from German's meals appeared there.

Slightly breathless she said into the receiver, "Hello?"

"We have to talk."

Her eyes widened in surprise. Unconsciously she put her other hand on the phone for support. "Ben?"

"We have to talk."

"I was just there. Why didn't you talk to me then?"

He sighed loudly but nothing more. She waited for him to continue.

"That stupid film was on television."

"What film?"

"The old comedy with Cary Grant and the dog, Mr. Smith. What a ridiculous name for a dog. It's so *clever*."

"You mean the movie where he shares the dog with his wife after they break up?"

"Yes."

"That was silly and not funny. We both thought so."

"I agree, but the guy on TV said that it was one of the 'great classic screwball comedies.' It was just on. As soon as you left, I turned on the television and that damned movie was playing. Ironic, huh? You walk out the door with our dog and that thing just happens to be playing on TV. Listen, really, we have to talk."

The movie didn't just happen to be on TV. Ling ran it on purpose to make Ben feel bad because the ghost was so angry with him for his idiotic behavior toward German. The two of them were sitting now at the kitchen table looking directly at each other. Ben didn't know that, of course. He just thought he was alone in the room, talking on the telephone to the woman he would have given half a universe to have back in his life again.

German answered decisively and the tone of her voice carried more than a little irritation. "We've talked about everything, Ben—over and over. There's nothing more to talk about."

"Yes, there is. There are . . . things."

She shook her head and bit a thumbnail. She frowned. She wasn't having it. Not this time, not anymore. "*Things?* That doesn't help me much, Benjamin." She was tired of his elliptical way of speaking, especially about things that really mattered. This subject exhausted both her head and heart.

But on the other end of the line Ling knew that something very big was going on. The ghost was paying full attention now. Would Ben Gould do it? Would he actually tell her?

"We really do *have* to talk, German."

Now it was her turn to sigh. He was beginning to sound like a broken record and it was strange. "You've already said that several times, Ben. But we've talked everything out till it's exhausted, you know what I mean?" She tried to keep her voice measured and kind, but it was difficult.

"No, this is different. This is very, very different from what you think. Can I ask for one last favor? Just one? Do I still have enough points for one favor?"

She looked up at the ceiling. "What?"

"I want you to meet me somewhere. Would you do that?"

"When? Where?"

"One eighty-two Underhill Avenue in an hour. Would you do that? Would you do it for me for what we once were?"

She hesitated, startled by the way he worded the sentence. There was no good reason to say no, so she reluctantly agreed. But unhappiness was very plain in the sound of her voice. She would walk Pilot over there because Underhill Avenue wasn't far from her apartment. At least they'd get some exercise. "All right, I'll be there."

"Thank you, German. Thank you very much."

• • •

Since the accident that should have killed her, Danielle Voyles had taken to reading the Bible. She did not make a big deal about it. Few people outside her family and some friends even knew she was doing it. Every morning before breakfast she read at least five pages. Then she closed her eyes and thought over what she'd just read. Thought hard. Danielle had never read the Bible straight through. The experience so far was mostly a combination of hard going or boring, but she was going to finish it. And when she was done, she wanted to read the Koran next. Until the accident, she hadn't spent much time thinking about God or the larger issues, but she was sure thinking about them these days.

One day Danielle and her boyfriend went on a picnic. They had been fighting a lot recently and needed some quality time alone to work things out. Otherwise they both knew their relationship was in big trouble. The picnic spot was a half hour's ride away by turnpike. The day was beautiful and the road was clear. When they were halfway there, Danielle saw something out of the corner of her eye. When she turned her head to look, she saw a small single-engine plane nosediving into a rocky field very close by on the side of the highway.

Afterward Danielle said the only thing she remembered were the sounds. First she heard a long loud *wooooom* as the plane made impact with the ground. Then the sound of different kinds of metal and glass smashing, snapping, and crashing. That's all, but it was a huge blessing because of what happened next.

Shattering on impact, the exploding airplane shot hundreds of burning fragments of metal, molten rubber, and everything else like bomb shrapnel in every direction. Some of it reached the road because it was so close. Two pieces hit their car. Part of a wing strut struck the front, tearing off a headlight and bending the fender. The second piece was the three-inch top part of a stainless steel ballpoint pen lying forgotten on the floor of the plane. Like a bullet, it shot through the car window into Danielle's forehead just above her right eyebrow.

There are wounds that should kill us but don't. Wounds, diseases, terrible accidents. When asked how that is possible, the greatest experts on earth can only examine the survivor, shrug like the rest of us, and smile uneasily. Miracles do happen sometimes.

After studying the grave head wound Danielle Voyles sustained in the accident, doctors were certain she would die no matter what they did for her. In an extremely dangerous six-hour operation, the large piece of pen was removed from her brain. None of the medical team expected her to live through the night.

Half a year later she was sitting on an exercise bicycle in the living room of her apartment, pedaling slowly but steadily while reading an article in a magazine about finding inner peace.

When the doorbell rang, she looked up in surprise. She was not expecting anyone because it was Saturday and she'd made no dates or plans. Getting off the Exercycle, she pulled up her sweatpants, which had a tendency to droop whenever she worked out. Walking to the door, her mind was still half in the magazine article, half wondering who might have come to visit. Danielle was a friendly woman. She opened the front door without thinking that whoever was on the other side might harm her.

Standing there was a very tall woman in a yellow baseball

cap, holding a leash with a dog at the end of it. Danielle had never seen either of them before.

"Hello. Are you Danielle Voyles?" the woman asked, and smiled hesitantly.

"Yes, I am."

"My name is German Landis. I'm sorry to disturb you like this, but I'd like to talk to you about your accident, if you don't mind."

"My accident?" Danielle reflexively reached up to touch the deep indentation and cruel purple scar on her head that would be her companions for the rest of her life.

"Yes. Can you spare a few minutes?"

German was not alone. Benjamin Gould stood next to her, but Danielle did not see him. She *could* not see him. She did not see him for the entire time that this tall woman visited.

She did not hear Ben when he spoke in a normal voice to German, telling her what questions to ask and, before Danielle answered them, what her answers would be, word for word. She did not see him wandering around her apartment, peering in open drawers, opening the refrigerator, and then saying loudly, "Yikes!" when he saw how little was in there. She did not see him when he sat down close to her on the couch so that the two of them were directly facing German.

An hour ago Ben and German had met outside Danielle's apartment building. It was a sunny day and both of them wore baseball caps to keep the sun out of their eyes. Ben had given her the yellow hat months before. It moved him now to see her wearing it and know she still used it. Pilot didn't react much on seeing Ben. He wagged his tail three times and then looked at a Labrador retriever puppy that was passing on the other side of the street.

German waited for Ben to explain why he'd asked her to come. Instead, he gestured for her to follow him to a park nearby. They sat down on a brown bench and he told her his story. Astonishing as it was, it didn't take long. After he had finished, she looked at him as if she had never seen Ben Gould before. She could not hide either her amazement or her dismay. He had expected that.

"That's mad. Benjamin, that is totally insane."

"I know it sounds like that, but it's the truth." He spoke quietly and with great conviction. He knew she was going to take a lot of convincing.

"Ben, this is creepy. You're scaring me now."

"Imagine how *I* feel! All I'm asking you to do is go to her apartment with me and see for yourself. Don't take any of it on faith. See for yourself."

She tugged on the brim of her cap. "You've said that twice."

He nodded. "I'll say it again: Go see for yourself. Knock on her door and watch what happens. I'll be right beside you."

They continued talking. The more she listened, the more confused she became because he was so convincing. It was without question the craziest thing he'd ever said to her, and Ben wasn't given to saying crazy things. But the way he described this, it became increasingly hard *not* to believe him.

"Who is she?"

"Just some woman. A stranger."

"How do you know her?"

"I *don't* know her, German. That's what I've been telling you: I have never laid eyes on this woman in my life."

"You're telling me that one day this just started happening with a stranger you've never met?" Her voice was wary and weary.

"Yes."

She brought a hand up to her bottom lip and kept it there while watching him. German once thought she knew this man well, but what he had just told her changed everything. It explained why he had ended their relationship. And why he had been acting so oddly for months. It explained everything and nothing. She wished to the bottom of her soul that she had never heard any of it.

"What am I supposed to do with this, Ben? What am I supposed to do now?"

"Meet this woman and see that everything I've told you is true."

She stood abruptly and walked away, pulling the dog behind her. Ben watched for a few moments and then followed. In front of the apartment building, German stopped and said without turning around to face him, "What should I say to her?"

"Tell her you want to talk about her accident. Say you're a journalist doing an article on posttraumatic stress. Or that someone in your family—"

"I'll handle it," she said curtly, throwing up a hand to cut him off. She didn't want to hear any more. She only wanted him to shut up.

When German rang the bell, Ben stood beside her. When Danielle opened the door, she looked directly at German and only at her. The expression on her face clearly said she saw only the woman and her dog.

"Hello. Are you Danielle Voyles?"

•   •   •

The first time it happened to Ben was the night months earlier when they saw the man stabbed at the pizzeria. After talking to the police and giving their separate testimonies, the couple went straight to a bar and drank themselves back to an uneasy calm.

Both of them liked sitting at a bar, never in a booth. High in a corner of this joint was a large flat-screen television mounted on a wall. It was tuned to a sports channel. They drank and talked and tried to regain their composure after witnessing the harrowing event earlier in the evening.

Now and then Ben looked up at the television to see what kind of game was on. A time or two his eyes lingered there while German spoke to him. It didn't bother her. They had known each other long enough now so that she knew he could be looking away but still listening carefully to her. It was one of her boyfriend's idiosyncrasies and didn't bother her.

The next time he glanced up at the television set, he frowned. Because instead of the Roma versus Lazio soccer match that had been on the screen moments ago, now there was a close-up of a glistening pink open mouth. It was undergoing extremely graphic oral surgery. Ben's first reaction was to exclaim, Hey, look at that! But he knew German hated blood or gore and they'd already witnessed a stabbing tonight. Narrowing his eyes for better focus, he continued staring at the TV.

At the same time that he was looking at the television set over the bar, Danielle Voyles was looking at a TV set in her living room. Both of them saw exactly the same thing: an oral surgery videotape. Danielle was a dental assistant who prided herself on being up on the very latest developments in the field. While recuperating from her operation, she spent a lot of time studying videotapes of oral procedures that her boss, Dr. Franz, had made.

While Ben watched in disgust, Danielle watched, ate cheese popcorn, and sipped from a can of Dr Pepper. Ben had been drinking vodka but suddenly his mouth filled with the distinctive tang of cheese popcorn. Which was then flooded away by the thick sweetness and bubbles of the soft drink.

The entire occurrence lasted only seconds. When it was

over he thought some part of his frazzled brain was playing tricks on him after the shock of the stabbing incident earlier. But in fact it was just the beginning.

In the days that followed, Ben Gould experienced more and more snatches of Danielle Voyles's life. Each time it happened, it was as if he literally *was* her for short periods of time. He saw through her eyes, tasted whatever she put in her mouth, and knew her every thought during the seconds he was inside her. Danielle was never aware of any of this. It was completely one-sided.

Frightening, fascinating, but always frightening again, he learned who she was, what had happened to her, what she believed, dreamed, and feared. He could not stop the experience from happening again and again. He would be standing at the kitchen sink in his apartment, drinking a glass of water. With no warning he'd suddenly be standing in front of a mirror looking at the reflection of Danielle's face, seeing it through her eyes. While she applied lipstick and stared at herself in the bathroom mirror, thinking about what to do that day, he experienced all of Danielle: what she saw, what she perceived, what she thought. At the same time, he remained separate and apart and always Ben Gould too. Just as suddenly the experience would stop and he would be back in his life. It had happened to him many times since the night of the stabbing. He told German Landis all of this while sitting with her on a bench in the park across the street from Danielle's apartment building.

This was what had made him increasingly odd and remote when they lived together. Of course, the freakiness of the experience impacted on his behavior toward German. Finally it became unbearable for her and she confronted him about it. But by then Ben was so afraid he was going insane that her alarm only exacerbated things and made him pull further away from her. A short while later she told him she couldn't stand their situation anymore and moved out.

Soon afterward, Ben went to Danielle Voyles's apartment for the first time. He knew her name and address because she had taken out her driver's license one day to prove her identity when cashing a check. He rang the bell and she answered but saw no one there on opening the door. She shrugged and closed it. He rang the bell again and she opened again, this time frowning. Seeing an empty hallway, she took three steps out into it to hopefully catch a glimpse of the prankster. When she did, Ben slipped around her and entered her apartment.

It did not surprise him that he was invisible to her. Previously he had tried every way he could imagine to communicate with Danielle while inside her. He had talked, whistled, and sung, but nothing worked.

"Hello," he said to her now in a normal voice from two feet away.

She closed the front door, shook her head, and went back to the program she had been watching on television.

"Can you hear me? Can you see me?"

Oblivious, she picked up the remote control and pressed the button to raise the volume.

Ben put his two index fingers together and blew an earsplitting whistle. Danielle pointed the remote control at the television. The bored expression on her face confirmed she'd heard nothing.

Hands in pockets, he walked around her small home looking at things he had already seen before, but only through her eyes. The apartment consisted of a living room, bedroom, kitchen, and bathroom so small that it could barely fit a sink and a shower. He made the tour in only a few minutes. Danielle had big-furniture-and-stuffed-animals taste. Each room was painted a different vibrant pastel shade. There were eleven stuffed animals scattered in various strategic locations. She owned a very good fountain pen that she used frequently to write long letters to friends. She hung her hand wash in the bathroom. She was an indifferent cook. In the silverware drawer were two knives, two forks, two spoons, a white plastic ladle, and a red Swiss Army pocketknife with lots of blades. She used them to cut bread and meat.

In the living room was an overstuffed yellow couch from a discount furniture store. Next to it was an almost matching yellow Barcalounger chair that she liked to sit on while watching TV.

After touring her apartment, Ben stood beside the couch with arms crossed, watching this woman for the first time from afar. A few days before, he had looked up her telephone number. He called and tried to talk to her. But when Danielle answered the phone she did not hear his voice. She heard nothing. After waiting a bit just to make sure there really was no one on the other end of the line, she put the receiver down. She thought about that now while watching her TV show: the phone call the other day when no one was on the other end. The doorbell rings today but no one's there. This sort of thing never happened to her. Were the events somehow connected?

The ghost found it all very amusing. Standing nearby, Ling watched both people closely. Mr. Gould was now getting a taste of what it was like to be a ghost. No fun, was it? Ling was invisible to both people. Ben was invisible to Danielle Voyles.

"You really can't see or hear me? This is insane. You *have* to know I'm here," Ben said, and then instinctively reached out to touch her, but his hand stopped halfway and dropped.

"She'll never see you," Ling said in a voice that Ben could not hear. "She can't."

There was a can of Dr Pepper soda on the table next to her chair. Ben wanted to grab it, shake it in her face, and shout, "Look at me! I'm right here." But if he did that and she saw only a floating can, the gesture would frighten her, nothing more. He didn't know this woman and had no desire to scare her.

At a loss for what to do, he crossed the room to the window and stared out at the street. Once when he was inside Danielle, she'd done the same thing, so he was already familiar with this view. While standing there he turned several times to glance at her. What could he do about this? Why was he invisible to Danielle Voyles? And why was he able to see the world through her eyes?

Ten minutes passed. Eventually she got up and went to the toilet. Ben took advantage of her absence and slipped out of the apartment. As he closed the door behind him with a barely audible click, he looked up and saw an old woman down the hall entering her apartment. She glared at him, her look saying, I know very well what you're doing, mister: I see you sneaking around. Not until she'd entered her apartment and closed the door too loudly did he realize this old woman *had* seen him.

And now here he was again in Danielle's living room. Only this time his ex-girlfriend and their dog were there, and those two could see him just fine. German and Danielle had been making small talk for a while. Ben had completed his latest tour of her apartment and was sitting next to her on the couch. German sat on the yellow chair, not knowing, of course, that that's where Danielle preferred to sit.

"Do you know a man named Benjamin Gould?" She kept looking in Danielle's eyes to see if they registered Ben's name or the fact that he was so near to her. They did not.

"Gould? No."

"You've never heard of him before?"

Danielle paused and looked at her hands, thinking, but in time shook her head no.

"Don't ask her that, German! I told you, ask about her accident."

Once again Danielle did not hear Ben speak. Back in her bedroom a telephone rang. "Could you wait just a minute while I answer that?"

German smiled. "Sure."

When they were alone again, Ben demanded, "What are you doing? Of course she doesn't know who I am—I already told you that! You've seen how she reacts: she doesn't know I'm here. How the hell is she supposed to know who I am if she can't see me?"

"What is this, Ben? What's going on?"

"*I don't know!* I swear to God I don't know. That's why I wanted you to come here and see it for yourself. This is what ruined us, German."

Returning a few minutes later, Danielle saw the tall woman talking animatedly to no one. Her head was turned to the right while she gestured with one finger and spoke to the emptiness next to her. Danielle tried to mask her surprise with a neutral voice.

"I'm sorry, but that call was from my mother. She's coming by in a few minutes and I have to go out with her. Maybe you can come back some other time."

German stood quickly and pulled Pilot toward the door. "No problem. I'll call and we'll set up another date."

"Good." Danielle opened the door. Ben stepped quickly through it.

Out in the hall again, German said to Danielle, "Can I ask one last question before I go?"

Because he was so eager to hear the question, Ben did not

notice the old woman down the hall who he had seen the first time he was here.

"That's him, Danielle. That's the man I was telling you about."

The three turned toward this neighbor who was once again standing twenty feet away near the door to her apartment. She had a broom in her hand and was pointing with it at the empty space next to German.

"Remember I told you about the man at your door that day? Well, that's him." Face set in accusation, the woman pointed again at invisible Ben.

Danielle was regretting ever having answered the door this morning. "Who are you talking about, Mrs. Schellberger?"

"*Him*. That's the man who was fiddling with your door that day."

Danielle couldn't see Ben, although the others did. Except for the dog, none of them saw Ling the ghost, who was also there. But Pilot didn't understand what the human beings were talking about. On the other hand, Ling saw everyone and understood everything. However, the ghost could do nothing to resolve this.

Maybe there was a way. Snapping its fingers to get the dog's attention, Ling said to him, "Run away."

Pilot tilted his head to one side, confused by the command.

"Run away. Create a diversion. *He needs your help*."

Now the dog understood and, without further ado, jerked his leash out of German's relaxed hand. He sprinted off down the hall toward the stairwell. Ben ran after him. Luckily, Ben was wearing sneakers, so his footsteps weren't really heard in the confusion of the moment. The three women watched Pilot run away. Only Danielle was surprised when German didn't go after her pet. Mrs. Schellberger wasn't surprised because she saw Ben chase it.

"Aren't you going to try and catch your dog?" Danielle asked.

Ignoring the question, German looked instead at the old woman, who appeared to be growing angrier the longer she stood there waiting for a response to what she had said. "Uh, yes. Yes, I am." Her eyes moved from Danielle to Mrs. Schellberger and then back to Danielle.

Danielle smiled thinly at her snoopy neighbor and then looked down the hall in the direction that the dog had fled. Nodding one last time at German, she went back into her apartment and closed the door.

"Well, excuse *me* for being a good neighbor," the old woman squawked, and marched away.

Ben didn't have far to go to catch the dog. It was sitting on the sidewalk in front of the building. Back to the door, its face was turned up toward the sun.

"How did you get out here?" Ben asked Pilot, as if he understood.

Standing nearby, fingers steepled against its chin, the ghost watched. Since coming here, it had constantly wondered when something like this was going to happen. Ben Gould had died. Granted, he was alive again because of that computer glitch, but he *had* died. And so had Danielle Voyles during the operation on her head. So the ghost assumed other people were also walking around on borrowed time.

"Ben?" German strode quickly out the door and walked straight through Ling.

Ben pointed to Danielle's building. "You saw what happened in there."

"Yes, I did."

He nodded, glad at least that she admitted to having seen it. "And what do you think?"

"You need help, Ben. I don't know what *kind*, because this stuff is way, way beyond me. I don't know what else to say except you frighten me.

"I don't know what's happening with you, but whatever it is has ruined us. If it's getting worse now, then you can't ask me to be here. You can't ask me to be in your life.

"I still love you and you know that. I *never* wanted to leave. I wanted you and me to be forever. But too bad: we're here now and here is impossible. No." She waved her hand in front of her face. "I can't do this. I love you, but I have to go. If you love me, too, you can't ask me to do this." With that, she strode away without looking back at any of them—the man, the dog, or the ghost.

Four

When German called Ben's apartment an hour later, no one answered the phone. No one answered when she called again one, two, and then three hours later.

Guilt, worry, and love gnawed on her heart. For so long she had puzzled and then agonized over what was going wrong with their relationship. But today, on finally learning the cause of all the trouble, her first reaction had been to run away.

Now when someone knocked on her door she rushed to answer it, hoping it would be Ben. Instead it was one of her landlords from upstairs reporting that garbage pickup day had been changed. As usual, the old woman wanted to hang around and chat. But German was in no mood for that and got rid of her quickly.

The shabby basement apartment did not help improve her frame of mind. In this time of doubt and confusion the place felt even smaller, darker, and unfriendlier than usual. Some homes are the perfect friend, womb, safe harbor, or hiding place when one is needed. Others are nothing more than spaces to sleep, eat, and store your belongings. The last and worst kind of dwelling doesn't even deserve to be called home because it offers nothing: no comfort, rest, or shelter. You get the feeling that if it were a person, it would not only resent your presence but would also turn you in to the authorities if you were in trouble. Bad moods darken in these places; despair grows like bacteria.

While pacing back and forth across the floor, German knew she had to get out of that dank cave right away. She would go over to Ben's apartment and apologize about before. All of it had been just too much; I couldn't cope. I'm better now, so let's talk some more about it.

But it turned out he wasn't home and neither was Pilot. When German moved out of his apartment, Ben had insisted she keep her key to the place. She used it now because no one answered her repeated knocking. It was the second time today she had been here but so much had happened in between visits. It felt as if a week had passed since she'd come by earlier to pick up the dog.

Once inside, she went from room to room searching for Ben or Pilot or she didn't know what. The word "clues" kept turning in her mind, but clues to what? Why Ben was invisible to Danielle Voyles?

It was such a great apartment. With no one around to distract her, it felt as though for each step she took in there another good memory surfaced. Everything was so clean, tidy, and bright. Light loved living there. It filled each room like milk in a glass. In depressing contrast, German couldn't drag light into her basement apartment even if she put a chain around its neck and pulled. She entered the bathroom and opened the medicine cabinet over the sink. She looked at the familiar bottles and tubes in there. She had used so many of them. When she saw his cologne she touched it, remembering the time she came into the room as he was spraying it on his neck. She came up behind him, took his chin in one hand, and licked the side of his throat because he smelled so delicious.

For obvious reasons, she saved looking in the bedroom till last. But a few moments after entering and seeing that it was empty, she heard the front door to the apartment slam shut. Ben was back!

Hurrying down the hall to meet him, German stopped short when she saw instead an old man, a complete stranger, standing just inside the doorway holding a slack leash attached to Pilot. The man was looking around with his mouth open in dismay. Even from a distance it was easy to see that he was confused and disoriented.

German approached cautiously. She was bigger than the man and undoubtedly stronger, judging by his age and appearance, but you never knew for certain. Seeing her, Pilot wagged his tail and padded over, pulling the leash out of the man's unresisting hand. This brought the old guy's attention back from wherever it was roaming and he focused on her for the first time.

German asked, "Who are you? How did you get in here?"

Slowly lowering his head, he looked at his hand, which was holding a brown key. He lifted it to show her, but German was only interested in watching his face. She could see he was trying to figure out how this had happened. His expression, a combination of consternation and surprise, said Why *am* I here?

Then he rubbed his nose. It was a most singular gesture; she had only ever seen one other person do it that way. Putting an open hand against the end of his nose, he patted it a few times and then rubbed it. Patted and then rubbed. It was ridiculous looking, the kind of gesture that, if she had seen someone else doing it, she would have smiled or even laughed.

Not now: now she froze. She barely managed to croak, *"Ben?"*

His hand stopped rubbing his nose. The old man's eyes, clearing now, looked at her. They were kindly and embarrassed. "I'm sorry, but do we know each other?"

"Ben? Is it really you?"

He looked at both arms as if checking to see if they were his. Then he smiled. "I think it's me. But are we talking about the same Ben?" His smile was cute and old-person gentle. "I'm Ben Gould. I'm really very sorry, but I have to admit that I don't remember you. Please don't take offense, though. I have Alzheimer's disease, or at least I think I do, and it's really made my brain into Swiss cheese."

German didn't know what to say. She didn't know what to think. She didn't know anything at that moment but the need to stare and deny. The old man continued looking and smiling at her but his eyes said No one's home.

Leash dragging behind, Pilot left the room unnoticed and walked toward the kitchen for a drink of water and a quick check of his food bowl.

The ghost was sitting at the kitchen table smoking a cigarette and staring at the drifting smoke. "What happened, Pilot? Who's that old man? Where did you get him?"

Instead of answering, the dog bent over and took a long drink.

"*Pilot?*"

"Wait a minute, willya?" He drank some more and then stopped. "I don't know what's going on. We were walking down the street and gradually started going slower. I didn't pay any attention until we stopped moving. I turned around and there *he* was."

"From one minute to the next he turned into an old man?"

"I guess so. I told you, Ling, I didn't see it happen. Suddenly there was an old guy holding my leash and looking around like he was completely lost. I led him back here and he let me. End of story."

The ghost put the cigarette out on the tip of its tongue. Then, after laying the butt carefully down on the table, Ling said, "This is not good news. Not good at all."

They heard the sound of footsteps coming down the hall toward them. German Landis entered the kitchen. She went to a cupboard and took out a teapot and two cups. After filling a kettle with water, she put it on the stove to boil. Opening another cupboard, obviously familiar with where everything was kept in this kitchen, she looked at the large assortment of teas arranged on the shelf. Ben and his teas: Ben and his love for good food. How on earth could that old man in the other room be him?

The dog and ghost watched intently as she moved around, preparing tea things on a tray. Before leaving the living room she had helped old Ben into a chair and said she would make them some tea. Afterward they could talk. The old fellow sat down with an exhausted groan and nodded gratefully at her offer. He looked so spent that she was almost afraid to leave him alone.

A few minutes later in the kitchen the three of them snapped to attention like an animal when it hears a piercing whistle. But a whistle didn't capture their attention: it was singing. Someone was singing in the living room, which meant it had to be the old man.

Rapt at the unexpected sound of his very good voice, all three of them listened to the singer.

"'A-live-a-live-oh,
A-live-a-live-oh,'
Crying 'Cockles and mussels, a-live-a-live oh.'

"In Dublin's fair city,
  Where the girls are so pretty,
  I first set eyes on sweet Molly Malone . . ."

Pretty as it was, the dog and ghost thought the singing was strange. German winced. The song was the Irish ballad "Molly Malone" and it was what Ben sang whenever he was happy. Often he sang the song when he wasn't even aware of doing it, such as when he was cooking something challenging. No matter where German was, whenever she heard Ben singing "Molly Malone," she knew he was content.

Leaving the tea tray on the table, she hurried out of the kitchen. She found the old man singing in front of Ben's bookcases. He was looking at an open book in his hands.

Glancing up at her, he said in an excited voice, "I know this one; I *know* this book!" He sounded so pleased, as if he had found the way home all by himself. He held it up for her and she saw the name John Thorne printed on the spine. Thorne was one of Ben's heroes. He loved to read to her from the writer's books on food and often tried the recipes in them if they weren't too exotic. German didn't like complicated food.

As quickly as his face had lit up, it shut down again. The hand holding the book trembled and dropped to his side. "It's horrible. Can you understand how horrible it is not to be able to remember your own life?

"When you're young, it's all about what you do with your life. When you're old, it's really only about what you remember. The only thing I've got left of my life is my memories, but now they're leaking out of my head. And there's nothing I can do to stop it.

"What's worse is sometimes I remember things very clearly. Like when I saw this book on the shelf: John Thorne. I know that name. I know his work. I once made his winter corn chowder. My mind blinks on and suddenly remembers everything just like it used to be. But ten seconds later or ten minutes or whenever, the lights go out again and I look at whatever I'm holding, this book or this memory, and I think, What's this? How did it get here?" He frowned. "At my age, you don't have *anything else* but your memories. I'm not trying to sound self-pitying but it's true. So when that goes away, who are you?" He sighed again. "What is your name? Would you tell me your name?"

"German. German Landis."

He nodded but showed no sign of recognition. "Can I tell you a story, German? Can I tell you something else I remembered today that made me happy?"

She dipped her head stiffly in assent because she was almost afraid to hear what he was going to say next.

"When I was very young, my family went into New York one day to attend a play. When it was over, we walked down Times Square and Forty-second Street. Somehow I got separated from the others. I could not have been more than four or five and now I was lost in what at the time was a bad part of Manhattan.

"I was so young that one of the only things I knew about survival was men in uniform could be trusted. So in the midst of all my fear and crying I went looking for a man in uniform, any kind of uniform, to help me.

"In those days on the long traffic island in the middle of Times Square was a military recruitment center. Four men representing the four branches of the military sat at four desks, backs straight, wearing beautiful different-colored uniforms while waiting for potential recruits to enter the office.

"Their small building was made of almost all glass. I looked in, saw those uniforms, and knew *that's* where I had to go.

They would help me. I crossed the street with the crowd and opened the door. The thing I remember most clearly now was one of the men looked at me standing there and said, 'You'll have to come back in a few years, sport.' All the men laughed at that. Then I told them what had happened to me. Like the super-heroes I knew they were, they somehow magically found and contacted my frantic parents. In what felt like minutes, my mother came flying through the door and snatched me up in her arms."

German had heard this story before. One day, when they were trading stories about their lives, Ben told it to her. But the incident had happened to his father fifty years earlier, not to Ben.

Ling entered the living room.

When old Ben saw the ghost he waved to it. "Hey there, how are you?"

"You can *see* me?" Ling said, startled.

"Of course I see you. I don't have much of a memory left but my eyes are still okay."

German turned around to see whom he was addressing. When she saw no one was there, she headed for the kitchen. "I'll just go get the tea things." On her way out she walked straight through Ling again.

They did not have much time to talk before she returned. The ghost could not believe that it was visible to the old man.

"How many fingers am I holding up?"

Old Ben counted and correctly said, "Twelve."

"Do you know my name?"

"Well, sure, Ling. Of course I know your name."

"How?"

The old man slid around on the large leather chair trying to find a more comfortable spot. He had hemorrhoids, which

were a real nuisance sometimes when he was trying to get settled. "We met at the council. Don't you remember? We were
introduced there."

The council was where the recently deceased met their
companion ghosts. Each person brought the ghost up to speed
on what his or her life had been like. When the newly departed
finished the account, the ghost explained what came next. As
soon as the relevant information was exchanged, the dead moved
on to the Afterlife and the ghost went to earth to clear up any
unfinished business the person had left.

Ling now asked, "How old are you?"

"Eighty-three," Ben said proudly.

Almost half a century longer than Benjamin Gould was supposed to have lived.

"How can you remember the council if you're still alive?"

Ben twisted in his seat. The ghost's question didn't appear
to faze him. "I remember a lot of things when my head is clear."
He closed his eyes then, or rather couldn't resist closing them.
He'd found the perfect spot now on the comfortable chair, the
morning's events had worn him out, and even on his best day
this old man had about as much energy as would fill a thimble.
"Let me just rest a minute and then we can talk some more if
you'd like."

But as soon as he closed his eyes, he was transformed back
into Ben Gould at age thirty-four. The metamorphosis took seconds. The process looked very much like a reverse time-lapse
film of a flower coming back to life, the old bent head swiftly
and sinuously lifting, its wilted brown petals paling quickly back
to white. A few seconds later this flower was fully erect, all of
its colors alive, vivid and distinct again.

Thirty-four-year-old Ben opened his eyes, looked dazedly
around at his living room, and rubbed his face with both hands.

He must have been really whacked-out tired to have fallen asleep in the chair. He had no memory of what had just happened. He was not aware of any change. The last thing he clearly remembered was watching German walk away from him when they stood in front of Danielle Voyles's apartment building. Now he was home again and everything was either a mystery or a mess. What was he supposed to do next? No wonder his psyche had demanded a short, coma-deep power nap. It needed to switch to screen saver to sort through all of the input that had arrived lately and see if any sense could be made of it.

"Can you hear me?" Ling the ghost asked now from across the room.

Young Ben could not hear or see the ghost. The dog entered the room but stopped on seeing the younger man sitting in the chair. Pilot looked from his master to the ghost. In response, Ling shrugged and threw up its hands. What was there to say?

As always, the ghost and the dog communicated telepathically.

"What's going on?" Pilot flicked his alert brown eyes from Ben to the ghost.

"See for yourself. *Poof!*—from one moment to the next, back to who he was."

"Yes, Ling, I see that. But how?"

"I do not know. It just happened. I stood here and watched." The ghost added unhappily, "This is all new territory to me, my friend."

"But that old man *was* definitely him, too, right?"

"I think so, yes."

"Well, how could he be an old man if he was supposed to die when he was thirty-four?"

Ling shook its head. "Because he obviously *didn't* die when

he was thirty-four. Look—there he is, very much alive although he was scheduled to die months ago."

"Is this supposed to be funny? Huh? Was all this your idea
of a big joke, Ben?" German stood in the doorway holding a tea
tray, fuming, staring daggers at her ex-boyfriend now turned
malicious prankster.

"German, hi! You're here. What a great surprise." He was
so pleased to see her that what she'd just said didn't register.

"You're a jerk, Ben. On top of everything else, you're a
nasty jerk." She put the tray down on the floor and turned to
get her jacket in the hall. She wanted to escape from this apartment as fast as she could.

Ben jumped up and hurried after her. "Wait. Where are
you going? Wait!" He grabbed her elbow from behind as she
moved away down the hall. Shaking his hand off, she whirled
around to face him and give him the full nuclear blast of her
anger, hurt, and sense of betrayal.

"Was it all a joke? Is this stuff *funny* to you? What happened
in that woman's apartment this morning and those stories you
told me about being invisible to her? Was that part of this stunt
too? Did you enjoy my reaction when we were there?

"I was *scared* for you. In spite of the terrible way you've
treated me, I was so worried about you. That's why I came over
now: because I was so scared for you and wanted to help.

"Then that old man who knew things only you could know.
Old Ben Gould. What a great touch: very clever. So where'd
the old guy go? Did you sneak him out the door while I was in
the kitchen making tea?

"You really tricked me, Ben. So bravo, if that's what
you wanted. Especially those stories about being invisible to
Danielle. And how she totally ignored you in her apartment

as if you weren't there? That was brilliant. Then back here for the coup de grâce with the old man, old Ben Gould. Wonderfully staged. You win today's Oscar for special effects."

She slapped his face and left.

•   •   •

Around midnight, the dog opened the apartment door with both paws as it had done many times before. First, Pilot carried a small oak footstool in his mouth from the living room to the front door. Ben had made that stool in high school shop class and often still sat on it while looking through his books.

Setting it down carefully on the floor, Pilot pushed the stool with his snout up against the front door. Luckily when German was living in the apartment she had replaced the original round doorknob with a horizontal stainless steel one from the 1970s she'd bought at a flea market in Stockholm. She had intended it to be a good luck charm for living with her new boyfriend. Installing it on his door exactly one month after moving in, she insisted that they hold a little ceremony for the new door handle, toasting it and their new life together with champagne. But when it brought no luck, she left it behind when she moved out. All one had to do to open the door was push down on the handle. Ben rarely remembered to lock it.

The trick was not in opening it so much as knowing the exact moment to jump away from the door as it began to swing open. At first, Pilot had a great deal of difficulty gauging this moment. Consequently the dog spent many failed tries getting it right.

Luckily the ghost was never around to witness any of this because Ling slept whenever Ben did. Or if it didn't sleep, it disappeared until Ben woke up in the morning or after a nap. Pilot asked about this but the ghost knew nothing. "I don't know where I go. I guess I sleep, like him."

The dog had its escape procedure down pat by now. Once out of the apartment and in the hall, it pushed the door closed until it was just barely touching the frame. Then Pilot anchored it there with a small thick piece of carpet he kept hidden in the apartment for just this purpose. Next, down the stairs to the basement and out through a window there that was almost always open.

On the street, Pilot looked both ways to make sure no human was around. When he was positive the coast was clear, the dog called telepathically for a guide, a useful perk all dogs had if they ever got lost.

Often—a little *too* often recently—the guide company sent something ridiculous like a Chihuahua to do the job. How many dogs on earth understood Chihuahua? Everyone knew the rule was you could only be guided either by your own breed or one that was at least part of your bloodline. The first time Pilot had called for a guide, an old beagle arrived panting as though it had just run back from the moon and was about to drop dead from exhaustion. The two dogs stared at each other a few long moments and then without a word the beagle walked away. Whatever was in charge of dispatch in this city apparently paid little attention when told what kind of dog needed to be led.

Down the street now a Rottweiler turned a corner and came trotting over. The two made eye contact and Pilot signaled that he had called for a guide. Luckily there was a bit of Rottweiler blood somewhere in Pilot's wild genetic mix, so this guide was fine.

Three feet away, the big black-and-gold dog stopped and said, "Are you ready, sir?"

"Yes."

The Rottweiler came up to Pilot and they started walking. "Nice night, isn't it?"

Trying to keep up with the dog, Pilot looked from side to side and nodded. "Yes. The breeze died down. It was a little windy before."

They chatted while the giant dog moved through town. Pilot had called for a guide tonight because he was unfamiliar with the neighborhood he had to visit.

Like human beings, dogs are creatures of habit. They pee on the same trees; they revisit the same places again and again to sniff. They're not as adventurous as people think. Dogs do not like surprises or change in general, no matter whether they are wild or domesticated. Follow a wild dog around for a while and you'll be surprised at how predictable it is. It follows familiar routes, forages in the same places for food, and only if none is found does it start exploring new territories. When Pilot lived on the street, he had a radius of about five miles he covered day after day. Of course that radius had been drastically reduced since he had been living with people and was walked on a leash. But Pilot didn't mind. So long as he was fed regularly and had a choice of comfortable places to sleep indoors, he didn't miss living free one bit.

"We've gotta slow down some up here because it can be tricky."

Pilot looked at the Rottweiler and asked, "Tricky how?"

"You'll see in a minute. Maybe there won't be anything, but you never can tell at this intersection. I wanted to warn you just in case."

Pilot did not like the sound of that but said nothing.

Soon trouble came at them from two different directions.

Cancer is pink, a pearlescent pink that moves swiftly and low to the ground like thin, beautiful fog. Dogs have the ability to see it but cannot avoid being touched by it if their time has come. Like most animals, dogs can both see and smell diseases.

They learn to recognize the differences between the deadly ones and the nuisances. Unlike humans, dogs also know that happiness can be as fatal as a melanoma. They know that happiness always comes in varying shades of blue, some fatal and others not. Like any illness, when happiness has run its course, time is needed to recuperate from it—sometimes an entire lifetime.

Almost to itself, the Rottweiler muttered, "Cancer coming."

"I see it."

"Let's hope it's not here for either of us."

"Right." The two dogs watched nervously as the colorful mist floated toward them.

Pilot said quietly, "My mother died of cancer. Or that's what I heard. I hadn't seen her for a long time."

When the disease was a few feet away, the Rottweiler unconsciously lowered itself to the ground. "It must be nice being a human being and not have to *see* these things, you know? If you're going to get cancer, then just get it. You don't need to see it coming down the street toward you and then climb up your leg. Damn. I hate this kind of suspense."

"Shhh, be still now," Pilot said.

The mist drifted lazily past them and was gone. Both dogs drooped, their relief palpable.

"When I was young, things like that never bothered me. I'd see cancer coming but never give it a second thought. I was young; it wasn't there for me."

While the guide dog spoke, Pilot peered around for signs of any other danger. Almost immediately he saw one coming. "Look at that! Let's get out of here."

As soon as the Rottweiler saw, it dashed off down the street, heedless of the dog it had been hired to guide across the city.

When any current moment is over, it immediately begins
to lose all shape and color. Like a fish pulled out of the water
and left to die on land, its colors pale and it flops helplessly
around until its life energy ebbs beyond a certain point and it
dies. However, there are some moments that refuse to die. As
they weaken, they stumble and lurch through the now, wreak-
ing havoc. Colliding with lives and events, they leave their mark,
aroma, their *scales*, on everything they touch.

Human beings cannot see or sense these rebellious pieces of
dying time, but again, animals can. They try to avoid them because they know any moment other than the present is at best a
distraction and, at worse, treacherous.

That is why animals behave so strangely sometimes. Why
they leap up from a sound sleep and run out of the room for no
apparent reason. Or they stealthily stalk something no one but
they can see. The truth is they're not stalking something but trying to escape without being seen. They know very well what
they're doing.

With his old, slow legs Pilot knew that he could not outrun
this thing, so the dog stood as still as possible and waited.

This particular piece of past time had no concrete shape
or color, which meant that it must have been dying for a long
while. Inside it, untold numbers of concrete and obscure images swirled. Seeing them, Pilot knew that he was witnessing
some part of history, but which one? The past is immense and
complicated. Encountering this small fading fragment of it was
like seeing a single piece of a jigsaw puzzle and trying to envision what it came from.

"Your name was Dominique Bertaux," the past said to Pilot
as it passed.

On hearing this, the dog's eyes widened in disbelief. He

had to hurry to catch up with the past as it drifted away down the street. "What? What did you say?"

"I *said* your name was Dominique Bertaux. You lived in Mantua, Italy, until you fell off your boyfriend's scooter, broke your back, and died. That was seven years ago." The voice of the past was cordial but plain. It spoke perfect unaccented Dog. "Would you like to see for yourself?"

Before Pilot could reply, the images inside the past slowed to reveal a grinning, ordinary-looking young woman riding on the back of a bottle-green Vespa scooter. She had long brown hair tied back in a ponytail and wore a sleeveless white dress that contrasted nicely with her tanned skin. A knapsack hung on her back while her arms were wrapped tightly around the waist of the scooter driver.

"That's you in your last life."

"I was *human*? That's the worst thing I've ever heard. It's a nightmare. You're sure I was human?"

"Yes. As I said, your name was Dominique Bertaux."

Aghast at this dreadful revelation, Pilot asked shakily, "But then, why don't I understand people when they speak now? I don't understand human language at all."

"Because you're a *dog* now. Dogs don't understand people. But that's about to change. After tonight you will understand human beings. You'll even be able to speak to them if you want."

"Why are you here?"

The past said, "Because I was sent to find you. They know about your sneaking out at night recently and the reason for those meetings that you've been attending. They don't like it. Animals are not supposed to spy on human beings. That's not why you're here and you know it. Besides, these people have been nice to you. Haven't they given you a good home?"

Alarmed at having been discovered and ashamed for his recent shifty behavior, the dog yawned to mask his shame. "Am I in trouble?"

"Yes, Pilot, I'm afraid you are."

• • •

Ben Gould woke with a shudder and then a startled gasp, something he almost never did. Heart thumping in his chest, his mouth was so dry that it felt as if his tongue were stuck to his palate with Velcro.

Blinking up at the dark, he kept licking his lips repeatedly, as if he'd just eaten peanut butter. He tried to will his galloping heartbeat back to normal, but it was difficult. What had he been dreaming about to have caused such a reaction? Ben didn't have big dreams. He didn't have many nightmares, either. He never knew if that meant he was dull or only well balanced.

"I woke you up. It was me."

Hearing an unfamiliar male voice registered somewhere in Ben's mind. But he was still sleepy enough not to understand that it made no sense because no one else had been in the apartment when he went to sleep: just him and the dog.

"Did you hear me? Wake up!"

Now it began to seep into Ben's head. His tongue stopped halfway outside his mouth as it was about to lick his lips again.

"We have to talk."

He turned his head slowly, slowly, to the left. Pilot was standing next to the bed.

"Right now," the dog said to him in a clear tenor voice. "There's all kinds of things I have to tell you."

Pilot had lived in the apartment a little over a month when he was forced to spy on the couple and the ghost. While out one day on a walk with German Landis, they encountered a Weimaraner and its owner. Pilot had never seen them before. At first glance the big silver-brown hunting dog appeared to be only another rambunctious, playful goofball. That irritated Pilot because he didn't like to play. After several attempts at trying to get the older dog to chase him, the Weimaraner walked straight up and asked in an arrogant know-it-all's voice, "Are you really so witless? I guess I had better spell it out then: Please follow me over to that corner so we can talk in private." Pilot was offended and disliked the other dog right away. But he went to the corner of the fenced-in dog zone nevertheless to hear what this wise guy had to say.

Their conversation lasted no more than two minutes. To human eyes it appeared as though they were just doing the familiar circle-and-circle-while-smelling-each-other's-butt routine. But the truth is dogs communicate thirty-seven times faster than human beings. We think when they sniff each other that it's only a hello-how-are-you thing. In reality it's their equivalent of reading every page of the *New York Times* Sunday edition.

The Weimaraner made Pilot an offer he couldn't refuse. The old mutt liked both Ben and German very much and was genuinely grateful that they had adopted and treated him like a canine king. They gave him free rein to sleep on whatever comfortable furniture he liked in their home. His bowl was regularly filled with yummy things to eat. Both people were loving, affectionate, and never unkind to him.

So why did Pilot betray them? Because the Weimaraner said, "Here's the deal: if you *don't* spy on them for us now, in your next life you'll come back as a human being again."

Aghast, Pilot immediately said yes because no fate was worse than that. When it walked back into Ben's apartment that day, the dog was a spy in the house of love.

Wearing only underpants and a T-shirt, Ben Gould followed

Pilot the talking dog now from the bedroom into the kitchen. It was three o'clock in the morning.

When they got there, the dog said to the man, "Open the refrigerator door. I'd do it, but it's easier for you."

Ben swung the door open. The single dim light inside was bright enough in the night-dark to make them both squint. Pilot peered into the fridge.

"Clear off that bottom shelf. We'll need it completely clear. Don't leave anything on it."

Again Ben followed orders without protest. When all of the food was either moved to other shelves or put on the nearby counter, Pilot walked up to the refrigerator and put his head inside. Ben thought the dog was going to take food but that wasn't it.

"Come over here. Put your head in here like me."

"I can't, Pilot, it won't fit. It's too big."

Pilot's tail wagged impatiently. "Then, put it in as far as it will go, Ben. Come on, get in here with me."

Ling stood two feet away, closely watching and listening. The ghost did not know what was happening. Like Ben, it had no idea what Pilot was doing. The dog had not said a word to it since waking Ben. Ling had been taken aback to hear Pilot speak the man's language and *to* the man, no less. While they were walking down the hall to the kitchen, Ling asked what was going on, but Pilot ignored his friend and kept moving. They had never been rude to each other, but this silence was unquestionably rude. That hurt Ling's feelings, on top of everything else. In any event, there was nothing the ghost could do at that point but watch, wait, and hope things would eventually come clear. But the dog held all the cards.

Ben got down on his knees and awkwardly slid forward on them up to the refrigerator. He felt like a complete fool, but what else could he do after what Pilot had divulged in the bedroom? The cold from inside the refrigerator was immediate, sending a shiver over his skin. Hesitantly, feeling ridiculous, he pushed his head forward until his face was almost all the way in.

But that didn't satisfy Pilot. "No, farther—as far as you can go. You've got lots more room."

From behind, it looked as if the dog and the man were worshipping the contents of the refrigerator. On tiptoe, Ling tried to see over their shoulders in case there was something inside the appliance that might explain everything.

"From now on, whenever we need to talk about this subject, we have to do it in here. They can't hear us when we talk inside a refrigerator. I don't really understand why, but I was told it has something to do with the chlorofluorocarbons in the Freon."

Ben turned his head slowly and looked at the dog. The deadpan expression on his face asked, *What* are you talking about?

Pilot saw the look and understood the other's consternation. "I don't understand it, either; I'm just repeating what they said. Whenever we want to talk about this, we have to do it in the refrigerator."

"Any refrigerator?"

"I guess so, Ben. A fridge is a fridge, right?"

"I thought maybe there was something special about this one because—"

"Can we drop that subject now and talk about more important things?" Pilot's voice was brusque; dogs often get frustrated with human beings.

Ben's eyes flared in anger. Suddenly he wanted to wring the dog's neck. How *dare* it be curt, especially after what it had just done to him. And what had it just done to him? Oh, only turned Benjamin Gould's world—his entire system of beliefs, his vision of reality, his perspective on the past, present, and future, God, the Afterlife, redemption, eternal damnation, et cetera—inside out, upside down, and everywhere else but loose. That's all.

Taking a deep calming breath, Ben stuck his head farther into the refrigerator and said, "Tell me the whole thing *again*, very slowly."

Pilot toned down his own impatience with the man and tried to choose the words more carefully this time. "All right: like I said before, in my last life my name was Dominique Bertaux."

Hearing her name again, Ben closed his eyes and kept them closed while the dog spoke. If there had been more room to maneuver in the refrigerator, he would have put his head in his hands.

Dominique Bertaux was Benjamin Gould's girlfriend when he lived in Europe. They met at a Van Morrison concert in Dublin and later she moved with him to Mantua, Italy, when he went there to study cooking. She was charismatic, wickedly funny, and as aimless as a door swinging back and forth in the wind. Ben was never in love with her but most of the time he loved being around her. Dominique was aware of his mixed feelings for her. Yet she chose to remain with him until the next someone or something caught her fancy and she hopped that bus on its way through her life.

Then one day Ben killed her. When they moved to Italy, he bought a brand-new Vespa motor scooter that he had been saving for for a long time. He always went too fast because it was so much fun and liberating to drive. Especially in Mantua, where the streets are ancient, windy, and narrow, and most Italian drivers consider any paved surface okay for motorized vehicles. The machine cost almost nothing to maintain, and having it allowed

Ben to revel even more in his European experience. As a joke, Dominique bought him a pair of cheap fake Ray-Ban Wayfarer sunglasses to wear when he drove the scooter to complete his "Mr. Cool" image. Ironically those sunglasses were the cause of her death.

Driving to lunch at a friend's house in the countryside between Mantua and Bologna, they whizzed past a field full of grazing cows. Dominique cried out loudly, "Ciao, cow!" The wild way she shouted it sounded hilarious. Ben snapped his head back, laughing. In doing so, he dislodged the sunglasses from his nose. When they started to slip down, he took one hand off the handlebars and grabbed for them. That caused the scooter to swerve violently. Dominique flew off backward because she had been waving at the cows with both hands instead of holding on to Ben's waist. The scooter was going forty-five miles an hour. When she hit the road, the impact snapped her back as if it were a pencil. She died before the ambulance arrived.

What Pilot said a few minutes before in the bedroom to convince Ben that he was telling the truth was "Ciao, cow." No one else on earth but Ben knew that those were Dominique Bertaux's last words before she died.

"Now I have to tell you something else," Pilot said.

"Something else? What *else* can you tell me?"

"There's a ghost standing behind you. *Your* ghost: the ghost of you." In a very human gesture, Pilot nodded in Ling's direction.

Ben turned but saw nothing. The ghost looked at the dog as if it had gone mad.

"Show yourself, Ling."

Shocked, the ghost adamantly shook its head no and crossed its arms over its chest for emphasis. The dog had no authority to order it to do this, even if the animal did have the ability to speak to humans now.

"I'm not asking, Ling. I'm *telling* you; it's an order. Show yourself." Pilot's voice was querulous and demanding. He spoke in English, so Ben understood everything that was going on.

The ghost thought, All right, if the dog wants to play things this way, then I can too.

Behind Ben, a new voice spoke from the darkness. "And who gave you the authority, Pilot? I'm supposed to show myself, which breaks every rule in the book, because a *dog* tells me to?" Whoever was in that darkness spoke clearly, their words precise and unemotional.

How often do we recognize our own voice when we hear it played back to us on a tape recorder? Too high or too low, it's almost never the familiar one we hear from inside when we speak. This happened to Ben Gould now on hearing the ghost speak in his own voice. He simply did not recognize it.

Pilot looked at Ben, waiting for a reaction. But after a few moments it was obvious that he didn't recognize the voice. The dog turned back to the ghost and said to it, "Stanley gave me the authority."

Whoever was in the dark gasped and then said, "*Stanley* told you that I should show myself? You actually met Stanley?"

"That's right, Ling. So please come out now."

•   •   •

Ben closed his eyes and slowly slid a forkful of egg into his mouth. Tasting it with eyes closed, paying attention to nothing else in the world but what had just arrived on his tongue, was the only possible way to do this food the justice it deserved. Because without question he had just placed another morsel of masterpiece into his grateful mouth. These were the greatest scrambled eggs he had ever eaten in his life. They were so transcendently good that they almost made him quiver with delight, despite the fact that Benjamin Gould had tasted many scrambled eggs in his life. Maybe they were so good because a ghost had made them for him. This female ghost, named Ling, had asked if he was hungry after telling him who she was and why she was there. She thought it was a good way to calm things down before continuing.

Chewing slowly, he again savored the rich and subtle flavors that somehow swirled and danced into every corner of his mouth. How on earth could a dish this simple taste so spectacular?

When this "Ling" put the first serving of scrambled eggs down in front of him—he was now well into his second and thinking seriously about having a third—he had been more interested in her than the food. But a single whiff of that hot food forced him to lower his eyes to the plate. He made a mental note to get back to her as soon as he had investigated this most remarkable aroma.

That was half an hour ago, and the eggs still held him in their thrall. Although tempted, he hadn't asked for either the ingredients or how she had prepared them. You did not ask a master magician how they performed an astounding trick. That was one of the things Ben loved most about food and cooking: with creativity and imaginative combinations, a masterful cook could make new worlds every time they prepared a meal. Or they could wholly reinvent something as simple as a plate of scrambled eggs.

"It's called Ofi."

Ben was in such a state of bliss that he didn't realize she was addressing him. His eyes remained closed as he chewed. If he'd been a cat he would have been purring.

She waited a few beats and then repeated what she'd said, only this time a bit more forcefully. "It's *called* Ofi."

She'd said the odd word twice now. Both times it sounded so silly that, out of curiosity, Ben opened his eyes to see what she was talking about. Directly across the table she stared at him.

"*Ofi*? What's Ofi?"

"The ingredient that makes those eggs taste so good. You were wondering—"

Straightening his back, Ben asked, "How did you know what I was wondering?"

From down on the floor Pilot said in an annoyed voice, "Because she's a ghost. How many times do you need to be told that?"

Ben dropped the fork loudly onto the plate—threw it down really. A clatter rang off every wall of that three-in-the-morning room. Aggrieved, he protested, "Excuse me! I would like to repeat one more time that everything I ever believed in my whole life has either been destroyed or hijacked tonight, okay? Every single thing. *Tutti*. And you, Pilot, are one of the hijackers. So if I'm not quite up to *speed* yet with female ghosts, being dead, talking dogs, and Ofi, then you'll just have to be a little more patient with me, okay? Okeydoke?"

"*Ofi*doke," Pilot said in a smart-ass voice, and then tried to catch Ling's eye. But the ghost was embarrassed by the man's rant and wouldn't make eye contact.

Ben had had enough. "What? What did you say?" Despite the heavenly meal, he was about to explode with frustration. The tone of his voice announced that loud and clear.

"I said *all right*, Ben, we'll go more slowly."

The air in the kitchen felt like the air in August just before a ripping thunderstorm: electric, loaded, and physically heavy. None of them wanted to speak first after that exchange between the man and the dog.

Eventually, Ling said gently, "You don't remember Ofi?"

Ben's eyes flicked over to the woman to see if she meant her question seriously. She almost flinched at the hostility in his eyes.

"No, I don't remember *Ofi*."

Looking at her hands, Ling thought, How do I say this without making things worse?

Ben watched her but kept an eye on Pilot, too, just in case the mutt had another trick up his sleeve.

"Do you remember Gina Kyte?"

"Yes, of course." Ben did not ask how this stranger knew about Gina Kyte, his first great love in nursery school. He could almost hear the dog say in a mocking voice, "She knows because she's a *ghost*."

"Well, then, do you remember when you used to pretend to hand food back and forth to each other when you were playing on the swings?"

Ben remembered those swings. He remembered the park they were in and the tall chestnut trees that brushed them over and over with summer shadows while they played together. He distinctly remembered the blue cartoon lambs on Gina's white sneakers and how her mother used to give them M&M's candies out of a big black-and-white bag. He remembered a lot about Gina Kyte and their many dazzling days together, but not this pretend-food part.

After he remained silent awhile Ling said, "Gina used to give you Ofi."

"What are you talking about?"

Down on the floor, curled around himself the way dogs do when they settle in to sleep, Pilot went *tsk*. How long was this going to take? Luckily the man was too focused to hear the dog's grumblings.

"Ofi was Gina's magical meal only for you. You know the way children play at things. Whenever you two played husband and wife or kitchen together, she made Ofi for you."

"What does that have to do with this?" Ben asked while pointing to his plate.

"You like those eggs so much because I put Ofi on them."

"But I don't understand what *Ofi* is!"

Ling said, "It's love and magic; it's a kid's imagination made real. Gina Kyte loved you and made up a name for her love: Ofi. Whenever she pretended to feed you something, she said it was called Ofi. You loved her, too, which is why you pretended to eat it.

"So I went back into your past, found her love, made it real, and sprinkled it over those eggs. *That's* why you like them so much—because you taste Gina Kyte's love again. Nothing is more delicious than childhood love."

Like a generous summer breeze that appears out of nowhere, cools for a few seconds, and then is gone, Ben had a moment's vivid memory of the blue lambs on Gina's favorite sneakers as they flew back and forth together on swings. Both kids were pretending to put food in their mouths and chew it. Gina reached over and snatched at Ben's imaginary food. He turned quickly away as if to guard it; his gesture made them both laugh.

When the memory ended, he said "Ofi" again. Picking up the fork, he touched it to the eggs left on the plate. "I don't remember that word, but I believe you. Gina was always making up crazy words for things. I remember that about her." Lost in a memory of lost times, Ben stared at the plate and didn't look up. He could not resist saying "Ofi" again under his breath. He blew slowly through his lips as if having just completed either a difficult task or a sad one.

Placing the fork gently and silently on the table, he looked up at Ling and asked, "Why are you both here? What is this all about?"

 •   •   •

"What do you see?" The woman asked the man as they stood side by side on the edge of the playground, watching the many children inside the enclosed area having loud fun. Two large chestnut trees in full summer bloom, planted long ago in the middle of the space, swayed luxuriantly overhead in the wind.

Off to one side was a set of swings, two of which were occupied by a little girl and boy.

The man watched them intently, but the expression on his face was neutral. "Are we allowed to get any closer?"

"No, this is it. No farther. You cannot have contact with them. It's not possible."

He accepted this and said no more. He was fascinated particularly with the little girl's shoes, which were covered in blue cartoon lambs. His mind tried to bring it all back into focus: what he was seeing, what he remembered, what he had been told.

The first thing that surprised, then amused, but finally touched him the most was how homely Gina Kyte was. Her large face did not have one distinguishing or attractive feature on it. A nose too flat, a weak chin, and eyes that were about as distinctive as two thumbtacks in a corkboard. You would not have looked twice at this girl if you saw her on the street. No admiring glances would ever have tagged along behind her as she walked through her young life. No one would ever say about her, "Wow, *that* little girl is going to be a knockout when she grows up." If anything, they would look at her plain puss and think, She'll probably look exactly the same when she's forty. And they'd be right.

Perhaps even worse was her voice. Although the two adults were standing at least twenty feet away from the kids, they could still hear the shrill semi-whine of Gina's voice whenever she bossed little Ben Gould around, which was most of the time. Do this. Don't do that. Give me that—it's mine . . . Her voice was all orders and gripe.

When Ling had pointed out the children and they had watched them awhile, adult Ben transfixed, he had twice asked if that really was the Gina he had known. He simply could not believe what he was seeing. *That* child over there was the little girl who had owned his heart so completely for years? It had been almost an entire lifetime since he last saw her, granted, and he knew any memory of a childhood crush was always backlit by time in loving colors. But, still, this little bossy shrieker was the one?

Surprisingly it was seeing Gina's mother, Mrs. Kyte, sitting on a park bench a few feet away from the children, that had convinced him it was true. Simply because Mrs. Kyte looked almost exactly as he remembered her. Was that how memory worked? The bit players in your life you remember as clearly as if they were figures in a photograph. But the main characters, the ones closest or most important to your soul, are frequently smudged or distorted by time and experience? How strange and wrong that was if it was the truth.

In a downcast voice he mumbled, "She was so pretty. I remember Gina as being so pretty." Ben turned to Ling while he spoke, as if it were imperative that she hear him say this.

The ghost hesitated and looked away in sympathy but did not respond. She could have. She could have said things that would have instantly lifted ten veils from in front of both his eyes and his understanding, allowing him to see a hundred miles into the distance. But she did not do that. She did not tell him those things. Ben had to figure everything out for himself or else it would be like breaking open an eggshell to help the chick inside get out. You could do that easily, but it did more harm than good.

"What do you see, Ben?"

"You asked that before. What am I *supposed* to see?" His voice was tight with frustration. If it had been a hand, it would have been a fist now.

Ling ignored the tone of his voice and spoke evenly. "Just tell me what you see."

"A playground. Kids. A park. Me and Gina Kyte as kids. Am I missing something?"

"Look some more."

" 'Look some more.' She tells me to look some more. Gina loved licorice. How's that? I just remembered it."

Ling didn't respond. Ben was stalling for time and both of them knew it.

He crossed his arms. "All right, so what am I supposed to be looking *for*? Is there any one special direction I should be looking in?"

Ling smiled mysteriously, signifying who knows what. Without another word she walked away from him and sat down on a bench.

Ben didn't know what to make of this woman but he sure wasn't going to make her angry. God only knew what ghosts did when they were mad at you. What he couldn't get over was how nondescript she was. All of his life he had passed women like Ling on the street and never given them a second glance. Why should he? She was mid-everything. Five foot three or four, mid-length hair the color of an old brown wallet, brown eyes that gave no sign of anything special behind them, and a body that had a few curves but nothing wowie. The only amazing thing about her was how well she could cook. *This* was a ghost? This was *his* ghost? This is what populated the Afterlife?

He had been sneaking peeks at her ever since she'd appeared in his apartment and revealed her identity, but he still couldn't get over it. *This* was a ghost?

A child walked up to the fence near Ben and, addressing him directly in a commanding lisp, said, "Stop wasting time thinking about that and look around you instead." Without another word, the child turned and ran back into the playground hubbub. Feeling as though he'd been caught in the act, Ben looked at Ling sitting on the bench. She widened her eyes and wagged a scolding finger at him, as if to emphasize what the little kid had just said. Get going—do what I told you. No more dillydallying.

He thought about all of the books and corny movies he had seen where this same scenario was played out ad nauseam: the novice commanded by the wise man (or woman) to look closely at the world around them and try to see through the surface of it into the heart of the matter. It was such a cliché. That's what this situation was: a living cliché. He wanted to walk over to Ling and say exactly that. But, judging by recent experience, she already knew what he was thinking. Maybe saying something confrontational would set her off. Then the ghost might do something grisly to Ben and he would never find out the meaning of all this.

So he did as he was told and looked carefully around the park. He did not know the names of flowers or trees. The subject had never interested him, so he had never made the effort to learn. He knew that the big trees in the center of the playground were chestnuts, but only because as children he and Gina had collected the nuts in their prickly green or yellow jackets after they fell from the trees. It was always one of the first signs that summer was ending. Accompanied by their parents every year, the two inseparable friends brought their full bags of chestnuts to the city zoo, where they were purportedly fed to the animals there. Neither child ever saw that happen, but they hoped it was true because it made them both feel useful.

Staring into the trees now, adult Ben put up a hand to shade his eyes against the sun dappling down through the leaves. Looking toward the playground again, he saw that little Ben and Gina were swinging high and hard side by side but staring straight ahead and not speaking to each other. Both of their faces were set and very serious. Most likely they were having a contest to see who could swing higher. He remembered that, too: how in the old days he and Gina were always competing for everything. Who could swing the highest, who could find more chestnuts, who could stuff the most potato chips into his or her mouth at one time without laughing.

For a few seconds, on the far periphery of his vision, Ben saw someone vaguely familiar. But the person didn't really register in his thoughts because Ben was too caught up in the scene close by.

Yes, he had seen this man before, but he didn't remember that. The memory was lost in the reality of what was happening right now. Ben Gould was in the presence of himself as a child. At the same time, he was trying to do what the ghost had ordered: see beyond what he was seeing.

Ling watched Ben watching the children. That was a real mistake on her part, especially since she knew she was supposed to be vigilant at all times when they were together. As a result, for too many valuable seconds the ghost did not see the man moving steadily toward them.

The bum's eyes were much clearer and calmer today than the night he had stabbed Ling's boss. In fact, Stewart Parrish looked altogether different today despite the fact he was still obviously a street person. That might have been one of the reasons that he didn't immediately register in either of their minds.

There are bums and there are *bums*. The worst look as if they are simply waiting for Death to pass by and notice them. If it's in a charitable mood, instead of dropping a coin in their filthy outstretched hands, Death will say, "Okay, you can come with me today." And these human fingernail clippings will be relieved. Because the only dim signs of life left in them by then are mutter, stupor, and stagger.

On the opposite end of that number line are the almost-bums, the ones who are either new to the role or still holding on tenuously to scraps of hope and tattered dignity. They've come to some kind of cul-de-sac in life, for sure, but they haven't given up yet. Not so far past the days of a real job, responsibilities, and a deserved place at the table, they still dress and act decently most of the time, albeit oddly. A good many of them carry combs that they use and wear their hats tipped at jaunty angles. They check their appearance in mirrors. If they have an odor, it is mostly from infinite numbers of cigarettes and the kind of cheap booze sold at the nearest market. It's a strong smell if you get too close to them, but not so bad.

These almost-bums often say funny or striking things when begging for money.

"Would you give me a hundred dollars, please?"

"A *hundred* dollars? That's asking a lot."

"Yes, well, I'm an optimist."

It's hard not to smile at their wit. More often than not you give them a few coins for having brightened your day an inch or two.

The last time Ben Gould encountered this bum now walking their way, Stewart Parrish had been an alarming wreck of a human being. Today he looked as though he lived just on the outskirts of normal. He was wearing a threadbare gray pin-striped suit that nevertheless looked pretty good and almost fit. A road-cone–orange shirt was buttoned right up to the top of his neck. Heavy-duty brown Red Wing work boots entombed his long feet. He'd had a haircut not long ago. He was not filthy, nor did he reek of fetid, sickening things, as he had the last time Ling and Ben had seen him. Most important, his eyes were clear: he was entirely present in the moment and not *persona non gravity*, as he had been that horrifying night in the pizza place. He was all here today and clearly focused on what he had been sent to do.

Both Ben and Ling smiled as they watched the two children leap off their swings together in mid arc. They soared through the air a short way before landing with the natural grace and elastic legs only kids possess. Next they ran over to Mrs. Kyte, who spilled M&M's candies into their small cupped hands from a black-and-white bag.

Ling was wondering what the candy tasted like when she caught a glimpse of Stewart Parrish. He entered her line of sight at a distance as he moved purposely toward them.

Seeing the bum, the ghost stood up and walked straight over to Ben. "We have to leave here right now. *Right now*."

"What are you talking about? We just got here."

"Listen to me, Ben: Remember the tramp who came into the restaurant and stabbed the guy? He's here now in this park and he's coming to get you."

"*Me*? Why? Where is he?"

She pointed toward Parrish, now only thirty or thirty-five feet away.

"What do we do? He'll be here in a second."

Ling said, "Tell me a place where you felt safe in your child-hood. We'll go there. It'll take them a while to figure it out and find us. By then we'll be gone. Come on, come up with a place."

Watching Parrish approach, Ben said, "Gina's basement. The Kytes' basement playroom."

Ling and the bum made eye contact and then she suddenly disappeared. That slowed him. He hadn't come for the ghost, though, but for the man. It took Ben several seconds longer to vanish, but he was gone, too, by the time Parrish reached where they had been standing.

Impressed, the bum rubbed his jaw and said a long "Hmm." Unfazed, he walked over to a bench and sat near where Ling had been only minutes before. From that vantage point he turned his full attention to the two children nearby eating M&M's candies, one by colorful one. Embroiled in a heated disagreement about who had won the swinging contest, they were completely oblivious to the shabby-looking man in the orange shirt.

Five

"This was not a good idea."

Ben blew out his lips in annoyance at the obviousness of Ling's statement. Still, he felt defensive about having chosen to come here. "I know. But how was I supposed to know, you know?"

"How long do you think they'll be?" Ling whispered.

"I don't know."

"Well, do you think you could at least move over a little and give me some more room?"

"Move to where, Ling? We're in a closet!" Ben whispered.

The basement playroom of Gina Kyte's house was decorated in a kind of combination pirate ship/tiki lounge motif. While in the Navy, Mr. Kyte had been stationed in Honolulu. He had tried to recreate the look of his favorite bar there in the basement of his house. He even gave it the same name as the bar: The Boom Boom Room.

On the walls were fake-flower leis, a hula skirt, a copy of a pirate hat expertly carved out of balsa wood, models of sailing ships, three loud Hawaiian shirts, lots and lots of bamboo, et cetera. The façade of the bar itself was a construction of coconut-shell halves glued together. It didn't look good but it certainly looked genuine.

Mr. Kyte prided himself on being an adept and creative drink "mixmeister." He spent many hours in his Boom Boom Room trying out different recipes for exotic cocktails.

"What is that awful music? It's giving me a headache."

"Don Ho."

"Don't be rude, Ben. I was only asking about the music."

"I was answering you: the singer's name is Don Ho. He was famous back then for his Hawaiian music."

"Is that what that is, Hawaiian music? It's terrible. What's he saying?"

" 'E lei ka lei lei.' "

"What?" Ling lowered her chin and looked doubtfully at Ben to check if he was joking.

He wasn't. "You heard me. I know those words by heart. That's the title to one of his most famous songs. Gina used to play this record all the time when we came down here."

Out in the playroom Mr. and Mrs. Kyte were sitting next to each other on a couch covered with a yellow and flaming red batik bedspread. They were sipping strawberry-banana daiquiris that Mr. Kyte had created from scratch and fresh fruit especially bought for this occasion. Both of them were naked. That is, except for matching magenta flip-flop sandals on their feet, which Mrs. Kyte insisted they wear because she was a bit neurotic about bugs that lived on basement floors.

The kids were in bed, the phone was off the hook, and their favorite music was playing in the background. The stage was set for the time both Kytes anticipated most all week: Pupu Platter Night in the Boom Boom Room.

On a wobbly bamboo table in front of the couch a platter

was filled to overflowing with a savory variety of hors d'oeuvres and finger food. Whenever they went to a Trader Vic's restaurant, the Kytes always ordered a pupu platter and this was their home version.

Grape-leaf *dolmadakias* and feta cheese fresh from the Greek grocer, little cocktail hot dogs in golden-brown rolls just out of the oven, potato chips and crinkle-cut carrot sticks for Mrs. Kyte's secret-recipe crab dip, celery stalks filled with cream cheese and dusted with their favorite Hungarian paprika . . . the couple had the fixings for their platter down to a science. Some of the things were specifically for her, some for him. Most of the selection they liked equally.

In the closet, Ling sniffed the air. Ben was squatting down with his face to the door, trying to see anything out there through the keyhole.

"What do you see?"

"Pubic hair."

"What?"

Twisting uncomfortably, he looked up at Ling. "The only thing I can see from here is their pubic hair. I have a perfect view of their crotches."

"Oh. Uh, we really do have to get out of here."

"Yeah, well, you're the ghost. How about a magic spell? Make us invisible or something."

She shook her head. "No can do."

"Why not?"

"It's technical. You wouldn't understand."

The rich unmistakable aroma of marijuana glided under the door and into their noses. *That's* what Ling had been sniffing before: cannabis.

Ben's eyes widened. "The Kytes are smoking grass! Gina's parents were potheads?" He rejoiced at this new revelation.

Don Ho stopped and was replaced on the record player a few moments later by the Moody Blues' classic album *Days of Future Passed*. Ben hadn't heard that one in years. Smoking dope and listening to the Moody Blues. Gina's parents toking up naked in the Boom Boom Room while Gina slept upstairs. Ben relished the whole picture. He was so glad to be here if only for this moment alone.

"You can't change anything when you visit it."

Ben's concentration was all on the Kytes when Ling made this statement. It took a while for his mind to change course and tack toward what she'd just said.

"What do you mean by 'change'?"

"I can bring you to any place in your history, any place in your past. But there are two conditions: Whenever you want to leave, you must find the way out of these places by yourself. I can't help you. The second condition is that wherever you do choose to visit, you can't have any contact with the people, and you can't change anything there, although you may want to very much. It's not possible."

"Did you just hear something?" Mr. Kyte asked in his stern voice. The music stopped and was followed by a long silence.

Next came the sound of frantic scurrying in the basement playroom as the Kytes tried to put on their bathrobes and erase all traces of the marijuana at the same time.

"What do we do now?" Ben mouthed the words silently to Ling. She held up a hand for him to be still and see how this played out.

Before the Kytes came downstairs, there had been fifteen minutes when Ben and Ling had had the Boom Boom Room to themselves. Ling sat on the couch while Ben moved slowly around, getting reacquainted with this landmark from his past.

His fingertips as much as his mind helped him to recall. He touched everything; he needed to touch everything.

"Is it like you remember? Is any of it familiar?" she asked.

"Most of it, yes. But some things are different, for sure. The smell is different. I remember there being a completely different smell in here."

"Or maybe it's the same smell but *you've* changed. Now you perceive it differently."

"True. That's possible. It was a long time ago." Carrying that thought with him, he continued to move around the room looking, touching, and remembering. As if he were visiting one of the many rooms of the Museum of Me.

Because he was so absorbed, Ben did not see the jolt of fear on Ling's face when she first heard footsteps on the stairs coming down to the basement. Her face relaxed when she heard the Kytes speak. When Ben heard their voices, he quickly pointed to the closet off to one side of the playroom. They hurried to hide in there before the couple arrived in their bathrobes and high spirits.

As children, Gina and Ben had played in that closet a hundred times. They hid treasures there. They hid themselves from the outside world. Secrets were revealed in the tiny room that otherwise might never have been spoken in the light of day. Calmed by the still, stale air and murk, Gina stopped being bossy and aggressive. It was another world in the closet for them, a stop-time zone where nothing happened unless they imagined it. The perfect place for hiding, dreaming, and pretending. When they were inside that closet, lions and dragons roared just outside the door, or bad guys searched for them everywhere but always to no avail. In there they were safe from everything.

Far off in the distance a doorbell rang again. It sounded much louder this time because the music was gone. Out in the playroom the Kytes looked at each other. Who came to the door at this time?

"Were you expecting someone?"

"At ten o'clock at night? No! Were you?"

Worried that the bell would ring again and wake the children, Mrs. Kyte hurried out of the room and up the stairs. Mr. Kyte took a fat carrot stick off the platter, dunked it deep in the crab dip, and followed his wife.

Back at the keyhole, Ben saw Mr. Kyte leave and heard him climbing the stairs. When certain the couple was gone, Ben opened the door. The playroom was empty and reeked of marijuana. They walked out of the closet and left the basement via an adjacent door that opened onto the backyard.

Once outside, Ling put a hand on Ben's elbow and held him. "I think something's wrong here. We'd better wait and see what happens to them."

"Do you think the person at the door is that bum?"

"I don't know, but it could be. Let's go around to the front and try to see."

Mrs. Kyte had answered the door but now was standing behind her husband while he spoke to Stewart Parrish.

"I knew it! I knew it'd be him. But how did he find you so fast?"

"Shh! I can't hear what they're saying."

Unfortunately for them, the others were too far away to hear their conversation clearly. They had to rely instead on watching the two men's body language toward each other and the faint smattering of words that drifted over to them across the evening quiet.

Stewart Parrish looked the same as he had earlier in the park: suit, orange shirt, work boots. Both hands rested in his trouser pockets. He appeared relaxed as he spoke to Gina's father.

"What if he stabs Mr. Kyte?"

"He won't. He can't mess around with your past or the people in it. He can only watch, like we're doing."

Ben wasn't convinced. "Are you sure, Ling? You didn't expect him to stab your partner that night, but he did."

The ghost frowned, because Ben was right. Even her boss had been surprised that it happened.

"Maybe *you* follow the rules, but obviously he doesn't."

"All right, Ben, I get your point. Let me think about this."

But she had no time to think because Parrish suddenly tried to shove his way into the Kyte house.

"He can't do that. He can't interfere with your past! He's coming for you in the past. He can't do that!"

"Looks like that's exactly what he's doing, Ling."

Mr. Kyte hit Parrish on the side of the head with what looked like a fast karate chop. The bum stumbled backward onto the front lawn, lost his balance, and fell down hard.

Delighted, Ling couldn't stop blurting a triumphant "Hah!" that was drowned out by Mrs. Kyte's loud wail to her husband to come back into the house and call the police.

The scene at the door froze. Kyte kept his arm raised while glaring at the stranger, ready to hit him again if he tried coming into the house. Mrs. Kyte cowered behind her husband. She wanted to run back inside to call the police but was petrified that if she didn't stay here, something worse might happen to her man. Parrish remained sitting on the ground, arms stretched out behind him to prop himself up. He grinned but his eyes were unclear, as if still gaga from the punch in the head.

Kyte pointed at him. "Stay away from my house. Get outta here right now."

Ben leaned over to Ling and said in a low voice, "Kyte knows karate. That guy better do what he says."

Ling snorted. "That *guy* is not afraid of karate, believe me. If he wanted to, he could turn Mr. Kyte into a chicken. Or an omelet."

"Can't you stop him?"

Ling shook her head. "I don't know."

Slowly rising to his feet, Parrish brushed off his hands on his jacket. Kyte and his wife tensed. Neither had ever dealt with a madman before.

Billie, the family's hyperactive cocker spaniel, came racing out of the house and onto the front step, delighted by all the people out there. He looked eagerly back and forth between his owners, hoping for a little love. When they ignored him, the young dog stepped down onto the lawn and wiggled over to Parrish. Mrs. Kyte started to say something but resisted.

The bum looked glad for the diversion. Bending down, he rubbed the caramel-colored animal with two hands all over its body. Billie loved that and wriggled like a hula dancer, licking the man's hands whenever they were within range. Parrish kept petting the dog and didn't look up.

"Hey, mister, did you hear me? Take off *now*, before I call the cops."

Parrish was rubbing Billie's back fast and hard, up and down with both hands. Suddenly he grabbed the fur on either side of the dog's neck and yanked it up into the air until it was as high as his head. Billie squealed and twisted, terrified that its world had gone from ecstasy to agony in seconds.

Parrish looked at the couple and then at their screeching dog. Amused, he watched the cocker spaniel writhe in the air in front of its owners. A small sign of what he could do, of what he just might do to these people at any second.

But then Parrish saw something and froze. His smile vanished. It was something on the dog. He saw a few inches of something on its body that instantly made him drop Billie and, to everyone's astonishment, run away as fast as he could. The dog ran back into the house.

Ling and Ben were as mystified as the others. All four of them stared in disbelief as the sinister Parrish sprinted out of the yard and tore off down the street. What they couldn't see and would have deepened the mystery even more was the look of fright on his face.

A minute or two passed. The Kytes gradually moved again. The man turned to his wife and asked, "What was *that* all about?" She began pulling on his sleeve to come back into the house. She was afraid the bum would return and the madness would start all over again.

But her stubborn husband wasn't ready to go inside yet. What the heck was going on? he wanted to know. One minute that lowlife was trying to push his way into their house, then he tortured the dog, and then just as suddenly he ran away.

"Please, Ron, please. For me, just come inside."

"But who was that? I want to know who the hell that was!"

Mrs. Kyte began to cry. She had reached her limit. She only wanted it to be half an hour ago again: the mood, the playroom, the music, them alone and safe and sexy. She wanted to be inside their house with the door closed, her family secure from scary out-of-control things like this.

Adding to the surrealism of the moment, a car drifted slowly by out on the street, its radio booming Gene Pitney singing "It Hurts to Be in Love."

"*Please*, Ron."

"All right, okay." His eyes swept the perimeter one last time, making sure no other threat was near before he went in. Ling and Ben crouched down so he didn't see them.

Trying to lure her man inside faster, Mrs. Kyte said, "I'll go downstairs and get the food. We can eat it in the living room."

"I'm not hungry anymore" was the last thing Ron Kyte said before the front door closed. Ling and Ben could hear the sound of locks being swiftly turned.

"All right, please explain that."

"I can't, Ben. I have no idea what just happened."

"Is he gone? Do we have to worry about him coming back?"

Ling shook her head. When she spoke, her voice was rattled. "I don't know. He was coming to get you but something really scared him away."

"It definitely had something to do with their dog. He saw something on the dog and that was it. *Voom*—he was outta here."

"Was it in the park? Was that dog with Mrs. Kyte when we were watching the kids?"

"Yes. It was sitting on the ground beside her. Mrs. Kyte loved Billie. She took him everywhere. I remember him always sitting on the backseat of their car yipping."

After making sure no one was around, they walked out of the backyard. The neighborhood was empty and silent. It was a Tuesday night in the middle of Benjamin Gould's childhood. The street was instantly recognizable to him despite decades having passed. He kept seeing things—unimportant details like a certain purple mailbox or model of car parked in a driveway—that made it even more real and familiar.

"Do you mind if we walk around here for a few minutes? I want to look at things, see what I can remember."

"Sure. Take as long as you need." Ling had barely finished saying this when the first one raced past very near to them on the sidewalk. Its incredible speed was what first grabbed their attention. Whatever it was was there and gone and then disappearing over the horizon all within seconds.

"What was *that*?"

"I don't know, but did you see how fast it moved?"

Another sped by in the same direction as the first, only this one ran out in the middle of the street. What they saw was white, stocky, and low to the ground, and appeared to be running on four legs. An animal? Was it possible any animal could move so fast?

Two more whizzed past and then two more. All were going in the same direction, all traveling at blur speed. Ben and Ling were better able to see this bunch, though, because they were watching the street now.

"They're dogs."

"No way, Ling. No dog can run that fast."

"They're dogs," she said with certainty.

Three more came next, moving side by side, rushing, flying by.

Before either Ben or Ling could say anything, yet another appeared. But this one stopped two feet away from them.

It was even whiter than they had thought. It was luminous, like the part of a white candle closest to the lit flame. It sniffed them the way any curious dog would. Sniffing their feet, it wagged its long, thin tail.

Their first impression was that it *was* a dog, but on closer inspection they saw they were wrong. The thick, muscular body probably weighed forty pounds. Its small head was square and formidable-looking, like a bulldog's, except there were no ears. None at all, not even holes. The eyes were set high and far apart on either side of the head, and they were too large for a dog. They looked like the eyes of a much bigger animal. The nose was flat and sand brown. Soundlessly it sniffed both of them for ten seconds straight.

The ghost and the man were spellbound. They stared in

wonder at its body as it busily smelled them. From head to tail the creature's white skin was festooned with thin purple veins. Ben longed to reach down and touch the skin, which was both so brilliantly white and scored everywhere with purple lines. Did that vivid violet rise above the skin or live flat beneath it? Although tempted, he didn't try to touch it because he was afraid doing that might scare the creature away.

His next thought was that its white skin was so thin and hairless, so translucent, that perhaps all of those purple veins were . . . but no: looking more closely now, Ben realized they were not veins at all.

It was writing—writing and what must have been hundreds of tiny, intricately detailed images. The white body was covered with what looked like *doodles*. The kind of mindless doodles one draws on a piece of paper while talking on the telephone. There were single words, all of them in English, numbers and individual letters, objects and faces. He recognized a lawn mower, a clock, a pineapple, and a sneaker. He knew this whatever-it-was animal would run off at any moment, so Ben tried to remember as many images as possible that were on the skin so that he could review them later. But that was difficult to do because the body was adorned with so many different things.

In the distance came a short keening sound that meant nothing to either person. But it did to the creature because it sped off as soon as it heard.

To Ben's surprise, Ling started moving too.

"Where are you going?"

She pointed forward. "That's where Parrish ran when he got scared, and now that's where they went too. Coincidence? I don't think so."

Ben joined her and they jogged along side by side in silence. He didn't want to go, but he didn't want to stay there alone, either, and take the chance of seeing the bum when he was alone. Choosing the lesser of two evils, he went with the ghost.

Several times along the way he wanted to stop and look longer at what they were passing. He remembered this street so well. Personal landmarks and places on it were old acquaintances or the X-marks-the-spots of childhood adventures he hadn't thought about in decades: the big white painted rock next to Olga Baran's driveway that had doubled as home plate whenever they played Wiffle ball. The house of horrible Mr. Shimkus. The small swimming pool in the Kellens' backyard that he glimpsed as they ran past it. Caroline Kellen's parents let the neighborhood kids use their pool in the summer so long as there was an adult in attendance to act as lifeguard. Somehow they always managed to find one.

Gina lived on Cinnamon Street, which Ben had always thought was the coolest address in the world. As an adult, on hearing a song called "Cinnamon Street" by the pop group Roxette, he was genuinely offended. It felt as though they had stolen that name from his memory. "Cinnamon Street" was not the name of a second-rate rock song to Ben Gould; it was an essential place on the map of his life.

At the end of the neighborhood the street dipped down and began a long curve to the right. The houses thinned out there as the road entered a small forest that led to the town elementary school. Street lamps lit the way. Just behind one of these lamps towered three giant elm trees that marked the beginning of the forest.

The white body lay beneath these trees.

On seeing it, Ben and Ling ran over and squatted down close by. Lying on its side, the animal looked asleep. Its eyes were closed and, strangely, those eyes appeared a good deal smaller now; they had shrunk. All four of its paws were curled in toward the body. The violet images on its white skin were fading. Soon every single one of them would be gone. Ears had sprouted on its head where a dog's ears are. Whatever this extraordinary being had been, in death it was transforming now into a dog. If anyone were to find its body by the side of the road, they would naturally assume the poor pup had been struck by a passing car. Probably trying to cross the road at night and unlucky. Just another road kill, nothing more.

"Where are the rest of them?"

Ben didn't care about the white animals at that moment: he cared about the bum. "I want to know where the guy is."

When she stood up, Ling lost her balance and began to teeter. Throwing back her head, she reached out a hand to steady herself by gripping Ben's shoulder. Once she was okay again, she continued looking up.

"What if he's still around here?" Jumpy at the possibility, Ben stood, too, and looked around the area in the false harsh light of the street lamp.

"You don't have to worry about him anymore."

"How do you know? If the guy can stab your friend and then kill one of these cute things . . ." He looked at Ling and waited for an answer. He hoped she had one. He hoped this ghost would say something in her nice manly voice that put his mind at ease.

Silently, Ling pointed up. She pointed toward what she had seen a moment before when she lost her balance. Ben's eyes followed the line of her finger but were off in his perception. He saw only trees and a lot of darkness.

"What? What am I looking for?"

"In that tree, there. Up towards the top."

In that tree towards the top was a bright orange man's shirt—an unforgettably loud orange. Although empty, it was still buttoned all the way up. The shirt was caught on two branches. With no wind blowing, it hung between them like a glowing flag or a caught kite.

If it had been daytime and they had walked around to the other side of the thick tree, they would have seen a pair of empty pinstriped trousers dangling from a lower branch. On the ground almost directly below the pants was one heavy work boot.

"Whoa! Was that his shirt?"

"Yes."

"You're sure, Ling?"

"I'm sure." Her eyes did not move from the tree.

"What did they do to him? Where'd he go?"

The ghost shrugged; it didn't care. "Whatever they did to him, he killed one of them first."

What lay on the ground nearby looked like nothing more than a dead white dog now, some kind of boxer/bulldog mix.

"I've heard about them, but this is the first time I've ever seen one. I'm almost positive it's a verz. That bunch of them came to protect you, Ben. They camouflage themselves as dogs until you need them and then they turn into that."

"Who sent them?"

Ling shook her head. "Honestly, I don't know. I know my bosses lied to me when they explained why they wanted me to come and keep an eye on you. Now verzes are here to protect you . . . I'm out of my league, Ben. Sorry." The mixed tone of despair and bitterness in her voice indicated she was telling the truth.

Ben asked, "What's a verz?"

· · ·

After so much excitement that night, even the cocker spaniel was tired. When the adults gently pushed the dog out of their bedroom and closed the door, he climbed the stairs to the second floor and made his way to Gina's room at the back of the house. Billie knew he was always welcome to sleep on the little girl's bed.

As usual her door was open because Gina didn't like the dark. She asked her parents to leave her door open at night so she could see the light burning at the end of the hall. She also liked it when Billie lay next to her. But the young dog was restless and almost never slept a whole night through. At some point he would invariably hop off her bed, walk through the house, drink some water, and sniff things; only after a satisfying walkabout would he climb the stairs again and get back into bed with the girl. Sometimes he did this more than once a night. But Gina was used to his fidgeting. She slept through the dog's comings and goings.

Walking into her room now, he leapt up onto a corner of the narrow bed, balled himself up, and prepared to sleep. But then he felt his stomach needed biting, so the dog raised his head again and went to work. He nibbled and licked as dogs do, stopped, and then went right back to it.

If there had been a light in the room and someone were looking closely, they would have seen bewildering things on a small patch of the animal's skin. About the size of a coin, very faint lines, designs, and drawings covered the dog's right inner thigh near its anus. But these markings were mostly hidden under fur and in an obscure place on the dog's body. Hardly anyone ever saw them because, unless you looked hard, they were almost impossible to see. But Stewart Parrish saw them and seconds later he was running for his life.

Satisfied with the biting work he'd done on his stomach, Billie curled himself into a dog ball and fell quickly to sleep.

Six

German Landis did not like to shop. She did not like walking into any store and having to choose. She didn't like being put on the spot. As a result, whenever she was forced to do it, she either came with a detailed list in hand of things to find or an exact idea of what she wanted.

German did not go to stores to shop; she went to buy. One size 34B white cotton bra, please. A half-gallon of orange juice and a dozen eggs. Two tubes of Winsor & Newton burnt-sienna paint. The day after her showdown with Ben Gould, she looked in her small refrigerator and knew at a glance that she must go to the market.

In the time that they had lived together, one of the things Ben taught her was that whenever you are upset, cook something delicious and difficult to prepare. Even if you end up giving it away or throwing it in the trash after you are finished, the effort and mental concentration required to make it will take your mind off the problem for a while. She'd watched him do this twice. Both times he emerged from the kitchen with a marvelous meal and a more peaceful heart. The food tasted great, but what she revered was Ben's way of resolving difficult personal issues. German loved physical work. She loved using her hands. She loved being with a man who, instead of brooding or sulking, put his hands to work when he was troubled to make something fine and worthwhile.

She decided that's what she would do now: buy some staples for her everyday needs and then some white beans, ham, chicken breasts, and garlic sausage for his cassoulet recipe, one of her favorite meals. German reasoned that if she made a big one, she could eat it for the rest of the week.

While dressing and preparing to go out, she thought of Ben's story about the time he ate the best cassoulet on earth in a small village in southern France. The name of that town was Castelnaudary. He pronounced the name so beautifully when telling the story that German made him repeat it twice just so she could hear the catch and roll of the word in his voice. She didn't want to think about him now but that was almost impossible. Joy, real joy, comes so rarely in life that we mourn the death of it a long time. In the beginning of their relationship she said to him, "Where have you *been*? Where have you been all this time? It feels like I've been holding my breath for years, but now I can finally let it out."

They were lying naked on the couch when she said this. To her great surprise and consternation, Ben got right up, walked into the kitchen, and started making her cassoulet for the first time. When she entered the room a few minutes later, bewildered by his having disappeared from her arms just like that, he started describing Castelnaudary and the time he had eaten this dish there. His back was to her while he spoke. When he turned, she saw that his eyes were filled with tears but he was smiling. "This is the greatest meal in the world, German. I have to make it for you right now. It's the best way I know how to show how I feel about you."

Only two weeks after she got together with Ben Gould, German told her closest friend in a nervous, giddy, and spooked voice that she thought she had found *him*. "My God, I really do think I found him." Her friend asked, "What, is it the sex?" German protested: "No, no, it's the *guy*. That's the incredible part: it's the whole guy. Even his hands are perfect. Have you ever met a man with perfect hands?" Her friend said, "Hands? Oh boy, you're in deep."

Because she was adventurous, German had experienced a large number of failed relationships over the years. She was at the age where she knew her chances of finding someone who sent both her heart and her hopes off the scale were rare. But then, one day in the library, there he was.

"I *don't* want to think about him now. Okay?" She said this out loud and very firmly, although no one was around to hear. German had a habit of doing that when she'd made up her mind about something. For her, saying things out loud made them final.

She missed Pilot. She missed taking his leash off the side table and asking in a normal, un-doggy voice if he wanted to go for a walk. She missed having another being in her life, especially now that once again the world felt so alien and large.

The supermarket was a short walk from her place. When German's life turned sad or strange, she tended to notice more of what was going on around her. She was the first to admit that when she was happy she drifted around in a dreamy cloud of inattention. Simply because there was enough in her head to keep her busy then: she did not need anything else to think about. But today was *a day after* and not a good one: the day after Ben's malicious tricks and surprises. A day after the galling realization of how wrong she'd been about someone she had once genuinely loved.

Walking along, she saw a young woman standing on a

corner, waiting for a traffic light to change. When the woman glanced over, her eyes were filled with equal amounts of suspicion and defeat.

German passed a forlorn-looking garage with no cars in the stalls or up on the hydraulic rack being repaired and none at the pumps getting gas. The only person around was the owner, who stood in the office door wiping his hands on a filthy rag. He glowered at German as she passed, as if she were to blame for the failure of this place and his disappointment.

Down the block the supermarket loomed, all bright windows and movement. Its parking lot was crammed with people and cars. Shoppers came and went pushing metal carts in and out of the store, to their cars, to the side, down the street toward home.

German was an inveterate snoop into other shopping carts. To her mind what people chose to buy said a great deal about them. She had often accompanied Ben to the market only because food shopping was such a pleasure for him and his enthusiasm was infectious. If she had not known him and were looking in his cart, she would have thought this man was either an interesting fellow or a food snob—or both. He never bought more than a few items at a time, usually only what he was cooking that day. His cart might contain capers and fresh dill, an eggplant, a bottle of ouzo, and two fat lamb chops he had given the butcher detailed instructions on how he wanted cut.

"Stop thinking about him!" she repeated too loudly while stepping onto the new black asphalt of the large parking lot. But German always thought of Ben when she went to a food market. There was no way to avoid it.

She picked up her pace and, zigzagging through both the parked and moving cars, crossed the busy lot toward the building. Often when Ben got to the door of a market he would stop and just beam in anticipation of the treasure hunt he was about to have inside. German noticed these things about him and they touched her. He could be so delightful. Even if it was over between them, why would she want to push away small, perfect memories like that?

Two Cub Scouts had set up a card table near the entrance. They were selling tickets to a raffle. As she passed they looked at her hopefully, but it was in vain. German never bought raffle tickets or lottery tickets or entered any sort of contest. She believed fully in luck but had her own theory about it. She believed luck chose you: it came to you but you could never go to it or win it or seduce it. Luck was stubborn, picky, and frequently recalcitrant if you bugged it too much with requests. It was the prettiest girl at the ball who could have her pick of partners. Woe to the boy stupid or vain enough to walk up and *ask* her to dance. Luck had come to German a few times in her life. For a blessed time she believed finding Benjamin Gould was the best luck she ever had.

The supermarket doors whooshed open automatically and she stepped inside. As usual, entering that cavernous place made her feel both physically small and incompetent: all the food displayed in there, the variety, the delicious possible combinations of ingredients that she was incapable of conjuring because she was only a mediocre cook and had no talent at it. Even when she tried her hardest, whatever German Landis prepared usually ended up tasting like airplane food. It was one of the things she had so enjoyed about living with Ben: he gladly did the cooking. She savored every bit of it and happily cleaned the dishes afterward, a job he detested. It was one of those small ideal arrangements, a perfect pact, that comes naturally in a successful relationship. How often does that kind of accord happen in life, especially with a new partner? How often are our weaknesses solved by the strengths of others, and vice versa?

Shaking her head at this unstoppable flow of Ben memories, German walked to the side and separated one metal cart from a large bunch there. She took the shopping list from her pocket and scanned it. Moving quickly, she could be finished and out of the store in fifteen minutes, which was perfect.

She got as far as the meat counter before being sidetracked. While trying to decide between two packages of chicken breasts—what was it Ben said about choosing chicken? What were those things he said to look for?—a colleague from the school where she taught walked over and began talking. German was drawn into a meandering enjoyable conversation about students, problems with stubborn administrators, and school life in general. She liked to talk, especially about her job.

German loved teaching, loved the energy and curiosity of her students. She loved how their impatience and enthusiasm kept her sharp and fully focused. Their reactions immediately told her when a project she'd assigned them was successful or a failure. Even when she frequently chattered on and on about it, Ben enjoyed listening to her school talk because she wore her affection and hope for the students on her sleeve. She spoke of the talented ones as if they were full-fledged artists, although they were only twelve years old. Even so, she believed that if they stuck with it, some of them could be professional artists when they grew up.

Although they were very different women, Ben felt that there were certain similarities between German Landis and Dominique Bertaux. Dominique had been sincerely satisfied with the rewards of everyday life, and German was, too. German didn't expect or believe that life held great things in store for her—which was fine—and neither had Dominique. Dominique had once compared her life to a beach after a storm: rarely was any treasure tossed up on shore there, but if you were a fan or collector of driftwood, bottle glass, or the variety of odd and surprising things that had been adrift in the ocean a long time, then you frequently found useful objects there to take home and appreciate. When German heard that anecdote, she nodded eagerly. She agreed with the analogy and told Ben that hearing it made her like Dominique even more. She could not imagine what it had been like for him when his girlfriend died, especially under those terrible circumstances.

"Excuse me?"

German was facing her colleague and hadn't noticed the woman approaching. On hearing the question, she turned and saw Danielle Voyles standing nearby, staring at her.

"Oh, hello." German introduced Danielle to her colleague. Then the three women stood there awkwardly in silence, each waiting for the others to speak.

Danielle had on a black cap pulled way down to cover most of the wound on the side of her head. She wore a black velour jogging suit and brand-new white sneakers. She looked sporty and at ease. But she wasn't at ease, as German was about to discover. With hesitant eyes but a resolute voice, she asked if it would be possible for them to talk alone for a few minutes. The coworker from school said good-bye and pushed her cart away toward the frozen-food aisle.

"I'm sorry to interrupt your conversation, but this is very important."

"It's no problem. How did you find me?"

"I looked you up in the phone book. You have such an unusual name that it was easy to remember. Then I went to your house. Your landlord said she saw you walking towards the market with a shopping basket, so I took a chance and came here."

German smiled sympathetically. "You went to a lot of trouble."

"Because we're *in* a lot of trouble."

As far as German knew, this woman had tricked her yesterday by pretending Ben was invisible when they visited her apartment. Still, when Danielle spoke now, German believed what she said. The fear that framed her voice was convincing.

"What trouble? What do you mean?"

"A man came to see me today. He looked like some kind of bum. He said his name was Stewart Parrish and that he knew you and your boyfriend."

"I don't know anybody by that name. Parrish? No."

"He said you'd probably say that. He told me to give this to you if you did." Danielle extended her arm toward German and opened her hand so the other woman could see what it held.

Usually at least once in a person's childhood we lose an object that at the time is invaluable and irreplaceable to us, although it is worthless to others. Many people remember that lost article for the rest of their lives. Whether it was a lucky pocketknife, a transparent plastic bracelet given to you by your father, a toy you had longed for and never expected to receive, but there it was under the tree on Christmas . . . it makes no difference what it was. If we describe it to others and explain why it was so important, even those who love us smile indulgently because to them it sounds like a trivial thing to lose. Kid stuff. But it is not. Those who forget about this object have lost a valuable, perhaps even crucial memory. Because something central to our younger self resided in that thing. When we lost it, for whatever reason, a part of us shifted permanently.

German Landis's lost object was a red stone. On one side of it was a clumsily painted picture of a clown face in bright yellow. One glimpse and you knew that an untalented child had painted it.

When she was very young, German was way too tall, klutzy, and plain as a potato. She wore boys' dungarees and T-shirts most of the time because they fit her better than girls' clothes. Besides, dresses made her self-conscious of her long, long legs. One cruel, clever classmate nicknamed her "Praying Mantis Landis" because she was so tall and thin and liked green jeans. At least once a day someone at school called her that name, always with a thick coating of disdain and derision on his or her voice. German was smart, sensitive, and talkative, although as a girl she had few friends to gab with. At that age she wanted nothing more from life than to either be accepted or shorter. If neither was possible, then she just wanted to fit in better than she did, despite her basketball-player height and big hands and feet.

Like every other girl in third grade, German had a crush on Rudi Paula. The blond prince of the schoolyard, Rudi reigned supreme at kickball, punchball, burping, and jokes. He was the focal point of any gathering. Even as a child he had the world on a string, and that was just fine with the world. Every boy wanted to be Rudi's friend, and every girl dreamt of receiving a Valentine card from him on February 14. Needless to say, he ignored German. She was convinced that Rudi didn't know her name, even though they were in the same class. If he did, he probably knew her as Praying Mantis Landis and only that.

One day their teacher told the class to find a rock and bring it in because they were going to paint them during art period. German brought in a big piece of quartz. When the time came, she went to work painting a complicated picture on the quartz that she had been designing in her head the whole day. When class was over and recess began, she wasn't close to being finished and asked if she could stay inside and continue working. The teacher agreed while the other kids filed out of the room.

Rudi Paula purposely waited until he was the last to leave. While passing German's desk, he gruffly, loudly plunked his still-wet red-and-yellow stone down in front of her. "*Here*. This is for *you*," he said, and then fled both the room and the implications of the gesture he had just made. Rudi Paula never said another word to her the rest of the school year. That summer his family moved to another town.

His stone was painted brick red and a yellow clown face was ineptly rendered on one side. For German Landis, however, it might just as well have been the Rosetta stone because of what it said to her. The only person she showed it to was her brother, who could not believe that the great Rudi Paula had actually given his glunky sister a present. Years later he wrote a song about it called "Rudi's Stone" for his band. Much to the adult German's delight, it was the only positive song in the Kidney Failure repertoire.

What Rudi's stone said to this tall, insecure girl was that she was all right. No, she was much more than all right: she was the kind of girl that Rudi Paula liked and gave presents to. It was her instant talisman: visible, tangible proof that life might turn out okay and she could end up happy. Some nights in the first year that she owned it, she fell asleep holding the stone in her hand. She kept it in a special place on one of her bookshelves. It never left her room because she was afraid of losing it. Although her parents were not privy to why a red stone was so important to her, they knew not to touch it, and they didn't.

As time passed and her life improved significantly, German would still flick her eyes over to Rudi's stone sometimes and smile, remembering the day and the exact momentous moment when he gave her his red gift of approval and hope.

Years later she looked up at the shelf one day and realized with a start that the stone had disappeared. She asked everyone in her family if they knew where it was, but no one did.

Surprisingly, though, the loss did not cause much reaction in her. Twelve-year-old German Landis had other things on her mind. There was the daily flurry of seventh grade, which she enjoyed very much. And a new intriguing boy in the school band who played the clarinet and said he would call her up one day maybe. She had a nice group of girlfriends now who took up much of the space in her head. Truth was, Rudi's stone now symbolized the loser she was embarrassed to admit she once had been. Like the girl wearing the stupid-looking party hat while mugging for the camera in an old photograph, German acknowledged the child who had once cherished and needed the stone, but that was no longer her. So when it disappeared from her life, only a small part of her was sad; an even smaller part wondered where the stone had gone.

Twenty-two years later she lifted it out of Danielle Voyles's hand and brought it up to her face for a closer look. Yes, that was it. There was no question. After all this time she once again held Rudi's stone in her hand.

Danielle asked, "Does it mean anything to you?"

"Yes, it means a lot, actually. This man gave it to you?"

Danielle nodded, her face tight and giving away nothing.

"What did he say?"

"He wants to know where your boyfriend is."

Despite what she held, German responded angrily, "I don't know where he is. And he's *not* my boyfriend.

"That's all? He gave you this stone and said he wanted to see my boyfriend?"

"No, that's not all. He said he had your dog and was going to kill it. Then he was going to kill me and you, unless you tell him. He said you two met in a pizza restaurant, where you saw what he can do."

. . .

Pilot woke when the front door closed. A loud *clack*, a normal sound; no one was trying to hide it or sneak into the apartment. The dog did not move from his comfortable bed. He watched the door to the living room, waiting for Ben Gould to enter. Time passed and Pilot continued to wait. Perhaps the man had gone to the toilet first. That would not be surprising. The dog could never get over how many times a day human beings went to the toilet. Neither could he get over the fact that in every dwelling he had shared with humans, they set aside one entire room for the purpose of emptying their bodies. In contrast, a dog used everywhere for its toilet and never thought twice about it. When you had to go, you went. The only reason a dog permitted itself to be housebroken was the trade-off: you give me food, shelter, and a million pats on the head and I'll leave your walls and floors dry. It was the best deal going.

"Pilot? Where are you?"

The voice calling out was not so different from Gould's. The dog had just awakened, so he mistook what he heard for Ben's voice.

"I'm in here, in the living room."

"The living room? Okay, I'll find you."

A strange thing to say, because this was the man's own home. Why would he need to *find* the living room? Pilot sniffed the air twice and waited. He was fully awake now, his senses heightened in anticipation. A light came on in the hallway. A few moments later a man's body was silhouetted in the doorway. Now the dog could smell him. It was not Ben Gould's smell.

"Pilot? Are you in here?"

The fur rose down his back. "Who are you?"

"Ah, there you are!" came the friendly reply. The light came on in the room and Pilot saw Stewart Parrish for the first time. The man stood there smiling with his hands on his hips. "Hello!"

How did this stranger know that the dog understood and spoke human language now? How had he found this apartment? How did he know Pilot's name?

Parrish continued smiling as he walked into the living room. Pilot lifted his head and sniffed the air more carefully. This man smelled of living outdoors. But he also smelled of closed rooms full of trapped, stale air and clothes stored in boxes a long time. He smelled of cheap food: lots of potatoes and bread, processed meat, sugary drinks, and . . . there was another odor emanating from this stranger that Pilot could not identify. It was mysterious, a wholly unique aroma that baffled the dog's sense of smell.

"It's a pleasure to finally meet you."

"How do you know who I am?"

Parrish answered eagerly, "Oh, I've been briefed. They gave me lots of information about you."

Neither spoke after that. Pilot waited, sizing the man up. Stewart Parrish appeared content to remain silent until the dog asked another question. He wore a pinstriped suit and an orange shirt. Human beings are wrong to think dogs cannot see color. They can, but colors are less vivid to them, less defined. For example, to Pilot, the electric orange of Parrish's shirt was the orange of a dead autumn leaf.

The man walked over to Ben Gould's favorite chair and sat down in it. He looked at his trousers and energetically brushed off his lap, although, from what the dog could see, there was nothing on it. Parrish looked at everything in the room as if memorizing the details. A wisp of a smile remained on his lips while he looked. He appeared to feel completely at home there.

"I had expected something smaller, to tell you the truth. This is a large apartment, from what I've seen of it so far."

Pilot waited.

"My name is Stewart Parrish. I've been sent to find out where Benjamin Gould is."

"Wherever he is, you can't go there."

Parrish leaned forward and put his elbows on his knees so that he was closer to Pilot now. "Yes I can. I just need you to tell me where he is and I'm off. You see, there are certain things I'm a little foggy about. Kind of like I just woke up from a nap and need to refocus my thoughts before they're clear to me again. I know things but I don't know them, if you get what I mean. I just need a little mental shove from you in their direction and off I go."

"Skillicorn Park." Pilot told the man the truth because the name was really the only thing he knew. He had no idea where the place was. The dog overheard Ben say the name to Ling when the two were talking. A moment later they both disappeared. To Skillicorn Park? Who knows? Who even knew where that *was*?

"Thank you. Good-bye," Parrish said quickly, and then he, too, disappeared into thin air.

Pilot looked at Ben's empty chair a long time and felt his heart grow hard and heavy. What's worse than being left out of things? The dog did not have the slightest desire to go to this Skillicorn Park or anywhere else. But that wasn't the point. What he resented was how everyone else seemed capable of going there with no fuss. Blink an eye and they were gone. Feeling once again like the last unwanted dog in the animal shelter, Pilot lay in his bed watching the rest of his world disappear to Skillicorn Park as if it were in the next room.

The dog rose slowly and walked toward the kitchen for a drink of water. Passing his master's chair, he paused and lifted a leg on it. A quick, short spurt of pee shot out and dribbled down the chair leg. No big squirt or anything—just enough to lodge a small wet protest against the Skillicorn Park gang.

Pilot was gone no more than five minutes. When he padded back into the living room, Parrish was once again sitting in Ben's chair.

"Surprise! Did you miss me?"

"Did you get lost?" the dog asked, but didn't bother looking at the man. He climbed back into his basket, circled twice, and lay down with a satisfied groan.

"Oh, no, I went there. It's a very nice park—lots of trees. But I arrived just as they were leaving: bad timing on my part. Do you know where else they might have gone?"

"I have no idea." Pilot closed his eyes, hoping the man would see, take the hint, and leave.

"Hmm. That's disappointing. You really have no idea?"

"Nope."

"Do you mind if I stay here and wait for them? I'll just sleep in this chair."

Pilot opened his eyes again and gave the man a dirty look. But human beings don't understand dog dirty looks, so it was lost on Parrish. "He may not come back tonight. He may not be back for days. I don't think he'd be happy if you stayed here for days."

"Fair enough. I'll make you a deal, then: I'll wait here for him tonight. If he's not back by morning, I'll leave. Is that okay with you?"

"Whatever." Pilot closed his eyes again and fell asleep quickly. He was an almost-old dog, bone tired from all the running around he had done recently. He assumed Parrish knew Ling the ghost because he had disappeared to Skillicorn Park in exactly the same way as the other two had done earlier. Somehow or other this stranger would find a way to reunite with them. But right now it was time to sleep.

•   •   •

True to his word, the next morning Parrish got up and prepared to leave as soon as Pilot awoke. "I'm on my way. I won't bother you anymore."

Shyly the dog asked, "Before you go, would you do me a favor? I don't know when they'll be back and I really need to pee. Would you take me outside for a short walk?"

"Sure, I'd be glad to! Do you have a leash?"

"In the hallway by the door."

"Then, let's go. We can take as long as you like out there."

Parrish clipped the leash to Pilot's collar and opened the front door. "Gee, I can't remember the last time I walked a dog. This'll be fun."

Thirty seconds after they were outside, Pilot jerked the leash out of Parrish's hand and ran away as fast as he could down the sidewalk. He ran faster than he had in years. He ran almost like a puppy, but that was because he was so frightened. His only idea was to escape from Stewart Parrish.

Pilot had waited a long time for the man to awaken. Whenever Parrish moved in his sleep in the chair, the animal quickly shut his eyes. He did not want the man to know he was awake and watching him. He did not want Parrish to know anything. If he did, there might be no escaping, and that thought worried the dog most because he knew now who the man was.

About five o'clock that morning Pilot had come half-awake so as to shift his position in bed. Because he was sitting so close by, Parrish's smell drifted over again. The dog hadn't been able to identify one particular part of his odor the night before, when they met for the first time. But in the mysterious place halfway between sleep and consciousness, the senses are tuned to a different, more obscure wavelength. *They* recognized the smell now. Shocked, Pilot came instantly awake, lifted his head in dire alarm, and only slowly, very slowly, lowered it again until it was resting tensely on his paws.

Dogs see ghosts. They see disease floating down the street like fog. They hear and smell the unimaginable. Yet dogs are indifferent to such things because they are simply part of their perceived world. Human beings don't gasp at flowers or think about the insect that lands on their feet. We accept what we know when we encounter it and go on with our lives.

At the same time, when we open a bottle of milk that has gone bad, pure instinct makes us rear back in disgust on smelling the rotten stuff. It wasn't Pilot's senses that now said, Run, run—get away! It was purely survival instinct.

Life and death do not mix. They could never dance together because both of them would insist on leading. They co-exist only because they are mutually dependent. In truth, they despise each other as the night despises the day and vice versa. If they were human siblings, they would have killed each other in the cradle. Each has its own distinctive odor. Everything alive has a warm ripe scent, organic, ongoing. Death's aroma is cold and unchanging.

Stewart Parrish smelled of both. That was impossible, according to everything Pilot had ever been taught or experienced in life. The dog had not recognized the odor earlier because it did not exist, or rather it *should* not have existed any more than cold fire or hot ice should exist. Nothing could be alive and dead at the same time. But Stewart Parrish was. Pilot knew now that any entity smelling of both was potentially the most dangerous thing he had ever encountered.

So Pilot ran. He flew. He moved as fast as his legs would go. While he ran his only thought was to run faster. Get away. Halfway down the block, the dog wanted to look back to see if the man was coming but knew he shouldn't slow down yet. Go farther. Get farther away because who knows how fast that man can travel if he wants to catch you?

Completely surprised by the dog's sudden lunatic dash for freedom, Parrish shook his head in amusement and sat down on the front stoop of the building. He watched Pilot run, black leather leash whipping back and forth behind him, until the dog was out of sight. Then Parrish reached into the breast pocket of his suit jacket and pulled out a pretty good cigar. He had been saving it for a nice quiet moment when he could sit someplace awhile, take it easy, and puff away in peace. Now that he didn't have to walk the dog, there was no time like the present. He would relax right here, smoke his cigar, and, after taking care of that one thing, eventually make his way over to Danielle Voyles's apartment, which was only a few blocks away.

The cigar was Honduran and had the slightly off-putting sweetness of all tobacco originally grown in Cuba but then transplanted to a climate similar to its origin but not quite. It was like Parrish himself: transplanted to new ground, he was similar to what he once had been but not quite the same. The result was a good cigar but not a great one. Just like me, Parrish thought with a snort: a good one but not a great one.

Half an hour later he took a satisfyingly long last draw on what little was left of the cigar. Bending his head back, he blew the smoke out all at once. The thick gray cloud was so dense that it hung unmoving above his head. Without looking to see if anyone was around to witness what came next, Stewart Parrish climbed up into that cloud of cigar smoke and disappeared once again.

Moments later he reappeared in German Landis's childhood bedroom. It was conveniently empty, which was nice because that gave him time to concentrate and do the job quickly without distractions, such as a little-girl German Landis asking, *What are you doing in my room?*

He walked around, picking objects up, weighing them in his hand as if they were fruit he was considering buying, then putting them down again exactly where he'd found them. Once in a while he muttered "Hmm" or "Nope," but for the most part Parrish remained silent while searching. Dolls, a pencil box, a Daisy Duck watch, and other objects were examined. He picked them all up, scrutinized each closely, put it down again. Eventually he saw the red stone on a shelf. Curious why something so nondescript would be up there, he lifted it from its place. He held it no more than a second or two before smiling and saying, "This is it." He pocketed the stone and left the room. Now he had to go find Danielle.

•   •   •

"Where is this man now?" German asked Danielle Voyles.

"At your boyfriend's apartment."

"He's not here? He's not waiting for you outside in the parking lot?"

Danielle shook her head. "No, he said he'd wait for us at your boyfriend's place."

An announcement over the supermarket's loudspeaker system cut off anything else Danielle wanted to say. Coca-Cola was on sale today at aisle seven. Stock up! The two women stared silently at each other while the announcement was repeated.

German looked at the red stone in her hand. How had he found it? How did he know what it meant to her? What did Danielle Voyles have to do with this?

"Should we go to the police? I don't know what to do."

"*Do* you know where your boyfriend is?"

"No. We broke up. I saw him yesterday but it was short and we didn't talk much." German wanted to say, "I saw him yesterday at your apartment, where you pretended not to see him," but the look on Danielle's face silenced her.

The two women walked toward the exit.

Danielle stopped and grabbed German's sleeve. "He told me something, the man. I asked why was he bothering *me* about this? I don't know you and I don't know your boyfriend, either. He said both of us were supposed to have died but we didn't. You know about my accident. But what happened to your boyfriend?"

German said, "Nothing. One of his *girlfriends* was killed a few years ago, but Ben? No."

They took a few more steps before German stopped and said slowly, as it dawned on her, "He fell. He fell and hit his head very badly right after we first met. He had to go to the hospital because it was bleeding in here." She pointed to the back of her head. "It was critical. For a few days it was very bad. But he didn't *die*."

• • •

Stewart Parrish was sitting in exactly the same place on the front stoop of Ben Gould's building when the two women showed up. He liked this spot. Liked being able to see the whole street and watch the neighborhood goings-on. He had spoken to an elderly man from Montenegro who was visiting his grandchildren. As soon as Parrish heard where the man came from,

he switched languages from English to Albanian, which thrilled
the old man. Then he chatted with a heavy teenager in a Puma
sweat suit on her way to aerobics class. Everyone he spoke to
was open and friendly. Even to a guy like him, who to all appearances was raggedy and down on his luck. Parrish liked that.
He liked that these people didn't judge his book by his cover.

He had just lit up a second cigar while sitting on the steps
when the landlord of the building came out to ask why he was
there. Stewart said that he was waiting for either Ben Gould or
his girlfriend German to return. He was an old friend of theirs
from school and expected them at any minute. Jovial and intelligent, his answers satisfied the landlord, who went back inside
and left Parrish alone.

It was turning out to be a nice morning. Danielle Voyles had
been no problem. He scared the wits out of her within the first
five minutes of their meeting. After that she needed no further
convincing. When he handed her Rudi's stone, she'd dropped it
because her hand was shaking so badly.

And now here they came, two smart-looking women
walking down the sidewalk toward him on this mild overcast
morning. German Landis was much taller than he remembered.
However, when Parrish saw her that first time months before, he
was in no state to judge anything. His mind back then was just a
garbage can full of disconnected fragments. When the women
were a few feet away, he stood up while at the same time ducking
his head in a sort of bow of respect and greeting.

"Hello."

Neither woman said anything. This was his show and all
three of them knew it.

"Danielle gave you the stone?"

German nodded.

Parrish's first impulse was to ask them to join him on the

stoop. But after what he'd done to bring them here, he knew they wouldn't want to do that. So okay, let's get down to business. "I need to find your boyfriend, Miss Landis."

"I don't know where he is. We're not together anymore."

The bum was truly surprised. "You broke up?"

"Yes."

"Woo, that changes things. But I still need you to tell me where he is."

Scared though she was, annoyance tightened German's mouth. "I just told you I don't *know* where is."

Parrish scratched his chin and looked at something over her shoulder. "That's not good enough."

Surprising herself, German dared ask, "Where is Pilot?"

"He's okay. But he won't be okay if you don't help me find Ben."

"Did you try his apartment?" She pointed toward the building. "Or his job? Do you know where he works?"

"Yes. He's neither of those places."

She raised her hands palms up. "Then I can't help you."

"I want to show you something." Parrish had already taken it out of his pocket when he saw the women approaching. Now all he did was turn his left hand over. They saw the sharpened kitchen knife lying flat against his open palm. "Remember this?" he asked German, and she nodded again. She assumed it was the same knife he'd used to stab the man in the restaurant that horrible night. She couldn't stand to look at it now.

"Good. Now, do you see the silver motorcycle way down the block? That brand-new Harley V-Rod? You like motorcycles, don't you, German? No, Formula One cars and old bicycles are more your thing, right?"

They looked but didn't see the motorcycle at first because it was parked so far away.

"I'm going to throw this into its front headlight." He flicked his hand forward. The gesture was haphazard; it looked as though he were trying to get something off his fingers. But the knife flew out of his hand like an arrow shot from a crossbow. Seconds later—much too soon—they heard a faint crash and tinkling.

"I hope the owner's got insurance on that machine. Danielle, would you go get my knife, please? You can tell us if I hit the light when you get back."

She touched the scar on her temple. "I'm sorry, but my head is really beginning to hurt."

"*Go get my knife!* You can sit down and rest when you come back. German and I need a few minutes alone together." Parrish didn't bother looking at Danielle when he ordered her to move.

She left after a fearful glance at German.

Parrish pointed to the top step. "Sit down."

When they were seated he said, "You don't know anything about what's going on with Ben, do you?"

"No . . . only what Danielle told me."

"That's all right. You don't need to know. Just help me find your boyfriend and you're finished."

"But I already told you—"

"I know what you told me, German. But you'd know better where he *might* be now than anyone else. So make a guess. That's why I came to you."

She thought. She really thought about it but could not come up with an answer for him. "If he's in the city—"

"He's not. He's back in his hometown."

Startled, she raised her voice. "What? When did he leave?"

Parrish ignored her question. "When Ben was a little boy, who was his best friend? I'm talking about when he was very young, like four or five, around then."

"Gina Kyte." German said the girl's name without thinking because when they lived together, Ben often told stories about Gina and their childhood escapades. His first love, he said it was also the purest love he'd ever known because there was nothing physical about it, only pure human adoration. He just flat-out loved Gina Kyte and woke up most mornings grateful that she was on this earth near him.

"Yes, Gina, that's right. Where did she live?"

"Cinnamon Street," German said, not suspecting this had any relevance.

Parrish slowly smiled. "You're joking."

"No, Gina Kyte lived on Cinnamon Street. Ben told me that several times."

"That is wonderful. What a name! Then Cinnamon Street it is. Thank you."

To her great surprise, Parrish stuck out his hand to shake. After a moment's hesitation she took it.

German waited for him to speak again but he didn't. She looked over. His expression was serene. He seemed content watching the street in silence. She remained quiet a little longer but eventually couldn't stand it anymore and had to ask, "What is going *on*? Why are you here? Why are you threatening us?"

He didn't look her way when he answered. "Benjamin Gould fell in the snow and hit his head on the sidewalk. He should have died but he didn't. Danielle Voyles was supposed to die when the piece of pen from the plane crash went through her head, but she didn't die, either. There are other people this has happened to—more and more frequently these days. Others who were supposed to die but didn't. Something's gone wrong with the system. I've been sent here to find out what it is and fix it."

"By stabbing people? By threatening to kill them? Who are

you? How do you know that they were *supposed* to die? Who sent you?"

"The Natural Order sent me, German. The way things should be and always have been. That's my boss."

Before his answer sank in, she stumbled on: "Why *did* you stab the man that night?"

"Because he was one of the bad guys: the guys who are letting things change that should never be changed. Believe it or not, we're the good guys here. You should be rooting for us."

"Rooting for death?" Her tone was snide.

Parrish went on in the same mild voice. "Do you like order? Are you an orderly person, German?"

Surprised by his question, she answered hesitantly, "Mostly, yes."

"Do you like pain?"

"No."

"Do you like it when things are chaotic or your life is out of control?"

"No." What was he talking about?

Danielle walked toward them. She held Parrish's knife away from her body, dangling between two fingers because it was something she didn't want to touch but must. All she wanted to do was take off, but the bum knew where she lived.

"Do you like being alive?"

German pulled back, thinking he might be about to do something to her. "*Alive?* Yes, I like being alive."

He shook his head. "*Why?* Life's chaotic, full of pain and suffering. It's unreliable and as disorderly as you can get. Nothing in life lasts, nothing's permanent, and there's not one thing that you can trust one hundred percent.

"Admit it: if a person had all those lousy qualities, you'd never want to be around them." His voice was measured and reasonable. He was not trying to convince her of anything, only stating some facts and making a very valid point.

But when she understood where he was going with this, she wasn't having it. "I know what you're saying: that's all Sigmund Freud's death-wish theory. I studied it in college." She raised an index finger as if preparing to recite something memorized for class. "Death means the cessation of pain, no more chaos, no more being controlled by things bigger or more powerful than you are, whether that happens to be people or fate or God. And nothing is more dependable than death because if you're dead today, you're going to be dead tomorrow. Mankind seeks permanence, not transience. Death is permanent."

"Exactly!" Parrish was pleased and impressed that she knew these things. It would save him time explaining. Yet what she said next threw him off.

"But you know what my professor said after he explained that theory to us? He quoted the writer E. M. Forster: 'Death destroys a man: the idea of Death saves him.'"

Danielle approached and was about to speak when she sensed the tension between the other two.

"Very poetic, but what is it supposed to mean?" Now Parrish sounded snide.

German said, "To me, it means life becomes even more beautiful and valuable once we *truly* realize we're going to die. But most of us never make that realization until we're told we're terminal by a doctor or whoever. By that time it's too late, 'cause all we feel then is fear."

Danielle enthusiastically added, "Like taking an ocean cruise but staying in your cabin the whole time. Only when the cruise is over and the boat's docking, you finally go out on deck and see how nice it is." After speaking, she was embarrassed by her outburst. But it was exactly the subject she'd been reading and thinking about like crazy in the days since her accident.

Parrish was disappointed. "That's so wrong. Neither of you has any idea of what you're talking about." He walked down the steps and onto the sidewalk.

Annoyed now, he looked at one woman and then the other. "You don't know how close you just came to . . ." His voice faded while he scratched his cheek. "The dog. I almost forgot the dog." Raising his left hand, he snapped his fingers.

Twenty-five blocks away, Pilot froze in place, but not of his own accord. He had been trotting along, still fleeing the half-dead man. But gradually his legs and joints began to sing pain, which slowed him considerably. Nevertheless, he had been moving at a pretty brisk pace until he was stopped in his tracks.

Next, the dog was lifted twenty feet off the pavement and flown backward in the direction he had just come from. Fighting against this with all he had, there was nothing the animal could do to resist. He was held by a force much stronger, stronger by miles, than he was. Pilot was entirely helpless and at that moment knew for certain he was about to die.

He flew back toward Ben Gould's apartment building so fast that it took no more than six or seven minutes to arrive. As he grew nearer, his body dropped lower and lower. By the time he reached the stairs where German was sitting, Pilot's feet were touching the pavement. The moment he stopped, he looked around in panic. He saw the two women and then the back of Stewart Parrish as the man walked away.

None of them ever saw him again.

Seven

The deeper Ben and Ling walked into the forest, the gloomier it got. What they had just witnessed hanging up in the branches of the tree didn't make things any brighter. Night and its entourage had arrived. The trees that surrounded them absorbed the dark like asphalt absorbs summer heat. Night sounds and smells are manifestly different from day. The man and the woman walked in single file along the side of the road that passed through the forest. The only lights they saw came from cars passing in either direction.

"How much farther is it?" Ling asked.

"To the school? I don't really remember. It's been a long time since I was last here." Ben walked in front. He spoke over his shoulder to Ling, who was following a few feet behind. The ghost didn't like any of this one bit. The roadside was extremely narrow and there was no real place to walk safely. Both of them wore dark clothes. It would be easy for a driver to miss seeing them. Ling had already said twice she didn't think this walk was a good idea. After the third time she said it, Ben couldn't resist asking, "Are you afraid of being run over and killed?"

It had been his idea to walk through the forest to the elementary school, even though it was night and there were no overhead lights on the road.

"Why do we have to do this now?" Ling asked when Ben was already several steps down the road.

He answered, "I don't know. I'm not sure, but I have the feeling it's necessary."

The ghost put her hands on her hips and frowned. "Necessary?"

"Yes. Don't come if you don't want."

"Ben, it's not like that: I *have* to come even if I don't want. You don't understand."

He stopped. "I don't understand because you tell me nothing, Ling. I'm flying blind here. If you're not going to help me with what you know, then I'm just going to have to trust my instincts, because that's all I've got. Right now they tell me to walk through this forest to the school. So that's what I'm going to do."

Fifteen minutes later, in what felt like the middle of the forest primeval, he turned left and began walking straight into the woods. Ling was glad to leave the dangerous road, but why here?

"Where are you going?" she asked his back.

He didn't answer but kept walking.

Ling followed. "Ben?"

No answer. She caught up and tried to get him to look her way, but he wouldn't. "You're not being fair, Ben. I can't tell you what you want to know because I'm not permitted to. They explicitly told me I couldn't. If it were up to me, I'd tell you everything—which, after what's been going on lately, doesn't appear to be much, believe me."

Without looking at her he asked, "Who's 'they'? Who told you that you couldn't tell me things?"

She half whispered, "I can't tell you that."

"Fine." He sped up and away from her. There was nothing the ghost could do but follow a few steps behind him.

The surroundings got darker and darker. Car noises from the road faded until they were barely a soft murmur from what sounded like miles behind them.

Unused to walking in the dark, much less walking in the dark through a forest full of stuff to trip over, Ling had a tough time. Not Ben, though: he moved at a steady pace, making it much harder for her to keep up.

In due course the ghost stumbled, staggered, and really whanged her left shin against a downed tree branch. "Damn it! This *sucks!*" Ling howled, learning yet another human emotion she would have gladly done without. They continued tramping along in silence. Ben led the way, although Ling didn't believe he knew where he was going in this darkness.

"Do you eat?" he asked.

"What?" Her shin was throbbing pain. She was trying to see where she was going without success. She wasn't sure she'd heard him correctly. His question came out of nowhere. "Eat? What do you mean?"

"Do you eat food? Do ghosts eat?"

"Of course we *eat!*"

"What, dead souls and bats?"

"Very funny. The other night I had a very nice pumpkin soup. I found the recipe in one of Nigel Slater's cookbooks."

"How do you know Nigel Slater?"

"I'm a ghost, Ben, not an illiterate. It just so happens that I like to cook, too, and I've tried many of the recipes in your books. You have very eclectic taste: a nice variety. Although you could use a few more books on Far Eastern cooking."

"Is that so?"

"In my opinion, yes."

"What kind of Far Eastern?" Although his voice was indignant, he slowed a little to allow her to catch up.

"Well, Thai for one. I didn't see any Thai cookbooks in your library."

Ben was offended. "I love Thai food, but where am I supposed to buy the right chilies for it? A real Thai recipe depends on very specific chilies, and they're impossible to find around here. Why buy a cookbook when you can't cook the dish correctly?"

Things between them became a little easier after that. While listening to Ling talk about cooking, Ben quickly realized she was an expert on the subject, and that obviously created a bond between them. Anytime we discover someone who shares our obsessions, they become a kind of instant amigo. While walking through the dark, the two cooks talked about the use of *yete* and *guedge* in Senegalese dishes, *santoku* knives, Bhut Jolokia chilies, and John Thorne.

"Thorne is one of my heroes."

She smiled and said, "I know that."

"Ling, how long have you been here watching me?"

"Almost three quarters of a year." She did not hesitate to explain exactly how it had happened: how she'd been informed of his imminent demise and subsequently ordered to earth to help him through his transition. When he died, she was to tie up any loose ends he'd left in his life, which was the only real purpose of ghosts. But then Benjamin Gould did not die.

"Briefed by who, Ling? *Who* briefed you about me?"

"I cannot tell you that. I'm sorry."

"It's all right. Go on."

"Wait a minute—did you just hear something?"

He had. When they both went silent, the sound of young

voices singing wafted over to them. But what children would be out here in the middle of the forest now? It was eerie and intriguing.

They walked toward the sound, not knowing what to expect. Both wondered almost at the same time if this might be some kind of trap, but neither said a word.

> *"Michael, row the boat ashore, hallelujah.*
> *Michael, row the boat ashore, hallelujah."*

They could hear the individual words now. The singing voices definitely belonged to children. The song itself was as familiar as morning.

"What are kids doing out here?"

"Singing, apparently."

As they approached and the young voices grew louder, both Ben and Ling unconsciously moved closer together. As if nearness might better protect them if something bad was about to happen.

A branch snapped loudly nearby. They stopped, because neither of them had caused it. Something moved in the dark. It was white and appeared out of nowhere.

"It's a verz."

One of the white creatures stood nearby, staring up at them.

"What should we do?"

"Michael, row the boat ashore, hallelujah . . ."

When she heard the singing this time, Ling made the connection. "It's here for the kids. It's protecting them." She looked at Ben and nodded, because she knew she was right.

Ben's voice was firm when he spoke. "You know who those kids *are*, don't you? Now I understand why my instincts told me to walk here." His question was rhetorical, because he knew who was singing. As sure of that as Ling was of why the verz was here. "It's *me* over there: me and Gina Kyte. Her father used to take us camping overnight in these woods. I just remembered that. He taught us how to pitch a tent and make a fire. He was a scoutmaster. He'd always go to sleep before us. We'd sit around the fire a little longer, singing till we got tired."

"Look—there's more of them."

Several verzes appeared nearby. They simply were there from one moment to the next. All of them faced the two adults but were not in any way threatening.

"Do you think we can keep moving?"

"Yes. If they were going to hurt us, they'd have done it by now."

Ben was right: as they walked forward, the verzes stepped aside. The flicker of a campfire was visible some distance away. They made for it without speaking. Ling kept an eye on the creatures at their feet, still not sure if they intended any harm. She had seen what they had done to Stewart Parrish.

Even in the dim light, the creatures all looked distinctly different. Some were larger, others smaller, some fatter, others thinner. A few had squarish heads, others' were more ovoid. None of the verzes had ears, and all had those distinctive big eyes.

"What do you think they did to Parrish?" Ling said, thinking out loud.

"The guy in the tree?"

"The *shirt* in the tree, yeah."

"I dunno. You're the ghost; you're the one who's supposed to have those answers."

"I didn't say much before because I didn't want to scare

you, but Mr. Orange Shirt had some seriously scary powers, Ben, believe me. But the verzes not only stopped him, they *evaporated* him."

"You said they're here to protect the kids. Because I'm one of those kids grown up and you're my ghost, maybe they're here to protect us too."

At the campsite were even more of them. Young Ben and Gina Kyte sat next to each other by a small campfire, singing. Gina's father wasn't around. The verzes were everywhere. Some were sitting up, others lying down; some appeared to be asleep, curled close to the campfire like pet dogs.

"Michael, row the boat ashore . . ."

The adults stood a few feet directly behind the children, watching the scene and trying to understand what was going on. Ben counted nine of the white animals and wondered if more were out there in the surrounding dark. Ling had already counted and was now wondering, if so many of them were near, how dangerous this situation was.

Even more troubling to the ghost was not knowing what to do now. Ling knew her powers could help Ben. She knew, too, how lucky they were to have avoided any kind of confrontation with Parrish. But other than knowing those things for sure, she was *lost*.

The ghost was so deep in dark thoughts that she did not hear the little boy when he spoke to her.

Ben nudged her arm to get her attention. "Answer him."

"What'd he ask?"

"If you like marshmallows."

"Huh?" Ling's brain stalled.

Adult Ben answered for her: "Yes, we like them very much."

"Do you want to roast some with us?"

"Yes, sure."

Neither child looked surprised by the appearance of the grownups. A few moments before, they had stopped singing and turned together toward the two adults.

"Gina likes hers really burnt on the outside, but not me. That burnt part tastes yucky."

"You don't even cook yours. They're probably not even hot inside." While speaking, Gina watched her marshmallow catch fire, bubble, and burn to black on one side. She drew it back and blew out the flame.

The adults walked over. They kept checking to see what the verzes would do as they approached the children. None of the creatures moved.

"You can sleep here with us tonight if you want. You'll be safe. But you'll have to sleep on the ground, because we get the tent." The boy said this without looking at them.

"How do you know that? How do you know we'll be safe here?"

Picking apart his marshmallow, young Ben ignored the question. Gina ignored it, too, while taking small, careful bites from every side of her marshmallow. When she'd finished that one, the girl reached into the large bag in her lap. Choosing a yellow one, she slid it onto the end of the stick. She handed that to Ling and moved over to make room for the ghost. No one made room for adult Ben. Standing by himself a few feet away from them, he felt awkward.

The boy finally answered the question. "I don't know it: *you* know it."

Ling looked at him. Gina ate another marshmallow out of the bag while staring at the campfire.

"I know *what?*"

"That you'll be safe if you sleep here tonight."

Perturbed, Ben asked, "How do *I* know?"

"Because I know it and I'm you." The boy stood up and looked at the man. "This is all yours: us, the forest, the fire—everything."

"What about the verzes? They're not mine."

The boy said, "They're only here to protect your memory, nothing else."

Ben looked at the ghost for help but she shook her head. He did not know how hard she worked to keep her expression blank. Ling knew how crucial this moment was. She did not want to reveal even one thing that might influence him.

Nevertheless, as if sensing some of what she was thinking, Ben said to her, "You said before it wasn't possible for me to talk to these kids. I could only watch them."

The ghost said nothing but could not resist slowly sitting up a few inches straighter.

"What's going on with Mary Helen Cline?" Ben senior asked the boy.

"I hate Mary Helen Cline," Gina said without looking up.

"Yeah, because she's a better kickball player than you are," the boy taunted.

"*No.* I hate her because she's stupid."

"Kickball."

"Stupid."

"Kickball."

The man interrupted, "You haven't told me yet about Mary Helen, Ben."

"I don't know what's with her. Why ask me?" The boy's voice slipped into grumpy.

"Don't lie: you know exactly why I'm asking."

The two Ben Goulds stared at each other, the older one grinning, the younger one glaring.

The older Ben walked over to Ling and gestured for her to follow him. "Come with me a minute. I have to tell you something."

Together they walked a short distance from the campfire—just far enough away so the kids couldn't hear.

"I remember this night, Ling. It came back to me just now. Seeing those marshmallows did it. Gina's parents never allowed us to eat them because they were bad for our teeth—all the sugar. But one time Gina snuck a bag along and we roasted them together after her father went to sleep. Earlier that day, Mary Helen Cline kissed me on the playground after a kickball game."

Ling smiled. "What are you saying?"

"All this *is* mine, Ling, just like he said. This is all part of my life. I was supposed to die months ago but I didn't. I wasn't supposed to be able to talk to my younger self, but I just did. The boy said the verzes are here to protect my *memories*. He said I knew that already and was only reminding me. Do you understand?"

Ling said no.

He hesitated, trying to figure out how to say this right. "I didn't die when I was *scheduled* to die. That's why they sent you: to take me up." He jabbed a thumb toward the sky, toward Heaven. "But when you came on schedule, I didn't die. Something inside me said, No, I'm not ready to go yet. *I'll* decide when it's time: *me*. Not the gods, or God, or Death, or whoever has been making those decisions until now.

"The same thing happened to that Danielle Voyles, I'm

sure. She was supposed to die when that piece of pen went into her brain. But she didn't die. That's why I was seeing through her eyes: because we had the same experience.

"*That's* why they sent the bum in the orange shirt to get me: I'm dangerous, because I didn't die when I was supposed to. Danielle too. And any other person this has happened to is dangerous to them too. I'll bet you a million bucks there are others.

"I've got to get access to as many of my memories as I can now. Because that's what this is all about: the answer to why I didn't die is probably in my memories." He sounded exuberant and totally sure of himself. He pointed at the boy. "I just talked to him. I was able to converse with my past, Ling, because now I'm beginning to remember the details. That could be the whole point: bring the memories of my life back into such clear focus that I can use them to figure this all out."

"But who sent Stewart Parrish, Ben?"

"I don't know yet; someone who wants me dead and silent. Someone who feels threatened by what's happened to me. Someone who wants things back the way they used to be. Back when whoever's in charge said 'Die' and you died. But something's happened and we're obviously part of it. Danielle and I are living proof of that. We're the Lazarus people.

"The more I remember of my life, the safer I'll be. I'm sure of it. When I saw the kids roasting marshmallows before, I remembered the night we went camping here and roasted them in secret after Mr. Kyte went to sleep. Next, I remembered Mary Helen Cline kissed me on the playground that same day. That's why I asked him about her before. You saw how he squirmed.

"That's *me* over there when I was a little boy, Ling. I talked to eight-year-old me. You said that wasn't possible, but I just did it."

"Yes, you did. But now you're going to have to figure out who's your enemy: who's out to stop you. And then how to get us out of here and back to your time."

Ben rubbed his hands together. "All of this is my time, Ling. What I have to do is figure out how to get back to that *part* of it. But the boy over there might be able to help."

Eight

"What's the matter with your dog?"

"What do you mean?"

"Look at him. He's been like that for minutes."

Pilot sat at rigid attention by the front door, just staring at it. As if someone had rung the bell and the dog were waiting to greet whoever came in.

German Landis and Danielle Voyles sat on the couch in Ben Gould's living room, discussing what had happened with Stewart Parrish earlier.

"Pilot does that sometimes when he knows Ben's coming home." Both saying this and phrasing it in the present tense made German feel strange. It was one of those small cozy details about living with Ben that she had forgotten. But now, having remembered it, the recollection made her feel even more alone than before.

"Is he?"

"Is who?"

"Do you think Ben is coming home soon?"

"I don't know. I have no idea."

Seconds later the doorbell rang. Pilot stiffened and his tail thumped on the wooden floor.

German stood and walked to the door. Opening it, she saw a little boy standing there. He looked from her feet slowly up her body until his eyes reached her face. He smiled until his teeth showed. Something about me must really amuse him, German thought. His face was dimly familiar but she could not place it.

"Hello there. Can I help you?"

Ignoring her question, the boy said with admiration, "He said you were tall but, man, you're *really* tall."

"That I am. Who told you I was tall?"

"You're name is German, right?"

"That's me."

"I came to help you."

"Cool." She smiled. Did he want to sell her Cub Scout cookies or something? Did the Cub Scouts *sell* cookies? He was much too young to be a door-to-door religious proselytizer. How did Junior plan on helping her? This boy was a few years younger than her students. Perhaps that's why he looked familiar: simply because he looked like her kids.

Standing on the other side of the room, Danielle called out "Hello!" to the boy.

He smiled but his eyes were on the dog, which stood at German's side and was intently watching him. Pilot was not the kind of slutty canine that threw himself at every person who entered the apartment and covered them with slobbery, promiscuous kisses. Oh, no, not Pilot. He was a watcher, a considerer. He took as long as he needed to check out a stranger. Only when he was convinced the person was okay would he walk over and give him or her a sniff or a bump hello with his head.

But this young visitor was different, and that made Pilot even more cautious. The boy smelled like Ben Gould. To dogs, a human being's odor is that person's one-of-a-kind fingerprint. It is singular, constant, and absolutely tamperproof. Splash on a bottle of cologne, take four showers in a row, die, it makes no difference: beneath any olfactory camouflage, people retain their own aromas, unique only to them. In its entire life the dog had never, ever encountered two people who smelled exactly the same.

"Is that Pilot?"

Both the tall woman and the dog jerked on hearing the boy say the name.

"Yes, it is. How did you know that?"

The boy ignored the question again and looked past her into the living room. "And are you Danielle Voyles?"

"Yes, I am. How do you know *my* name?" She came over and stood just behind German.

"Because I'm here to help you too."

"But who are you?" she asked in a pleasant voice.

Instead of answering, the boy said to German, "Your favorite song is 'Under My Thumb.'" Turning to Danielle, he said, "And your favorite song is 'What if I Can't Say No Again,' right?"

Simultaneously the women scowled, because he was correct. They had just been talking about their favorite music a few minutes earlier. Anything to take their minds off what was going on.

Still looking at Danielle, he continued, "You snore at night but it's a nice sound. It's funny, because it sounds like a quiet growl. That's what your boyfriend said."

The boy asked for a glass of water.

German wanted to stay and ask him questions, but at the moment she was so flummoxed that she was glad for an excuse to go. A round trip to the kitchen now would give her time to regroup her thoughts.

Walking through the living room to get the boy his drink, she passed one large window and then a second. On the ledge of the second window were three photographs in stylish walnut frames. She had given them to Ben when they lived together. Before that, the pictures they held had sat inside cheap red plastic frames he'd bought years before at a dime store. Every time German saw them it annoyed her, because she knew how important those photos were to her new boyfriend. One day she bought three expensive frames, placed the pictures inside, and without any ceremony returned them to their places on the windowsill. Ben noticed immediately. She was surprised at how touched he was by what she considered a small gesture. He loved those photographs, but even more he loved her thoughtfulness and the way she made the change without bringing it to his attention. Danielle had looked at each of the pictures earlier and smiled.

The first one was of Ben's family sitting around a picnic table. It was raining and they all wore rain gear. The second was of his beloved grandmother a few years before she died. In the picture she wore a blue Chicago Cubs baseball cap. The third photo was of Ben when he was nine years old at summer camp. He was holding a bow in one hand and an arrow in the other.

German was several feet past the photographs when she stopped suddenly, blinked rapidly several times while processing certain information, then sort of moonwalked backward to look at one of them again. What she saw made her bite her lower lip and shudder all the way down her body. This picture and what had happened with Stewart Parrish earlier that morning said logic was now dead and all bets were off.

Two minutes later she was back at the front door. Handing a full glass of cold water to the boy, she asked, "You're Ben, aren't you?"

"Thank you. Yes, I am."

"How old are you?"

"Eight." He drank all of the water in a few loud glugs.

"Where's Big Ben?"

Danielle looked at German as though she were crazy.

The boy stepped into the apartment. "I have to come in if I'm going to help you."

•   •   •

Half an hour later he said he was hungry, so German made him a fat peanut butter sandwich. She remembered to put it on white bread and cut off the crusts, because Ben disliked bread crusts. There was also a can of root beer in the back of the almost-empty refrigerator, because all his life he had liked the drink, so she gave that to the boy too.

They all sat at the kitchen table, the two women watching little Ben Gould devour the sandwich and unself-consciously belch his way through swallowing soda much too fast. He seemed very pleased with himself after every burp.

"So, Ben, how did you get here?"

Through a very visible mouthful of gummy tan peanut butter, he managed to say, "I rode a song."

"You wrote a song?"

"No, I *rode* a song. That's how I got here: I rode a song."

"I don't understand."

He shrugged, as if to say, "That's your problem."

Working to keep the impatience out of her voice, German asked, "Could you explain it to me?"

He put the sandwich down and took a long swig of root beer. "You like that song 'Under My Thumb.' When it came on the radio, I rode it here."

"But how? How do you ride a song? What does that mean?"

"I don't know; you just do it. It's real simple."

"Where did you come from? Where were you before here?"

"Crane's View."

German had earlier told Danielle that that was the name of the town in upstate New York where Ben had grown up.

"You *rode* a song from Crane's View to here?"

"Yeah, I already told you." He pushed the last piece of sandwich into his mouth and shook the soda can to hear if there was any more left inside. "You want me to show you how to do it? Have you got a radio here?"

"On top of the fridge."

Although he'd been talking to German, the boy turned and looked at Danielle. "Turn it on and find a song you remember. One from when you were little."

Danielle shoved her chair back and stood up. She walked over to the refrigerator and switched on the radio. Twisting the round dial, she surfed quickly across a sea of stations while German and little Ben watched her.

"What am I searching for?"

"A song you remember from back when you were a little kid."

Because her back was to them, they didn't see Danielle smirk at the slim chance of *that* ever happening. As a child, she was almost never allowed to listen to music in the house. Her parents were devout Jehovah's Witnesses who firmly disapproved of "the sound of other singing." As a result, the family radio was turned on only so that they could listen to worship services broadcast from California that her parents particularly enjoyed. The only song Danielle really remembered from her childhood besides the ones in the *Sing Praises to Jehovah* hymnbook was the famous spiritual "Oh Happy Day."

As she kept surfing through the radio channels, she thought what a wild fluke it would be to find that one song on the radio right now.

After waiting awhile, German turned her attention back to Ben. "How did *you* do it?"

There was a loud crash in the living room. Glass—a huge crash and tinkle of breaking glass. The three looked at one another with expressions that asked, What was *that*?

They didn't have long to wait. Seconds later, a white animal charged into the room and went right for the boy. Little Ben screamed but the women were too amazed to do anything.

The boy leapt from his chair, ran across the kitchen, and climbed straight up a wall. Like a spider, he scuttled up the smooth surface on all fours. To cross the room, he'd had to brush past Danielle, who was standing next to the refrigerator, her hand still on the radio dial. She could still feel his touch long after he had climbed the wall.

The white dog—or was it a dog?—stood directly below young Ben and gazed up at him as if he were dinner. Neither of them made a sound. The boy's eyes staring down were hot with rage and fear. The dog's large eyes were calm. It did not have ears.

Danielle sidestepped away from the refrigerator and moved slowly back toward the table and German. All three sets of eyes were on the boy perched high up on the wall. His eyes darted back and forth between them but always returned to the white animal.

In time, little Ben began to move farther up the wall and then out onto the kitchen ceiling. On reaching the middle, he stopped. Dropping his head back, he looked down at them again.

Pilot chose that moment to enter the kitchen, curious at all the racket. After the craziness earlier with the half-dead man, running away, and then flying back, the dog had gone into the bedroom to take a restorative nap while the humans talked. What he saw now was the two women, a white verz, and the boy who smelled like Ben hanging upside down from the ceiling. Pilot had never seen a human being hanging from the ceiling before. The dog exchanged glances and a silent hello with the verz. Pilot did not need to smell the other animal's behind to obtain information. He already knew that all verzes' behinds smelled exactly the same. Neither did he need to ask why the thing was there, because verzes were like ambulances: they appeared only when human beings were in trouble and needed outside assistance. What Pilot did not yet realize was that the women could see this verz. *That* fact would amaze the dog.

The hanging boy said something in an eerie, silky, sibilant language that neither the dog nor the women understood.

Pilot asked the verz what the kid had said.

"He knows I'm going to kill him and asked if he could choose how to die."

"Can he?"

The verz dropped its eyes from the ceiling and looked at Pilot. "Not a chance."

German was torn between wanting to flee and trying to do something to help little Ben. What made her hesitate was having seen the boy climb a *wall* and hang from the ceiling like a bat.

"How did you know I was here?" the boy asked.

Verzes speak through their eyes. "I saw you sneaking around outside. I assumed you'd try something like this, so I just followed you."

Upside down, young Ben smiled. "You're clever. But it was a smart idea of me to come here, you have to admit: pretend I was the boy and win their confidence. It got me into this apartment.

In a few more minutes they would have been eating out of my hand. If you hadn't arrived, I would've gotten Danielle."

To the others in the kitchen it sounded like a bunch of gobbledygook, lots of "s" sounds hissing down from the child on the ceiling.

"Now what happens, verz?"

"Now you fall down and I kill you."

"I have a better idea."

"Really? What's that?"

"Let me go and I'll tell you a secret."

"Tell me the secret first and I'll consider letting you go."

The boy grinned. "You're lying."

The verz blinked twice. "You too."

"You're definitely going to kill me?"

"Definitely."

Little Ben asked in a sad voice, "If I am going to die, answer one question, because it's really been bugging me: Why did they send a ghost to help *him* but not one for *her*?" He nodded toward Danielle Voyles.

The verz said, "Because she doesn't need help. She's going to figure this all out by herself. Why do you think I came? Because she already sensed that something was wrong with you."

"You think?" The boy sprang from the ceiling. Twisting gracefully in the air like an expert gymnast, he landed in a coiled crouch near Danielle. The move was unexpected. The verz was taken completely off guard. It was unable to stop little Ben when he sprang again, this time for Danielle's throat.

Instinctively throwing up her arms, she crossed them in an X in front of her face. That quick gesture blocked the boy for precious seconds. And in those seconds, the being masquerading as young Ben Gould transformed back into what it really was.

Death is what humans fear most, although everyone has a different idea of what it'll look like when it comes for him or her. But Danielle Voyles had already seen her death once. Seeing it now for the second time only made her angry.

"Oh, no you don't." She threw the radio at the thing with all of her might and hit it in the face. Then she sprang five feet straight up in the air and landed on top of the refrigerator. None of it was thought out: her body screamed *Jump!* and she did. Crouching on the refrigerator, she tensed to jump again if the beast came after her.

But the verz was faster. Charging forward, it sank its teeth into what moments before had been the little boy. But by then the "boy" had metamorphosed into something unrecognizable.

Fearsome jaws clamped tight around it, the verz stepped slowly backward while dragging the squirming being along with it. The verz wanted to get the thing out of the kitchen because it did not want the others to see what it was going to do next.

Not that they *wanted* to see. Pilot didn't move. German Landis stepped back fast to avoid touching either creature when the verz passed her.

Danielle stayed perched up on the refrigerator and watched the action down below. From that safe-for-now vantage point, she wondered, How'd I do that? How did I jump so high? Her mind was split between watching with awe as the verz dragged the whatever-it-was out of the room and puzzling over how she had leapt to her present location. What she didn't realize yet was that she had only copied the boy. She had done exactly as he had to escape.

While crossing the floor, the verz suddenly slid on something slippery and lost its balance. For an instant it opened its mouth in surprise and the thing wrenched itself loose. Darting across the room, it went straight for Danielle again. She saw it coming, leapt off the refrigerator, and skittered high up on the wall, just as the boy-monster had done minutes before. Up there on the kitchen wall, she glared at her new enemy a few feet away on top of the refrigerator.

Down below, the verz sprang for the monster. The monster sprang for Danielle. Like a fly, Danielle waited till the last second and then easily jumped from the wall and across the kitchen, landing near German Landis, who stared at her in wonder.

The monster followed but this time it was cut off in midflight by the verz, which caught it by the throat and pulled it brutally to the floor. Together they landed on top of the dog. Pilot was not quick enough to scramble out of their way.

Frightened, desperate, pinned down, and unable to move, Pilot instinctively bit whatever was nearest, and that happened to be the verz. The white animal had one job to do: protect Danielle Voyles. Nothing else mattered and nothing else could interfere with that task. Without hesitation it raked its claws down the dog's side, drawing blood.

Pilot howled and thrashed around, almost freeing himself in the process. The verz saw this and moved slightly to allow the wounded dog to escape. Held tightly between the verz's teeth, the red thing was losing energy now. The verz could feel the slackening through the muscles of its jaw, but it would not let go until it was sure the thing was dead.

"Stop!" Danielle shouted.

None of them really registered the command, because so much was happening at once. The world around them was havoc.

"*Stop!* Don't kill it."

They heard this time and turned to Danielle.

"Don't kill it. Let it go. You have to let it go."

The verz immediately opened its mouth and let the beast drop to the floor.

It was red now, russet, almost brown. The red was not blood, though, but the true color of its skin. Mortally wounded, it had no energy to move. Its neck was broken. The little oxygen it could draw in did no good.

Showing no fear or hesitation this time, Danielle walked over and squatted down close by. Even as it lay dying, the thing's drooping eyes followed the woman. Extending both hands, Danielle grabbed hold of its body and dug her fingers deep into its skin.

The eyes rolled up into its head. It made a sound that could have been a sigh or a gasp. Squeezing and squeezing and squeezing, Danielle began kneading its skin like bread dough. After some moments the red body sagged visibly in her hands. It was dead by then but that didn't matter, because moments before it expired, Danielle had found what she was searching for inside it and brought that back into her own body. It was alive inside of her now. It was the reason she had told the verz not to kill the beast. She needed to take this thing from it while it was still alive.

Standing, she could feel that new element moving inside her while it searched for its proper place: the place of its origin. Not a pleasant feeling for Danielle. It felt like an icy wire sliding down the inside of her chest. Perhaps it wanted to escape. Perhaps these things cannot return to us once they have left our bodies—once we have *allowed* them to leave. Despite that, Danielle waited, and in due course it did stop moving. She touched the small of her back and said, "It's here. It stopped here." The others did not know what she was talking about.

On the floor the dead thing began to fade. Within seconds it had disappeared. Both hands still on her back, Danielle looked at German Landis and pointed with her foot to the place on the floor where it had lain. "What I took out of it was once part of me. I lost it when I was little. No—*I gave it away* when I was little. I did it; it was my choice.

"That's what all people do when we're frightened: we give away parts of ourselves. We do it on purpose. No one steals them or forces us. We give away our best parts: the ones that make us whole and right. Piece by piece we give them up until finally . . ." Danielle stopped and put one hand to her forehead. "I have to sit down." She crossed the room and sat again at the kitchen table.

Danielle put a hand flat against her chest. "We're born with everything in here—everything we need to be happy and complete. But as soon as life starts frightening us, we give away pieces of ourselves to make the danger go away. It's a trade: you want life to stop scaring you, so you give it a part of yourself. You give away your pride, your dignity, or your courage . . .

"When all you feel is fear, you don't *need* dignity. So you don't mind giving that away—at the moment. But you regret it later, because you'll need all those pieces. By then they're gone, though; you can't use them to help.

"Do you have a piece of bread? I'll show you how it works."

German took a dinner roll out of the wooden bread box on the counter and handed it over. Danielle placed it on the table. "This is how we look when we're born: complete and whole, every single person." She began pinching small pieces off the roll. In seconds it was pitted all over and looked like birds had been pecking it. Dropping the pieces on the floor, she covered them with her foot and pressed down. When she lifted her shoe again, the squashed bread bits had turned into dirty shapeless blobs. Some were stuck to her sole.

Peeling one off, Danielle made to fit it back into the roll. When that didn't work, she held out the dirty bit to German and said, "Imagine this is a part of myself I gave up once when I was frightened. They took it, changed it, and sent it back looking like that." She pointed with her chin toward where the dead creature had lain. "When that thing began to die, I suddenly saw through its body to the heart. I recognized it had once been part of me. I gave away that part. They changed it into the heart of a monster and then sent it back to get me."

Exasperated, German shook her head. "How do you know this? How can you *know* these things?"

Danielle's face was clear and serene. In time she said, "I saw through the skin to its heart. It was beating slower and slower. As soon as I saw it, I knew that heart was once part of me. So I reached in and took it." She touched the area on her lower back where it was now. "You can always take back the lost parts of yourself if you can find and recognize them."

• • •

Benjamin Gould awoke breathing through fur. After opening his eyes, several seconds passed before his brain grasped that he was sort of breathing, sort of suffocating. However, it wasn't a frightening feeling; it was more uncomfortable than anything else.

The first thing he saw was a large white something directly in front of him—not a few feet away but inches. And heavy. Whatever it was lay across the lower half of his face so that it covered much of his mouth and nose. The more awake he became, the more smothered he felt. Plus, the thing covering his face and chest was *heavy*. Ben shoved it off and tried to sit up—unsuccessfully, because when he put his arms down to brace himself on the ground, both hands sank into warm fur on either side of his body.

Panicking, he gasped, "Get off! Get *off* me!" and pushed and squirmed and got up off the ground. The four verzes that had been sleeping on and around him didn't like being disturbed but remained silent. They weren't supposed to say anything because their job was to protect this man at all costs. If he told them to move, they moved.

"You were sleeping on my face!" he said muzzily while wiping his hand back and forth across his mouth. Shivering, Ben rubbed both cold arms and stared at the small tent nearby where the children and Mr. Kyte were sleeping. It looked a lot more appealing than it had a few hours ago when he'd gone to sleep curled up beside the campfire. In his mind now Ben saw himself lying in that tent, cozying up inside a thick goose-down sleeping bag. Green. It would be a forest-green goose-down sleeping bag that covered him right up to his toasty-warm neck. He imagined himself inside that sleeping bag without large numbers of earless fat white animals lying on top of him as if he were a rug.

He was hungry and cold and did not know what to do. By the look of things, it was the middle of the night. Not even Ling was around to talk over the situation.

Because he was out there alone amid darkness, bewilderment, and muddle, Ben said in a soft voice, "I want to go home right now. I just want to go home. That's all."

A heartbeat later he was standing in front of the brightly lit bathroom mirror in his apartment, looking at the reflection of his face. Ben touched the mirror above the sink to assure himself that it was real and not an illusion. He pulled his hand back and touched his face. He opened the door of the medicine cabinet. The bottles inside were familiar products that he remembered buying. He closed the cabinet and picked up the damp bar of soap on the sink. He smelled it: bitter almonds. That was right too. For his birthday German had given him an expensive box of milled almond soap. What had just happened? How had he managed to return home in an instant from the forest in

Crane's View? What had he done to make that happen? He looked again in the mirror.

The door behind him opened. German Landis stood framed in the doorway wearing one of his sweatshirts and underpants. She was so tall that the shirt came to just below her belly button. She had on women's white cotton boxer shorts, her favorite kind of underpants and the ones that always twisted Ben's guts whenever he saw her in them. Her face was flushed and puffy with sleep. He only wanted to kiss her. That's all he thought then: Just let me kiss her and feel that smooth skin again. I don't care about anything else. One kiss. Let me kiss her and smell her hair. Let me do that and I'll be okay again.

"Hello there," he said gently.

She said nothing and did not react, only stared at him. What was she doing in his apartment? As had happened the first time, Ling again materialized, standing on top of the lowered toilet seat in Ben's bathroom. But now German witnessed it. She saw a small, nondescript woman emerge out of nowhere, standing on top of the toilet with arms crossed over her narrow chest like a genie in a Sinbad movie.

Ling recognized immediately that German Landis could see her. She only wished she'd known earlier that it was going to happen so she could have put on some makeup.

Very coolly German stated, "There's a woman standing on the toilet seat."

Ben looked and nodded.

Ling stepped down and walked over to German with her right hand extended to shake. The moment she had dreamed of for so long had arrived. She was about to meet the woman she loved. "How do you do? My name is Ling."

German Landis looked at the ghost the way you never want to be looked at by the object of your affection. German looked at Ling as if she were a postage stamp, a bottle of ketchup, or an out-of-date movie schedule. Her eyes said nothing, they only took in data. "Who are you?"

For the first time since materializing, Ling looked at Ben to see how he wanted her to answer this question.

"Tell her."

The ghost started to speak but Ben put up a hand to stop her.

"Wait a minute."

The two women, both impatient, looked at him.

"Something's wrong."

"Gee, Ben, no kidding."

He shook his head. "That's not what I mean." He stared straight ahead, as if seeing something important in the space directly in front of him. His eyes flicked over to German. "She's in trouble. Danielle Voyles is in trouble." He hurried out of the bathroom. What else could the women do but follow?

"Pilot?" he called down the hall. "Pilot, where are you?"

The dog lay in his bed fully awake, dreading what he knew would be coming at any moment.

"Pilot? Pilot, where *are* you?"

Maybe he won't find me, Pilot thought as he lay there. Maybe he's in such a tizzy now that he'll forget about me and go by himself. He knew Ben needed his help to save Danielle.

The bedroom door swung open and behind it a blast of hall light swept in and over the animal. "There you are. Let's go."

"I old too am."

Already half turning to go back out the door, Ben stopped. "What?"

Pilot said something completely unintelligible this time. The two stared at each other.

"I don't understand you." Ben could feel his brain trying to untwist the dog's words into recognizable order. Now he understood he was not entirely back here yet, caught somewhere between his past in Crane's View and home now.

"He says that he's too old to go with you," Ling translated from out in the hall.

Ben walked across the room, grabbed the dog by the scruff of the neck, and hauled it out of bed.

Ling didn't think this was a good tactic but she remained silent.

When the mutt was standing, Ben got down on all fours so that they were eye to eye.

Ling was prepared to hear him rebuke Pilot. When he spoke, though, she didn't understand a word he said. But the dog apparently did because it stiffened and began wagging its tail furiously. When Ben stopped speaking, the dog ran out of the room and down the hall to the front door.

"What did you say? What language were you speaking?"

Ben stood and walked past her. "Wolf."

Nine

A man, a dog, and two understandably disgruntled women were walking down a sidewalk. One woman was a ghost, the man should have been dead, the dog was the reincarnation of the should-have-been-dead's girlfriend, and the last, the tall woman, was an innocent bystander who had the bad fortune of loving two of the others.

Three of them were asking the man how he did that.

"How did you know where we were?"

"How did you get back here without my knowing it?"

"How did you know the wolf language?"

Ben ignored them all and kept walking. He did not know the answers to any of these questions, so he thought it best to remain silent but look resolute. Hopefully his demeanor would make them think at least for a while that he knew what he was doing.

When they realized he wasn't going to talk to them, the women began a conversation. Naturally, German didn't know that this short woman walking alongside had been observing her for months. She didn't know that Ling could have made impressively detailed lists of what German Landis liked and didn't like. Or that Ling was in love with her and, as a result, had studied her the way ardent church scholars study obscure religious texts.

Now that Ling could actually talk to German, she was bursting to tell her a whole slew of things. And to ask a million questions that she had been storing up since that unforgettable moment months ago when she looked at the tall woman sitting in a chair reading and realized with a woozy thump that she loved her.

"You really don't know what's happened to Danielle?" the object of Ling's affection now asked, walking fast.

"No. I'm limited to Ben." Ling hurried to keep up because her legs were so much shorter.

"What do you mean by 'limited'?"

"I only know what's happening to him. I can see what he's thinking but no one else." Ling failed to mention that she could see into other peoples' future, as she had the day she saw German for the first time and checked to see how much longer the woman would live.

"Then what *is* he thinking? Why won't he answer our questions?"

"He's trying to figure out how to save Danielle," Ling lied. She didn't want to upset German any more than she already had. The distressing truth was that, since returning here this time, Ling could no longer read Ben's mind at all.

Yes, it was a dream come true that she could communicate with German now, but that wasn't her job. How was the ghost supposed to help Ben when she didn't know any more about what was going on in his head now than his ex-girlfriend did?

"If you're a ghost, why can I see you now? And why can I understand what Pilot is saying?"

Hearing his name spoken out loud, the dog turned to see if German needed anything.

Ling did not know the answers to those questions, either. But she could guess and try to make it sound convincing. "Ever since Ben refused to die, more and more strange things have been happening to him and around him. And they keep changing. Nothing in his world is fixed anymore; nothing's stable. The fact you can see me now and understand what your dog says may change tomorrow. It's like we're all in his force field but it's unstable. We're affected by whatever changes happen to him."

A few feet in front of the women, Ben said to Pilot, "You know what you have to do when we get there?"

The dog said nothing.

"Pilot?"

"I assumed that was a statement and not a question," the mutt muttered mutinously.

Understanding the animal's discontent, Ben said more softly, "I'd do it myself and let you stay at home, but I don't know how to talk to verzes."

The dog remained silent. Then Pilot decided he did want to say something. "There could be monsters over there, you know."

Ben could only agree.

"There could be monsters and killers and other deadly things. But you're still making me go. I don't care what your reasons are—it's not fair. I'm way too old. I thought we were friends."

"Come on, Pilot, you are the only one here who can speak to verzes."

"And she can't?" Both of them knew Pilot was referring to Ling.

Leaning over, the man lowered his voice so only the dog could hear him. "She can't do anything anymore. But she doesn't know that yet."

"Well, thanks for sharing *that* reassuring piece of information. It makes me feel much more secure now."

Ben had no response. What do you say to a sardonic dog?

"So, Master, let's review: you've got a useless ghost, an old dog, and a girlfriend who doesn't have a clue. Hey, but you don't have a clue, either, so you're useless too.

"Still, us four losers are supposed to go and rescue this Danielle woman from monsters and killers."

"Maybe there won't be any when we get there."

Pilot wasn't having it. "Fine. Do you want to go first?"

Because Ben was avoiding the dog's eyes by looking down and to his right, he was the first to see the pink fog a hundred feet away moving toward them. It was a remarkable sight: absolutely candy-pink fog roiling and floating down the sidewalk at ankle height.

"Jeez, what's *that*?"

Pilot saw the fog and stopped, his right front leg still up in the air. The women did not see anything, although both turned to look in that direction after hearing Ben exclaim.

"What is it? What do you see?" Ling asked.

Pilot didn't know what to say. Should he tell the truth: that this fog coming toward them was cancer? That if it stopped and enfolded any of them, they were doomed.

With his new heightened awareness, Ben could see the fog but did not know what it was. How could such a thing exist? *Pink* fog? How come he had never seen it before in his life?

"What is it? What are you looking at, Ben?" German asked.

"*That!* Don't you see it?"

"See what?" Ling asked.

"The fog: the pink fog there."

German looked at Ling. The ghost's face was troubled, because of course she knew about this fog but could not see it herself now.

And then it was upon them. Pilot thought about trying to run away, but that did no good. You could run all day, but if you were fated to be touched, the fog would find you anywhere. He remembered the last time he had seen it when the Rottweiler accompanied him that night. The other dog had said it wished it were human so it would never have to see this fatal stuff when it appeared.

It drifted along the sidewalk and then slid across the tops of Ben's sneakers. He felt nothing. The man and the dog watched the fog move. Ben thought it looked like pink cigarette smoke. Nothing happened until it rose slightly off his shoes and a tendril of fog glided up beneath his jeans. When it touched the bare skin of his leg, Ben immediately said a very tough *"No."*

Taken aback both by the force of the word and the man's nerve to even say it, Pilot was impressed. He could only watch to see what came next while hoping against hope that the fog had not come for him.

Reaching down, Ben grabbed the pink smoke with one hand as if it were a living thing—an eel or some sort of a snake. Holding tight, he yanked it hard. The piece that had drifted up his leg came right out of his pants.

"No. No. No," he kept repeating calmly. As he spoke, Ben began pulling the fog with one clenched hand through the other. By doing that, he squeezed the formless stuff into a kind of translucent rope. Once it had passed through his hands, it lay unmoving on the sidewalk beside them.

"Ben, what are you *doing?*" German demanded to know, because she could see only the peculiar actions of his hands but not what they held. Ling did not see it, either, but the ghost knew something significant was happening. She remained silent but fully attentive.

Ignoring German's question, Ben snapped his hands apart. The pink fog broke in two. The part that was still only fog— what he had not yet touched with either hand—evaporated instantly. What he had touched lay whole and formed at his feet.

Amazed, Pilot looked at Ben with new eyes. All his life the dog had seen cancer fog floating through the air on its way to finish something off. It was the final boss of every living thing, the sheriff that took no prisoners. But now this average man had stopped it and then broken the fog in pieces. How was that possible?

"It came for me, Pilot. You don't have to worry because it wasn't after you," Ben said to the dog, and picked the motionless pink rope up off the ground. Working gracefully with both hands, he curled it round and round his arm. "It came for me. It'll keep coming, too, but it's nothing to worry about. Really. At least not now." He formed a half smile that withered quickly.

German approached and started to speak, but Ben shook his head at her. "Don't ask questions now. I'm trying to figure this out and it's hard if I'm distracted."

She went ballistic. "Don't say that! Don't dismiss me like that, Ben Gould. Why did we stop? And what just happened? What are you doing there?" She looked at his empty hands doing their mysterious winding and looping.

Without another word, he took the section of pink rope he was holding and slid it down the side of her face.

Although it looked as though nothing was in his hand when he touched her, German felt something warm and liquid on her cheek. Then whatever it was entered her face, her neck, and sped throughout her body. It moved as fast and powerfully as lightning.

While Ling and Pilot watched, the tall woman relaxed. Not only her body but her entire demeanor calmed. To all appearances she gave the impression of someone who had been injected with a powerful sedative. Her body swayed, wobbled, and only just righted itself before collapsing. Later, on reflection, German recognized the feeling was akin to the joyous helplessness of her body during orgasm: no control, but no desire for control either; the joy of falling because there was no fear of hitting. While it happened, her vision blurred and her body felt weightless. Her body was gone, really, but she didn't understand that until much later when things had been explained.

By touching her with the pink rope, Ben had touched German with death. But because it was not her own death, she was immune and could experience it purely for what it was. What she felt was what every single being feels in the first moments after it has died: unimaginable peace, weightlessness, and the jubilant freedom of the soul leaving a body that has been its burden for so long.

The elation she felt did not show on her face. It went far, far beyond the facility of facial expression. She looked stunned, yes, but only that.

"You touched her with the fog, Ben! How's she supposed to understand that? Really, how is she supposed to understand?" Ling demanded.

"She has a right to know some of this, Ling. I've forced her into the middle of it now, and you know that."

Putting his arm around German's shoulders, he held her until he felt some strength return to her body. She looked at him vacantly but not with any ill feeling. She looked at her ex-boyfriend as if he were a light pole.

There was a car parked nearby. He led her over, thinking it was better for her to rest against something solid awhile before they continued.

Pilot came over and asked the ghost, "What's wrong with what he did, Ling? Why are you angry at him?"

"He showed her something she should never have seen."

"By touching her with the pink fog?" Pilot assumed she could see it too.

Ling nodded. "Yes. It was his death, so that couldn't hurt her, but still, he should never have done it."

"What happens when you touch fog meant for someone else?"

Ling said, "Do it to Pilot, Ben. Let him know. He's as involved in this as she is."

After making sure German was okay, Ben left her leaning against the car. He picked up the rope on the ground nearby. Bringing it over, he glanced at Ling once more to make sure she meant what she'd said.

"Yes, do it."

He touched Pilot on top of the head with the rope and stepped back. The dog whimpered and collapsed.

"Now me. Touch me with it too."

"Why?"

"Do what I tell you!" Ling put out her arm. He touched it with the pink rope. She felt nothing. She had no reaction. Looking straight at him, she didn't even blink. "Nothing. I knew that would happen. I can't feel anything and I can't see anything, either. I can't see the rope. Why, Ben? Do you know? If you do, tell me. I need to know."

He held nothing back. "Because your powers are gone, or most of them. You're almost a normal person now. I knew it the moment I saw you appear in the bathroom before. If you do have any leftover powers or whatever, they'll be gone soon. You can't depend on them anymore."

Ling didn't react to this news. She only wanted to know the truth so she could adjust to it. "How do you know these things?"

He put his hand on the top of his head. "*I* don't know anything; some part of me does. A part I don't know or control. It brought me back here from the woods in Crane's View. *I* didn't do that. I didn't have anything to do with it. I'm positive it's the same part that stopped me from dying when I hit my head last winter.

"I don't know what it is or where it is in me. And I have no idea what it's going to do next. But it's taken over; it's the boss now. It's me, it's *mine*, but I'll be damned if I know what it is.

"That's how I knew before that Danielle was doing something now that could be bad for her: it just came over me, like a cloud in front of the sun. I did nothing."

Ling answered in a steady, confident voice, because she was sure what she would say was correct. "Your will is going in front of your consciousness."

"What do you mean?"

"Your will has taken over. It decided it's time to take action. And now it has."

He considered this. "Can't you tell me something ghosts know that might help now?"

Ling grinned. "Not anymore, pal. You just said I'm no different from you now. But I'm sure what I'm saying is true. I'm sure I'm right.

"You can talk to ghosts and dogs now, Ben. You understand our languages. But there's so much more." She held up a hand

and counted off each achievement on her fingers. "You stopped your own death. You traveled through time to get back here. I took you to the park in Crane's View and Gina Kyte's basement, but you brought yourself back to the present.

"What more proof do you need? Something inside you that was dormant till now woke up, stepped forward, and said, 'Enough is enough. Let's go.' I believe it's your will: the part of Ben Gould that sees a problem, determines what needs to be done, and takes action."

"And even stops death?" he asked.

"Yes, and even stops death."

Ten

Danielle Voyles picked up the lip balm and turned it around and around in a hand held up close to her face. She examined the object as if it were a precious artifact from an ancient civilization. The product was called Carmex and came in a small white-and-yellow plastic jar. It was empty and had been for many years. Nevertheless, she always kept it in a prominent place on her vanity table. Once after moving to a new apartment she thought she had lost it, which made her extremely upset. She had been thinking about this small container ever since German Landis explained the significance of her red "Rudi" stone earlier in the day.

When Danielle got home after the madness at Benjamin Gould's apartment, she went straight to her bedroom to make sure the Carmex was right where it belonged, because that little empty jar was *her* important talisman. It was the first thing Danielle Voyles had ever stolen.

She loved stealing things and was a skillful thief. But until she was twelve years old she had never known how gratifying it was. One day, on the spur of the moment, she stole this jar of lip balm from the neighborhood drugstore for no reason other than she wanted it and no one was around to see her snitch it. That impulsive act changed her life in many ways.

Being the child of religious parents, Danielle had suppressed any sensations of exhilaration or adrenaline rushes throughout her body. The best she had experienced was the joy, the intense joy, that she felt every time she took a risk and walked down a street afterward with whatever she had put in her pocket, hot in her hand because she hadn't let go once since lifting it. Hot from the heat of holding it too tightly as she walked, poised but petrified, out of a store, the object now hers forever for free because she'd been wily and careful about stealing it just right.

Over the years she'd stolen so many things that she became a thoroughly adept and blasé thief. She rarely stole anymore, true, but if she needed something and the circumstances were right, she still simply took it and never thought twice about it.

While in the hospital recuperating, Danielle began wondering if her freakish accident had been some kind of cosmic punishment for her lifetime of petty theft. What goes around comes around. In her case it had come around in the form of a plane crash that shot a metal splinter into her skull.

That's why she began reading all those religious texts afterward. What if God finally got around to her case and, having reviewed the facts, had begun His retribution? Could that be what was happening to her now? Looking at the Carmex container in her hand, she speculated once again: What if I hadn't stolen this goop that day? Would any of this be happening to me now? No pen would have punctured my head. And no earless creature would be dragging a dead red monster across a kitchen floor right in front of my eyes.

Turning the empty jar around and around in her hand, she could not stop thinking, What if? And the third time she thought it, the chance to find out arrived as silently as a cat walking into a carpeted room.

When Danielle looked up and focused on her surroundings, she saw that she was standing inside a small drugstore. Not a mammoth place with aisles that stretch forever and carry a hundred different varieties of aspirin and vitamins. At first glance one could easily see this was a mom-and-pop business with just enough of everything to keep the neighborhood happy. Intermittent shelves were half-empty because the owners hadn't gotten around to restocking them yet. Some of the products in there she hadn't seen, much less thought about or used, since her childhood.

Twelve-year-old Danielle Voyles now appeared at the other end of the aisle. She wore a simple navy blue dress that the adult recognized immediately. The girl's hair came to just below her ears. She was a sweet-looking kid, not this and not that. The most memorable thing about her was the beat-up man's leather briefcase she carried. It looked wholly out of place in her small hand. It looked as if she were holding her dad's bag because he was somewhere nearby and would be joining her at any moment.

Walking down the aisle, the girl now looked at adult Danielle but plainly didn't see her. Dawdling here and there, picking things up and putting them down again, she moved slowly toward her older self.

Adult Danielle watched the girl with delight and only a little apprehension. Seeing her actual twelve-year-old self living, breathing, moving, humming now, and not as a faded, frozen image in an old photograph was just too exciting and surreal not to be wonderful. The girl was humming . . . Yes! She was humming the song "Oh Happy Day."

At that moment, though, something went wrong, and it began with the buttons.

Her mother had made the blue dress for her when she was eleven and had her daughter choose buttons she liked. Watching this girl in blue walk up the aisle toward her now, Danielle looked at them and remembered the day she'd bought them. But while focusing specifically on the large round white buttons, they began to change from white to yellow and finally to green. They changed shape too. While she watched, they went from round and white to banana yellow half-moons. A few seconds later the half-moon buttons transformed into green frog buttons. All this while the girl walked toward her adult self.

In her late teens, Danielle had owned a sexy dress with banana yellow half-moon buttons on it. In her closet at home now was a housecoat she changed into after work. It had green frog buttons down the front.

Upset, she shifted her gaze from the morphing buttons to the face coming toward her. It was no longer a twelve-year-old's face. The body remained the same but there was a flickering around the edges of that countenance and it became a much younger girl this time: Danielle at five or six.

This child, this six-year-old Danielle Voyles, stopped at a shelf and took down a small yellow-and-white jar of Carmex. After making sure no one was around, she twisted it open and stuck her finger deep into the middle of the ointment. She smeared the pungent stuff back and forth across her small lips. Then, screwing the top back on, she moved to put the jar back on the shelf. Halfway there, her arm slowed and stopped. Again checking to make sure no one was coming, the girl slid the Carmex into the front pocket of her dress.

While watching the theft, the adult suddenly grasped two previously unknown facts about herself that changed her self-image forever.

The first revelation was this: although she was twelve when

she stole for the first time, it was actually the six-year-old Danielle who had committed the theft. Not the seventh-grade, just-recently-discovered-boys, embarrassed-to-have-to-use-her-father's-old-briefcase-in-school girl. No, *that* Danielle was not a thief.

True, her body was twelve when she stood in the drug-store aisle and heard something inside her scream, *Steal it!* But it was the six-year-old, elated by the danger and risk, who pushed aside any doubts and took it.

For the first time in her life, adult Danielle realized it is all of our selves that have lived up until this moment that decide what we do: not only the me who is living right now.

And there is no saying which one of those selves will pre-vail.

Out of that revelation grew the second: all of our selves—past and present—determine what we do every minute of our lives.

Danielle Voyles did not start stealing when she was twelve. She started stealing when her six-year-old self ordered her twelve-year-old self to do it.

Having realized these things, the woman's hands began to shake. She was twenty-nine. She'd had a so-so life. Some of it had been her doing, some not. But how much of her middling life had happened the way it did because the wrong Danielles had made the wrong decisions? How many times should the last decider have been younger or older, more cynical or more trust-ing, than the one who'd had the final say?

Of course six-year-old Danielle was still alive in the twelve-year-old. She was alive in the twenty-nine-year-old too. The six-year-old was part of her history, one of the first rings of the Danielle Voyles "tree." But what the adult had never known un-til this minute was that child not only continued living inside but had also played a significant role at least once in determining her later destiny.

Feeling a tug on her sleeve, Danielle looked down and saw that the twelve-year-old in blue was now standing beside her. The adult started to nod but stopped and shook her head no instead. No, she did not understand this. No, it was not all right. Time passed before she grasped the significance of the fact the girl had touched her: she was now visible to her younger self.

"I'll meet you outside," the girl said, and turned around and walked toward the front of the store. What else was there to do but follow?

Through the windows she saw that it was drizzling outside. But, approaching the front door, she also saw that despite the wet weather, some kind of event was happening in the drugstore's small parking lot. There were only two cars parked out there on opposite sides of the lot, which was good, because set up directly in the middle of it were four picnic tables. All of them were full of people. Women. Every table was full of females of all ages. Danielle thought it must be a meeting of the Girl Scouts and their mothers or a women's club and their daughters.

Because of the wet, gray day and her physical distance from the group, she did not get a clear view of any of the faces at the tables out there until she'd pushed the door open and stepped outside. The drizzle was warm and pleasant, despite the fact it was coming down steadily. The delicious smell of grilled meat hung in the air, together with the smells of wet asphalt and trees.

She scanned the tables for the girl in blue but did not see her. What Danielle did see was her self sitting at the picnic tables. Her self and her self and an assortment of other versions of her self were sitting at the four picnic tables. All of the women sitting together, young and old, were Danielle Voyles at different ages in her life.

Once able to comprehend what she was seeing, she could not resist walking toward the group. None of them paid attention to her. They were eating grilled spare ribs and potato salad, talking, and laughing. Two girls who looked only a few years apart were playing a spirited game of patty-cake together. One woman of about twenty-five was scolding a very young Danielle whose face was smeared with chocolate. A girl in her late teens sat alone at the end of a bench reading a fat romance novel— Danielle still loved to read fat romance novels—while playing unconsciously with the ends of her long hair.

"Would you like some food? Are you hungry?"

Tearing her eyes away from the scene, Danielle turned and saw the girl in blue offering her a paper plate piled high with delectable-looking spare ribs and potato salad. In her other hand was a cup filled with a brown bubbly drink. Danielle guessed that it was Dr Pepper, her favorite.

Without speaking, she took both and followed the girl over to the tables. Again, no one there paid attention to her other than to slide over and make room. After the girl sat down next to her, she helped herself to a large rib off Danielle's plate and quickly began eating it. She got a smear of barbecue sauce on the left side of her mouth because she ate so fast and sloppily. Wiping it away with the back of her hand, she went back to gnawing the rib. It was clear the girl wanted to eat and not talk, so Danielle began eating too. It was better that way, because it enabled her to focus on the women around them.

Everyone's voice was different. One was high and irritating, while another's was slurred and mumbly. She tried to concentrate on specific women and see if she could match the voices to the faces. It was interesting how infrequently they fit together. One girl who could not have been more than ten had a startlingly low voice. Only after listening awhile did Danielle realize the kid had a bad cold. Of course! Since her childhood, whenever she fell sick, her voice dropped an octave into what she called her frog voice. Boyfriends had said it was sexy and they liked it, but she thought it sounded as if she were croaking. This girl who spoke now in that low frog voice sat two Danielles away.

A little girl sitting directly across the table put down her paper cup and let out a long loud burp. No one paid attention to the sound. Neither did today's Danielle, because even now she burped out loud when she was alone, especially while drinking soda.

She recognized their clothes, she recognized their hairdos. She remembered the purses they carried, the dolls in their laps, the titles of the books they were reading, a yellow pencil with a fat funny white clown eraser on the tip. A cheap brown Walkman with black headphones that she had owned a few years ago and played Chely Wright tapes on over and over again because the music perfectly fit the heartbreak she was experiencing at that time.

She saw a woman in a black silk bathrobe, her head wrapped in thick white bandages like some kind of macabre cocoon. The bandages covered her eyes and nose right down to the nostrils. This bandaged woman ate very slowly, carefully raising the fork to her mouth. Danielle had bought that black bathrobe at a Victoria's Secret store to impress her boyfriend right before her accident. It was one of the most expensive pieces of clothing she had ever owned. It was stolen from her hospital room right before she was released. A very small girl stood next to the mysterious-looking robed woman, staring with her mouth open in wonder at this chewing mummy in black.

Danielle continued eating her delicious meal in the warm drizzle while sliding her eyes back and forth across the different versions of herself. She grew calmer. She listened attentively to the others' conversations. Someone told the great old joke about the gynecologist and the eggplant. She loved that joke but had forgotten it many years ago. When they said the punch line now, it was exactly the way she had when she used to tell it. Nearby yet another Danielle described how her boyfriend needed a new car and was thinking seriously about buying a Subaru. That was the car she was in when the plane crashed nearby. She listened, watched, and ate.

Soon, too soon, she began hearing things she did not want to hear. Lies, stories she knew were untrue but she had told anyway, excuses she'd made up for her bad decisions, bad behavior, and bad moods. She was surrounded by various versions of herself at different times in her life. Most of these women and children were flawed, insecure, undistinguished, and not particularly brave. Almost all of them dreamt that life would pick them out of the crowd and place a crown on their heads. But in their hearts they knew that wouldn't happen because they didn't deserve it. Nothing was special about Danielle Voyles, no matter what age she was. This child, this teen, this woman, lied and postured, preened and pretended to be someone she wasn't, on many occasions just so that those who knew her, whether they were schoolyard or church pals, prospective boyfriends, or work colleagues, would find her prettier, smarter, funnier, more everything than she actually was.

Her whole life she had wanted to be more than she was in just about every way. But she did not have the smarts, the looks, or the resources to achieve it. Danielle Voyles was not nearly as interesting as the picture of herself she tried to sell to the world.

Try as she might, lie as she did, she was only moderately successful at both her ruse and her attempts to improve.

"Excuse me, do you mind if I sit down here?"

She looked up and saw herself. More than any of the others at the picnic, this woman was her mirror image in every respect: clothes, hair, shoes, everything.

"Yes, of course." She slid over on the bench, forcing the girl in blue to slide over too. The second Danielle, this identical twin, this clone, had a plate full of the same food she had been handed minutes before but which was now almost gone with the help of the girl.

"What's it like?"

"Excuse me?"

"What's the future like?"

Danielle looked at her twin and assumed she was joking. "What's it *like*? Aren't we the same person? Aren't we the exact same age? We're dressed alike. We look alike . . ."

"Yes, but there's a ten-minute difference between us."

"Ten minutes?"

"I'm ten minutes younger than you. Look at my plate: it's full. Look at yours: empty. I'm just beginning the meal you've already finished."

"This is a joke, right?"

"No. Look around here. Every one of us is you, obviously: you at different times in your life. I just happen to be the closest in age. And all I'm asking you is what is our future like?"

"That's ridiculous! I'm right here; this is the future: this picnic table, me talking to you. Do I look different? Does *anything* about me look different? We're exactly the same. What could I possibly know that you don't?"

The other Danielle looked at her as if she were the dimmest

person on the planet and said, "You are six thousand seconds older than me. Do you realize how many thoughts and ideas and decisions and questions have gone through your head in those six thousand seconds? We're different. Believe me, we're different.

"You're the future of every single one of us here." She pointed and pointed and pointed to each table. All of the Danielles were looking at Danielle now. "You know what happens to us. Wherever we are in life right now, you know what happens next. *That's* what makes you different."

She pointed to the bandaged woman, who was also turned their way, her hands crossed in front of her on the wet table. "See her? All she does is worry about what her face will look like when they take the bandages off. Will her sight be all right? Will her hearing? She hasn't told anyone yet, but sometimes she has trouble hearing. Will that continue or will it get worse?"

Next she pointed to the little girl in blue. "And what about her? Will she go on stealing things now? Is the cat out of the bag and her real self finally set free? Or was taking that Carmex only a onetime thing? She wants to ask you if she's eternally damned now in God's eyes."

Danielle looked at the girl whose small face was now scrunched up with worry. The girl nodded at her: what the other woman had said was true.

A middle-twenties her stood up and asked, "I think I'm pregnant. But I'm afraid to buy one of those home pregnancy tests from the drugstore. I'm too afraid to find out."

Danielle remembered. At twenty-two she'd met a sexy red-haired guy in a club who was the greatest lover she had ever known. They made love all the time, everywhere. She had never reveled in sex so much in her life. Although she took the birth control pill, there were three traumatic weeks when she was increasingly convinced she was pregnant. The constant worrying in that time shrank her world down to the size of a pebble.

Looking at her now, Danielle shook her head and said loudly, "You're not pregnant. You don't have to worry. It's just that your period is really, really late."

The other's face lit up. She clapped her hands together very fast like a child.

"Almost all of us have questions. If you wanted to, you could go around and answer them."

"Which ones don't? Are there any 'me's' here who *don't* have questions?"

Her twin smiled and nodded approval. "Good question. Yeah, the ones who like where they are in life."

"But why can't *you* answer them? You're only ten minutes younger than me. You know what happens to every one of them."

The other answered fast, as if she'd been anticipating that question. "Who you are now is different from who you were ten minutes ago. You might know something I don't. Or maybe you figured something out that still confuses me."

Danielle looked again at the young woman who'd thought she was pregnant. She was talking to a neighbor now, laughing and lively in her relief. Danielle knew that soon Mr. Sexy would dump her in a sudden cruel way. She wouldn't be able to decide what hurt more, his rejection or the fact they would never have sex again. Six months after it was over, she would receive a text message on her cell phone from him suggesting (his word) she take an AIDS test because he had just tested positive for HIV. At the end of a ghastly weekend alone and terrified, she would take the test and find out that she was not infected.

Should she tell her that now? Walk over to this ebullient, relieved young woman and say, Wait, the ordeal is not over yet?

Not by a mile: This guy you're with now will soon change the way you look at and interact with men forever. After him they'll never be the same to you again. He'll create a hunger in you that won't be satisfied by anyone else. In the end he'll smash your heart with a hammer and later scare you right down into the marrow of your soul. It will make you hate men, hate sex, hate yourself—

"Well? Are you going to answer their questions?"

"I don't know. I haven't decided yet."

In the end she did it. But cautiously, leaving out certain things with every question she answered. Editing, shaping, and censoring, she would listen to a question and then try to remember what her state of mind was at that age. Could they handle this information about their future? Was it all right to tell them this or that? She divulged what she thought would help them to know but nothing more. When their questions had bad or painful answers, she would steer her response as diplomatically as possible in a different direction.

The girl who thought she was pregnant asked if her present boyfriend was "the one." Danielle said no, but that was okay because she would discover several things about him she didn't like. If she were to marry him, she would regret it later. Danielle suggested the girl enjoy the wonderful sex they had together and just accept the guy for what he was for as long as things worked between them. No more and no less.

She told the bandaged woman she would recover fully. When the bandages were removed, she *would* have a scar on her head from the accident, but not such a bad one and nothing more. Her hearing would return completely. And although it was difficult to believe, something good would result from this terrifying experience: she would learn to value and savor life more than she ever had before.

But Danielle did not tell the wounded woman about the hideous nightmares and acute anxiety attacks she would have for months after returning home from the hospital after the accident. Nor did she tell her about the paranoia that would seize her sometimes when she left the apartment or rode in a car. Nor did she describe the feeling of impending doom that hung over hours of her day much too often and kept her home in her safe little apartment where things were familiar and the treacherous world out there was a few walls away.

She spent a long time going from table to table answering their questions, soothing their fears, assuaging egos. The drizzle kept coming and so did their questions. What Danielle found most interesting about the experience was that not one of them asked about the long run, the big picture, or years from now. Every Danielle wanted only to know about something going on this moment in their lives or, at the very most, next week or month. None of the children asked, When I grow up will I . . . None of the older ones asked, In a year . . . For all of them, life was right now.

"My turn."

Tired out, she was finally alone, eating a piece of pecan pie with a white plastic fork. Her twin sat down nearby and said it again: "My turn."

Danielle slid pie into her mouth and chewed. Biting down hard on a fragment of pecan shell, she squinted one eye almost closed. Fishing around in her mouth with her fingers, she found the guilty shell and placed it on the edge of her paper plate. "*You have a question?*"

"Yes, I do."

Amused, Danielle cut off another slice. As she was about to put it in her mouth, she said, "Go ahead."

"Why didn't you ask them any questions?"

"Huh?" Taken completely by surprise, her mouth stopped moving and she stared at her twin. Was this a trick question, or did the other woman expect an answer? "Why *would* I ask them questions? They're my past. What good would their answers do me now? The past is past."

"Don't you want to remember who you were? Or what it was like back then? Don't you want to remember details you forgot? It's your life: Don't you think it could help you now?" The twin's voice grew louder and sharper as she spoke. Her last sentence wasn't a question but a demand.

This wasn't interesting to Danielle, and she went back to her dessert. It had almost been interesting because the initial question was so odd. But now she felt her twin was splitting hairs, and that didn't interest her.

"Whatever."

"That's not an answer."

"Whatever."

In response, the twin swiped her hand across the table. Danielle's pie plate flew off and hit the ground some distance away.

"Hey!"

"Wake up. You are just *not getting it*. Look around, dummy. Your whole life is here in front of you. But not *once* have you shown any curiosity about it. You answered their questions but didn't ask any—not one. How can you be so uninterested in your own history?"

Stung, Danielle shot back, "What am I supposed to ask, huh? What am I supposed to ask her?" With a flip of her wrist, she pointed randomly at the teenager still sitting alone on a bench reading a book.

Walking over to the reader, the twin asked if she would join them for a minute. Closing the book with a dramatic sigh, the girl said, "All right." When the three of them were to-gether, the twin asked the girl several trivial questions about her-self. She answered, but it was obvious she just wanted to get back to her book and be left alone.

"And what was the worst dream that you ever had? Do you remember?"

The girl perked up at the question. She spoke as if she couldn't get the words out fast enough. "Yes, completely. I had a dream when I was little that was so gross that I still remember it. I dreamt I was in a car crash. Well, not really a car *crash*, because what happened was, we were driving down this road when sud-denly a plane, like, crashed in a field right next to us. All these things came flying off it at us and one hit me in the head. It was like we were under attack. I got really messed up."

Danielle stared in disbelief at the teenager, then at the other woman. She repeated what she'd just heard to verify she'd heard it. "You *dreamt* you were in a car when a plane crashed next to you?"

"Yes. And a piece from it hit me here." The girl pointed to her temple.

Danielle looked at her twin, ignoring the girl altogether. "This is true? I dreamt the accident when I was young?"

The twin nodded. "That's why I said you should have been asking all of them questions."

"I *dreamt* that accident?"

"Down to the last detail."

• • •

What the others told Danielle finally made her weep. In the middle of someone else's answer, her head dropped to her chest and she began to cry. So many of their stories and memo-ries she had forgotten. The amazing, beautiful dreams. The fears and hopes, even the questions. It felt as though she had forgotten everything interesting and important.

"How could it happen? How could I forget so much of my own life?" She addressed the question to a stable and mellow twenty-five-year-old version of herself. Uncomfortable with the question and the pleading tone of Danielle's voice, the other woman gave her a sympathetic look and walked away.

Danielle turned to her twin standing nearby and asked again, "How come we forget so much?"

The woman answered, "The question's not how: the question is *why*."

"Yes, okay, then: Why?"

"*Ty krasivaya.*"

"What?"

"*Ty krasivaya.* Don't you remember that?"

"No."

"It's Russian. It means 'You are beautiful' in Russian."

Danielle wiped rain and tears off her face. "*Tee* what?"

Her twin repeated the phrase slowly, as if she were a language teacher getting every bit of the pronunciation correct. "*Ty krasivaya.*"

"No, I don't remember that."

The twelve-year-old had been tagging along the whole time. Now she said, "It's what Mr. Malozemoff says. He says it sometimes when I go to his store to buy gum or something."

That brought on a new torrent of memories of life at twelve for Danielle. Going to the candy store owned by Mr. Malozemoff, the thin Russian who always seemed to be standing in the doorway to the place, smiling and smoking. Sometimes he spoke Russian to the kids because it made them laugh. He liked and pitied Danielle. He'd heard that her parents were very strict and religious, plus it appeared she had few friends. So he once told the plain-looking girl that she was beautiful in Russian. *Ty krasivaya*. When he translated the phrase after she asked what it meant, she blushed. The next time she went to the store, she shyly asked him to write down that phrase for her. From then on, he would sometimes repeat it when she came in, but only if she was alone, because he didn't want to embarrass her. In Danielle's whole life he was the only person who ever told her she was beautiful. But, as is so often the case, long ago she had forgotten Mr. Malozemoff and his small, important kindness.

"How could I forget these things?" She paused to slow her breathing. "How can I remember them again after they're gone?" She looked at her twin and something dawned on her. "And how did *you* remember Mr. Malozemoff? If you're me ten minutes ago, I didn't remember him then."

The twin said, "Because I'm history now: *your* history. After your time is finished, you become just another part of Danielle Voyles's history. You join all the other parts. Then you know everything they know."

"So there's me living now"—Danielle held her right index finger with her left hand—"and there's all of you. There's a wall separating us. You remember everything because you're all part of my past. But I only remember little bits and pieces because I'm living now."

"Right."

Mulling that over, the image of fireflies came to her mind. Danielle was not a person who thought in metaphors, but now she pictured her memories as fireflies. Those lovely summer evenings when she was a girl running around the backyard, catching some in a jar. Keeping them for a few minutes to watch up close before releasing the dots of soft light back into the night. They never seemed to mind. But sad now to think that all she remembered of her life—her entire *life*—was like a few flickering bugs in a jar. "Lilacs."

"What?"

"Lilacs. Every spring Mr. Malozemoff's store always smelled of lilacs. He kept a big bouquet of them on the counter so long as they were in season." Danielle was pleased to have remembered this detail.

"You mean those kind of droopy purple flowers he has in his store? Those things are lilacs?" the girl asked.

"Yes. He kept a vase of them in the same place on top of the cigar counter. I remember that now. I want to remember more. I want to remember my life. How do I do it? How do I bring things back?"

Her twin pointed toward the women sitting at the four picnic tables. "Talk some more to them."

Eleven

"Something's wrong."

"Now he tells us."

The three stood on the sidewalk in front of Danielle Voyles's apartment building. Pilot had been with them until a few minutes before but then wandered off.

"Ben, this was your idea. You said she might be in trouble and that's why we came here. Now you say something's wrong. What are we supposed to do, go in and see if she's all right or not?"

"I'm telling you, something's wrong. Something else is *wrong* here. I don't even know if she's in there now. Coming over here, I was sure and I knew we had to help her. But now I don't know. Maybe that's why I thought she's in trouble. Something's changed. Something's different."

"Great, that tells us a lot: 'Something's different.' "

"Cool the sarcasm awhile, willya, Ling? Let me figure it out."

She started for the door. "We're wasting time if she really is in trouble. I'll just go in there and see."

Ben reached and stopped her. "That's a bad idea. You can't do what you could before. Going in there could be dangerous."

The ghost sneered. "What could happen—I might die?"

Still holding her arm, Ben pinched it hard.

"Yow!" Ling snatched the arm away and rubbed it. "Are you crazy? Why'd you do that?"

"To show you what pain is like. Which means it's the same for you, too, now. Yes, Ling, you *could* die, and it might be hideously painful. Do you know where old-ghosts-turned-human go when they die? I don't. Did they tell you that before you came here?

"Ben?"

He ignored German and continued staring at Ling to make sure she'd gotten his point.

"Ben."

"What?"

"Look." German was pointing down the sidewalk. Pilot was standing together with two other dogs, two cats, and what looked like several large rats underneath a street lamp. They appeared to be conferring.

The group of animals broke up and came toward the people. But a few feet away they veered off and made for the apartment building. Pilot passed closest but said nothing and didn't even look in their direction. When he was almost to the front door, he stopped, turned around, and came back. He spoke to Ben.

"We're going inside to look around. It's too dangerous for people in there now. Wait here till we come back."

"Pilot—"

The dog turned around and trotted away.

All of the animals were from this neighborhood, so they knew Danielle's building well. First the rats went around back and entered through a small broken window in the cellar that they had used for a long time. After getting the all-clear from the rats, the cats followed.

Pilot stood halfway up the front yard watching to make sure they got into the building okay. That accomplished, he barked the signal to the others to proceed. Standing together on the front lawn specifically under one open ground-floor window, the other two dogs immediately started fighting. Loud and ferocious, they made it look and sound as if they were really trying to kill each other. But up close you could see that their bluster was feint-and-fake; they weren't doing any damage.

Soon the landlord of the building threw open the front door and came charging out, brandishing a broom in his hands. "Get outta here, ya mutts! Get away from my building!"

The dogs moved a little closer to the street but did not stop fighting, although the landlord was now trying to push his broom between them. When Pilot was sure the man's whole attention was turned the other way, the dog sidled into the building through the open door.

• • •

Rats and cats think differently. Rats are much smarter animals but also awfully greedy and can be distracted by anything that is in their immediate self-interest. In contrast, cats generally take a more distanced view of things. They stop eating as soon as they're full. When anything bores them, they walk away without hesitation or concern for others' feelings. They are not diplomatic and do not suffer fools gladly. Felines find life both amusing and pitiable in equal measure. They don't see that as a contradiction, either. Isn't it possible to smile and sigh simultaneously?

When the rats entered the basement of Danielle's building, the first thing they searched for (although they never would have admitted it) was something to eat. Despite what they had promised to do for Pilot, they remained true to their rat-ness: eat first, investigate second. They hit the basement floor sniffing for snacks and not Danielle Voyles. They had been in this building only a few days before but knew from long foraging experience that there was always the chance juicy morsels might have been dropped, forgotten, discarded, or left behind in the intervening period.

By the time these rats had covered the nooks and crannies of the basement, looking for treats, the cats were already on the staircase up to the ground floor. When all of the animals spoke together earlier out on the street, the rats had said that this landlord usually left the basement door open a crack so that his own cat could get in and out. They also said the man detested dogs, so a big rowdy dogfight on his front lawn was sure to draw him out of the building.

Both rats and cats have uncommon senses of smell but use them for distinctly different purposes. Rats are down-to-earth, nuts-and-bolts smellers: they sniff the air only to detect imminent danger, food, or the potential mate. Right now is enough to them and the only thing that matters. If a male's horny and desires a certain female that recently gave birth, he'll eat her young and solve the inconvenience that way. Life's tough for a rat. Get used to it. Use your nose to find what's important, get it, and then get out, because everybody else hates you and wants you gone. No animal can smell danger or a threat faster or better than a rat.

Pilot knew this when he called on them to help. He also knew, however, that he had to supplement their tunnel-vision pragmatism with the aestheticism of poets, and that's why he'd put out a "calling all cars" to any cats that happened to be in the neighborhood and willing to help. Cats smell the air the way professional wine tasters sample wine. They sip it in small bits and then whish it around in their heads while thinking about it. Only after due consideration do they exhale. Both kinds of animals can smell and distinguish many different elements contained within one slip of air. But rats aren't interested in making those distinctions if they don't lead to immediate gain. Cats take individual odors so seriously that sometimes they'll pretend to be cleaning themselves thoroughly when in truth they're taking time to mull over a smell before coming to a conclusion about it.

Because he had already visited her apartment once, Pilot knew exactly what it and Danielle Voyles smelled like. He had described the smells to the others and asked them to find out if those scents were alive when they entered her place. Another major difference between animals and mankind: Animals can discern both a present and past tense for a smell. They know immediately if something is still there or not just by its odor in the air. That's why Pilot had asked both species to help. No animal smells hazard faster than a rat. But if Danielle was *not* in her apartment or was in danger, then Pilot wanted to hear the cats' conclusions after smelling the lay of her land.

Customarily cats, rats, and dogs despise each other. But Pilot had brought this group together today by formally issuing a call for "universal peace to overcome chaos," or UPTOC. No animal in this part of the world had requested an UPTOC for generations, which was exciting. Because no matter what happened today, this event would cause waves all the way up to the highest levels of the animal kingdom. Some said the first call for an UPTOC had happened on Noah's ark. Otherwise, how else could so many different breeds of animals have survived together in such a small space without ten kinds of catastrophe and carnage and the direst consequences of survival of the fittest? Others believed that UPTOC began much earlier, perhaps in the age of the dinosaur. No one could be certain.

When they are young, all animals are taught how to make the call. But few have done it because it is too risky and dangerous. An UPTOC made at the wrong time or for the wrong reason could reveal to mankind one of nature's great secrets: animals— *all* animals—understand one another when necessary. At birth, every species is taught two languages: its own and the universal. Only mankind forgets this universal language by the time it is old enough to speak.

The old woman was coming out of her apartment when she saw the first cat down the hall. She did not like cats. She did not like animals. She did not like much of anything on this earth, but particularly not cats. They were dirty, wanton, and loud. They were moochers. They took everything from you and then they died. It was the same thing with men. But at least men spoke the same language as you and once in a while they were nice to cuddle with. Who wanted to cuddle a ball of furry dirt?

"Get out of here—scram!"

The cat looked at the old woman, Danielle Voyles's snoopy neighbor, in the stuck-up way cats do that makes you want to strangle them. The woman's voice got louder, more commanding: "You heard me—*get!*"

Another cat appeared near the first, an even uglier one. Black and orange, it looked like a Halloween leftover. How had two stray cats gotten into her building? It must have been the landlord—him and that flea-infested cat of his. Maybe he'd invited these two characters over for dinner. Maybe they were all going to make a night of it: cat food for dinner and then a few hours of TV together.

Not if she had anything to say about it. As she took a firm

step toward these trespassers to show them who was boss, three big fat rats came into view behind the cats. All of the animals now started moving toward her like a bunch of bad guys in a cowboy movie. Rats she didn't mind. They were clever and nasty and knew what they wanted. Sort of like her. She admired them for their grit, but not now. Five animals were coming at her, and who knew what nefariousness they had planned. Everyone knows how dangerous animals in packs can be. It didn't matter one bit to her that this pack consisted of two cats and three Norwegian rats. Five animals with teeth were five animals with teeth. Fumbling the key back into the lock, she threw open her door and scurried inside.

None of the animals cared that she had seen them. They would be out of the building in minutes and, short of attacking them with a weapon, there was nothing she could do in so little time. They continued down the hall until they reached Danielle Voyles's apartment. All five got down low and put their noses against the crack at the bottom of the door. Almost as one, they inhaled deeply.

About that time, Pilot climbed the last stair and was on their level. He had just caught sight of the group down there when every single one of them turned from Danielle's door and came racing as fast as they could toward the staircase and Pilot. The expressions on their faces were pure terror.

"Wait!" was all Pilot managed to say before they blew by him, down the stairs to the basement, out the hole in the window, and right the hell out of there as fast as their legs could go. Racing down the sidewalk, one of the rats was so frightened by what it had smelled that it had a heart attack and died. His temporary comrades didn't even bother looking back at the twitching body as they ran.

Standing on the sidewalk in front of Danielle's, the three

people saw the animals race out of the building and watched silently as they fled into the distance. Except for the rat that died in flight from fright. Fortunately, that happened too far away for them to have seen it drop dead, scared to death. The two dogs that staged the bogus fight on the front lawn had left as soon as they knew the others had gotten into the building.

"Pilot's still in there. I wonder what happened."

"Me too."

"Should we go in?"

"He said to wait out here."

"Yeah, but that was before them." Ling pointed toward the stampeders.

Ben asked, "What do you think, German?"

When it came, the sound was piercing but not possible to recognize or define. None of them thought it was a scream or a cry for help. It was loud, disturbing, and mysterious.

"What the hell was *that*?"

The sound stopped German from answering Ben's question. They looked at the apartment building and then at one another with the kind of danger-alert eyes that silently asked, What *was* that?

Then it came again but was still unrecognizable. It could have been many things, only one being a dog crying out. The only sure thing was that the sound came from inside Danielle's building.

Too bad Ling was no longer a fully empowered ghost, because if she were, she would have recognized the sound. And then she would have run away even faster than those other animals had.

But Ben sensed something after hearing the sound a second time. He quickly touched the back of his neck as if he'd been stung there. "You two wait here. I'm going in there."

Neither woman protested, but it wouldn't have mattered.

Whatever it was that he had sensed grew stronger now and had his full attention. Distracted, he repeated what he had just said, "You two wait here," and then walked toward the building without looking back.

German called out a halfhearted "Ben," without really knowing what to say if he turned around. But he didn't. She was left with his name on her lips and the image of him walking away in her eyes.

Without thinking it might be locked, Ben turned the knob on the front door and it opened under his hand. He stepped inside to complete silence and shadows. He was not afraid, only curious.

Where were all of the people who lived here? There was always noise of some kind or other in an apartment building: comings and goings, the sound of conversations or laughter behind closed doors, TVs or music playing. But inside there now it was completely silent. Not a peep. Why? Where was the landlord? Minutes ago he'd been out on the front lawn, yelling at the fighting dogs. Where was he now? Which one was his apartment?

Ben walked to the staircase at the other end of the hall. Danielle lived on the first floor. That was where he would look. The silence around him continued as he climbed. The only sound was the *shuff* of his sneakers on the carpeted stairs.

On the first landing he stopped and looked both ways to see if there was anyone around. No. He started moving down the hall toward her apartment. Halfway there, music suddenly blared out from somewhere. It was a disco tune from the eighties that he recognized because it had been a favorite of his sister's: "My Forbidden Lover" by Chic. The music appeared to be coming from an apartment a few doors down from Danielle's. Walking slowly toward it, he remembered the snoopy old woman who'd made trouble when he was last here. Could it possibly be the music came from her place? An old grouch playing Chic?

Warily approaching the door to her apartment, he saw that it was open a crack. Because there was no other noise, he was certain the music came from in there. When he got close he tried to peek into the place, but the crack was too narrow. With the tip of his foot he pushed the door open a bit more for a better view.

In the middle of a cluttered living room an old woman was dancing naked. Her back was turned to him. Ben saw the back of an old woman dancing naked to disco music. And she was really shaking it down. No Goody Two-shoes prissy gavotte/ waltz/cha-cha-cha trash from her. At the moment he caught his first glimpse, she was dancing a difficult combination of the Bus Stop and the California Hustle. She was dipping her shoulders and rolling her hips. She added a little shing-a-ling thing with her hands. That move was her very own invention. She had created it one night while listening to Gloria Gaynor sing "I Will Survive" live at the Flip Flop Club in Bakersfield. To this day she swore Gloria had seen her doing that special move and nodded her approval of it *from the stage*.

That had been the greatest night of Brenda Schellberger's life. She was with Howard Smolakoff, the only man she had ever truly loved. When they got back to his apartment after dancing until three, Howard begged her to take off her clothes and dance just for him the same way she'd been dancing all night long at the club. She felt so sexy and alive, desired, and in tune with the cosmos that she didn't need to be asked twice. Dropping her clothes where she stood, she waited with fidgety hands on naked hips while Howard put on his one Donna Summer record. For the next fifteen minutes she danced nonstop without once looking at him to see his reaction. She didn't care. She didn't need an audience because she was dancing for herself, ecstatic, right in the center of the absolute center of the happiness of her life. She didn't need Howard's approval or appreciation or desire, although it was even better that he was there to share these glorious minutes.

She thought about that one-of-a-kind night for the rest of her dull life.

It was her touchstone, her one concrete assurance that splendid things can and do happen sometimes, even to people like her.

In the end Howard turned out to be a weak, phlegmatic mama's boy, unable to commit to anything, and who in time slunk out of her life. But the Howard at the end wasn't the same man she danced for that night. *That* night they were only a third of the way into their relationship. At that moment she was certain she'd found her man and was still basking in the glow of them working so well together. Everything was ideal that night; everything was sexy, triumphant, and right. The congruence of great things was beyond compare. That was why she repeatedly thought about those few hours for years to come. What Ben Gould witnessed through her partially open door was old Brenda Schellberger reliving the pinnacle of her life. After which it was all downhill.

The same thing was happening to every person in the building. No matter what their age, every one of them was in one way or another reliving the single greatest time they had ever known. And it would never end now because they never *wanted* it to end. Seeing that was what frightened the animals away minutes earlier. It was also what had made Pilot cry out so bizarrely when he grasped what was going on. All of this was Danielle Voyles's fault, as Ben was about to learn.

•   •   •

Of course it was the quiet one. But it's generally that way, isn't it? The quiet girl sitting alone at the end of one of the picnic tables, reading a fat paperback book. The one who had dreamt the accident so many years before it took place. Danielle came back to her and asked the girl again if she had any questions about her life to come. The teenage reader closed the book on a finger and promptly replied no. Danielle was impressed because the others had had at least a few pressing questions and insights about their shared life. But not this one. It was plain from the look on her face that she didn't want to talk about the future, ask about it, or know more than she already did. The only reason she had stopped reading now was good manners, not because she was curious—like all of the other Danielles—to discover what her future held.

"There's *nothing* you want to know? You don't have any questions?"

"No."

"Jeez. Why not?"

"Because I'm so happy now. I don't want anything to change. I know it will, but I don't want to hear about it." She shifted her book and a piece of paper dropped out of it, a photograph. The girl gasped and snatched the picture out of the air before it touched the wet ground. She checked to see that it was okay and then pressed it tenderly to her chest, as if to give it back some of her body heat.

Intrigued, the older Danielle asked if she could see. The girl handed it over. The woman recognized the person in the snapshot immediately. She looked from the picture to the girl. The two women smiled very much the same smile at each other.

Danielle looked at the picture one more time. Returning it, she said the magical name: "Dexter." The girl nodded and slipped it back into her book.

Dexter Lewis was the great love of Danielle's young life. Sometimes as an adult she admitted to herself that relationship was the best she ever had. Dani and Dex. Dex and Dani. Love forever. Senior year in high school: Had she ever been happier or more content?

"I don't want to ask you questions because I don't want to know about my future. I want things to stay exactly like they are now and not move an inch." The girl held up her paperback. "I have books, Dexter loves me, and things are perfect. I don't want it to ever change. But you'll say that it will, won't you? You'll tell me Dexter's going to leave, or something terrible will happen to me, or him, or my family. I don't want to hear it! I don't want to hear about what happens tomorrow. Why? How could tomorrow be better than right now?

"See these other women here now? I haven't asked any of them even one question about their lives. Not one. Nothing you or they know about my future could make me happier than right now. You'll only spoil it, no matter what you say."

The girl was 100 percent correct. Dexter did leave eventually, bad things were going to happen, and nothing in her future *was* ever as perfect and fulfilling as her life was then.

"Has he taken you to the Lotus Garden yet?"

The girl's eyes softened. "Oh, yes! We went there two weeks ago for our three-month anniversary. It was the best meal ever. The food was so good. We ate in their beautiful garden with all the colored paper lanterns? It was like a dream."

The lanterns. Danielle had forgotten about the delicate paper lanterns hung from the trees that swung in the evening breeze. She sat down next to the girl on the bench. "Would you tell me about it?"

"Why? You already know. You did it; you were *there*."

"Yes, but it was so long ago. I've forgotten most of the details. I forgot about the lanterns. I'd love to hear about it again. Would you tell me?"

The teenager was glad to recount the whole story of the best night of her life. "I was standing at my locker in school. Dexter came up and said our anniversary is this weekend. What should we do to celebrate?"

Because the memory was so recent for her, the girl remembered almost everything: the colored paper lanterns in the restaurant's garden, the waiter without a tooth, and her lame jokes about the Chinese music playing in the background. She remembered Dexter explaining to her that the word for "crocodile" derived from the ancient Greek words *"krokē-"* and *"drilos,"* which meant—

"Pebbled worm," adult Danielle said, remembering. Her younger self nodded and continued.

The more the girl talked, the more the adult recalled. And the more she remembered of that brilliant night, the less her present mattered. The adult Danielle completely immersed herself in the girl's details. It was like walking into a swimming pool, shallow end first. When the water rose over her head, she welcomed it; she willingly sank down until it engulfed her.

In reexperiencing it with the eyes, heart, and history of an adult, the woman was able to relish the romantic evening as much if not more than the girl did. Adult Danielle knew too well the betrayals, disappointments, bad luck, and mediocrity that later filled her days. So she knew this date was an extraordinary oasis in an otherwise arid life. The girl, on the other hand, saw it as only a sample of all the amazing things that were to come in the future. Dinner with Dexter was just a taste, an hors d'oeuvre, before the grand main course that was sure to be her adulthood.

In high school, Danielle's English class read the play *Our Town*. She never forgot the famous last scene where the dead character Emily is permitted to return to a random morning in her youth to witness her family eating breakfast. Despite its ordinariness, she is overcome by the richness and simple beauty of the mundane event. Eventually, Emily cries out to her family to recognize and treasure this moment and all moments like it in their lives. In vain, of course, because the living cannot hear the dead.

Danielle was not dead, but her night with Dexter Lewis at the Lotus Garden was. Yet, like Emily in the famous play, she was also given the opportunity to revisit that earlier experience. But, unlike the character, the adult Danielle was soon entirely part of the event, not just outside looking in. The more she listened to the girl, the less it was memory and the more it was now. Gradually she began to taste the warm spring rolls and smell Dexter's English Leather cologne. The more things were described, the more real the experience became for her. And as that happened, the life she had been living half a day ago faded.

Our "now" is so boring and forgettable most of the time: Sit at your desk. Walk to the kitchen. Take a pee. Take a walk. Take a nap. Take your time, because it's so uninteresting that nobody else wants to take it. We remember few things about what we did with our days, since most of them are like air with no fragrance. What did you do in the afternoon two days ago? When was the last time you laughed out loud? Or ate something that made you close your eyes and groan with pleasure? Naturally we remember the perfume times because there are so few of them.

Given the chance to experience again a past occurrence when everything was so perfect that we never wanted it to end, who would say no? And what if reliving it could somehow go on forever? Dinner with Dexter indefinitely. Would we choose to remain inside that past paradise as long as possible, or opt to return to our daily ho-hum now, when typically the only thing to look forward to is the weekend, a favorite TV show, so-so sex now and then, or going to bed at night? Like those incomparable dreams in which we meet the people we have longed for all our lives. They are perfect. Everything is perfect, and to our surprise the dream keeps getting better as it continues. But then we wake up, and immediately think, No, no, not yet, a few minutes more, please! Let me finish the meal, the kiss, that walk on the beach at sunrise with them. We fight to go back to sleep to try and recapture the moment, the person, and perhaps, most important, the exquisite feeling of being swept up in life rather than swept aside by it.

Almost everyone has come close to actually living dreams like those once or twice in their lives. Maybe it was that perfect date when you were twenty, or one magic afternoon in Istanbul, an hour, a meal, a dance, a walk by a lake in the rain you wouldn't trade for anything. How tempting if it were somehow possible to go back to those experiences and live them forever.

"What are you thinking about, Dani? You look so far away."

For the first time since falling into this memory, she actually heard Dexter Lewis's voice rather than imagining it. She was no longer an adult listening to the girl. She and the girl had literally become one, having that once-in-a-lifetime dinner again at the Lotus Garden.

She inhaled deeply, blinked, and looked across the table at eighteen-year-old Dexter Lewis. He had bad skin but not too bad. She had forgotten that. She did remember he liked black shirts. She remembered the black one he wore now. He'd unbuttoned many of the buttons to make it look cool. But Dexter was too skinny to show that much neck and chest. She felt a burst of love for him for trying to be something for her that he wasn't.

Without thinking, she answered, "I was thinking about my accident. It just flew across my mind. I don't know where the thought came from."

Dexter looked confused. "*What* accident?"

Part of her, the girl, asked the same thing inside her head. "What accident?"

Upset that she'd been careless enough to blab this, the woman sat up straight. Thinking fast, she muddied her statement as best she could. "The accident. *This* accident: the fact we met the way we did. That's an accident. It was such a coincidence, you know? What were the chances of it happening like that?"

Dexter still looked perplexed. "We met in American history class, Dani. What's so accidental about sitting next to each other in class?"

• • •

While Danielle sculpted her words and thoughts to fit that teenage world she now inhabited, Ben Gould walked slowly down the hall toward her apartment. After the initial shock of seeing the dancing old woman, he stepped forward and gently pulled the door to her apartment closed. He had no idea why she was doing it but assumed that, whatever her reasons, the old bird would not like strangers to see her dancing in her birthday suit. But he was wrong. The woman would not have cared because she was no longer part of the present by then. She inhabited a world and a time far removed from this one.

If Ben had been able to see behind the doors of every apartment in that building and understood what was going on in them, he would have been astounded. Because every single occupant of 182 Underhill Avenue who happened to be home at that time was somewhere else in his or her life. Like Danielle at the Lotus Garden and the old woman dancing naked for her boyfriend, the only part of the tenants that was physically present in the building was their bodies. Every other element was living somewhere in their pasts.

As soon as Danielle chose to move completely into the evening at the Lotus Garden restaurant, the allure of the past she freed from within became so overpowering that it moved out of her apartment, into the hall, and then throughout the rest of the building like an irresistible aphrodisiac. The few people inside at the time were all doing the same old nothing and therefore were particularly receptive to its magic.

One man sitting in one-hundred-times-washed Bermuda shorts and an undershirt was staring into a cup of coffee. He began thinking again about his time in the Marine Corps at Camp Lejeune—one summer day in particular. He was twenty-seven then and just married. It was hot that day and he loved the heat. He loved his new wife and felt her love for him whenever they were together. How had he lived so long without her? He liked his job and was good at it. He knew what he was doing with his life. His profession was important and meaningful. Unless things went very wrong, he would remain in the Corps until retirement and then join a small-town police force somewhere.

He remembered the smell in the air all that summer: the ripe lush smell of North Carolina in August. He remembered the sleeveless gray-and-purple dress his wife wore that morning when he left their apartment. He remembered the color of the bottle of her nail polish on the pine kitchen table. All of the windows were open and breezes were blowing through them, lifting the curtains.

His red-and-white Chevrolet Impala SS convertible was almost new. Soon, when he had time off, they would drive it to the ocean at the Outer Banks: drive right up to the water at night with the top down and sit there together, watching shooting stars blaze trails just for them. Standing in the military base parking lot, he slid his hands into his pants pockets. Looking into the cornflower-blue sky, he daydreamed a few moments about going to the ocean for the first time with his new wife. Right then, that moment: that was it—the pinnacle of his life.

Thirty-one years later, staring into a half-empty cup of stale coffee, he moved straight into that memory as soon as he realized he could and never once looked back.

Jumping on a trampoline with a long-dead twin sister, sitting in a tree house during a snowstorm while sharing a bologna sandwich with a fiancée, learning the intricacies of watchmaking from a Belgian master in Brugge . . . throughout that building, one by one the residents unhesitatingly traded their dull nows to return again to the best times of their lives and stay there.

"Help."

Ben heard it as he was about to touch Danielle's doorknob. Looking to the left, a few feet down the hall he saw Pilot flicker in and out of view. Like a faint signal on the radio, the dog was visible a few seconds, then gone the next. Visible, gone.

"Help!"

"How? What do I do?"

Pilot tried to speak but disappeared. When he shimmered

momentarily back into view, all he was able to say to the man was "Make a verz" before disappearing again.

"What? Make a what?" Ben asked no one because no one was around but him. He looked at the space where Pilot had been, waiting and hoping for the dog to reappear, but he didn't.

Make a verz.

The dog creatures with big eyes and no ears. Purple words and doodles on their white bodies. Make a verz.

Me?

•   •   •

Outside the building the two women waited apprehensively, unsure of what to do. Ling knew that without her powers she could do little to help here. She didn't know if it made her angry or exhilarated. In a way, everything was now new to her because she was only human and that was exhilarating.

The front door of the apartment building suddenly banged open and Ben came rushing out toward them. The way he was moving, both women thought he would go right by and down the street like the animals, but he didn't. Running over to them, he grabbed Ling by the arm and pulled her hard to follow: "Come on. Come on."

"What? What are you doing?"

"You've got to come with me, Ling. Right now." He hesitated and then said to German, "But you should stay here. I don't know what's going to happen in there, so please wait here till we come get you."

"Go to hell, Ben. I'm coming too. Let's go." She didn't wait for him to respond before she started moving.

Ben had lived with her long enough to recognize both that tone of voice and her don't-mess-with-me body language. German Landis had regularly beaten up both her brother and sister when they were children. She was not a person to challenge when she was angry or sure she was right.

The ex-ghost watched their exchange and fell even more in love with German. What backbone! Even Ling was hesitant about going inside the building now without her powers and some idea of what was going on there, but not German. Boom—full speed ahead, girl.

Inside, the three walked up the stairs to Danielle's floor. On the way, Ben described to them the naked dancing woman and the disappearing dog. It sounded funny but it wasn't. It sounded insane but it was true. Neither woman said anything. They wanted to see for themselves.

Seven steps up the staircase German started thinking about doughnuts. Big fat freshly made golden glazed doughnuts right out of the box. The gloriousness of eating them for breakfast along with a cup of blazing hot coffee.

Why was she thinking about doughnuts *now*? Because Ben walked in front of her. She looked at his back as they climbed the stairs and for no reason it reminded her of an occasion when they were living together. One Sunday morning in the middle of winter, he walked into the bedroom still wearing his heavy gray overcoat. He was carrying a tray with two smoking cups of coffee and a peach-colored box full of warm fresh doughnuts that he had gone out to buy while she was sleeping. The night before, after making love, German talked about how much she liked doughnuts for breakfast, and now here they were. She could smell the pungent coffee and the just-baked doughnuts from across the room as he approached. Neither of them spoke while he lay the tray down on the bed and shifted things around so that it all looked just right. She was so charmed and touched by his thoughtfulness that she was wordless. Ben opened the box and tipped it up her way to show the treasure inside. She blew him air kisses with both hands and then reached for one. He stopped her, lifted the first one out, and offered it to Pilot, who had come over from his bed in the corner. The dog had never seen a doughnut before and was curious but cautious, as was his nature. To show the dog they were safe, Ben took a small bite out of this one and then offered the rest to Pilot, who took it like a gentleman.

"German?"

She heard the voice but it sounded far away—three rooms away, half a house away. She didn't recognize Ben's voice.

All three had stopped on the stairs because German had stopped and wouldn't move. Ling looked at Ben and shrugged.

He said her name again but this time more tentatively: "German?"

They thought perhaps she was frightened and had stopped to pull herself together before going on. But despite Ben's saying her name twice, German stayed where she was and did not move.

Why should she? She was in a perfect moment: They were all eating doughnuts together on a cold Sunday morning. The food was delicious, their love was new, they were safe in his warm bed, and Pilot was adorable in his seriousness.

Staring at her and trying to figure out what was wrong, Ben saw something strange in her right hand. Looking at it, he squinted to better focus because what he saw there made no sense. German was holding a doughnut, a golden doughnut. He craned his neck forward to make sure that was what it was. Where had she gotten it? Had she had it with her the whole time? A *doughnut*?

"Ben, she's fading!"

He saw it happening to German's hand, but it didn't register in his mind until Ling spoke. Her hand was becoming transparent. The hand, the doughnut it held, and her whole body were fading. She was leaving. Danielle Voyles's nostalgia had reached her now too. German wanted to be back in bed with Ben that cherished winter morning, eating doughnuts forever. Not here.

"What's happening to her, Ling?"

"I don't know. I really don't."

Throughout that apartment building, all of the tenants were fading: back to happier pasts, to days when things made solid sense and were so much more right. Where for a brief immaculate time, life had been faultless.

"Make a verz." Pilot had said that before he faded too. Ben did not know how to do that. But he remembered Ling had recognized and named them as soon as she saw them at Gina Kyte's house. Ling knew what a verz was. Would she know how to make one?

He looked at her and in that fraught moment identified something for the first time that he had never seen before. Climbing down the stairs to her, he put both hands on Ling's shoulders. When she made to speak, he stopped her.

An instant later his hands on her bare skin began removing what she *did* know. Like a bee extracting nectar from a flower, Ben first took Ling's ghost knowledge, or what few traces there were of it left in her. She wasn't aware of it because it lay inactive in her unconscious and in the most remote corners of her mind. But Ben found it all. He took everything he needed, knowing he was leaving her perilously little to build the rest of her life on. But he took it anyway because he knew that what he was doing was more important than any one life.

He emptied her first of her ghost knowledge and then of specific elements of her newly gained human knowledge. All of what she was and what was left of what she once had been entered Ben's hands, and he took whatever he needed of it.

This took only seconds. When he was finished, he stood still and put one very warm palm against his stomach.

Ling reeled. As she was about to fall, he grabbed her and helped her sit down. She looked at him with empty eyes.

Ben walked back up the steps to where German was still standing and bit her.

He took her hand holding the doughnut and bit it high up on the wrist, hard enough to draw blood. More important, he bit German hard enough to make her shriek in pain, pain that brought her back to the present. She jerked her arm away, hitting him in the mouth as she did. Most of her mind was still so anchored in her past. The bite was like being shaken violently awake from the deepest sleep.

He watched until he was absolutely certain that German was back here, now, completely in the present. Then he hurried toward Danielle's apartment, not sure whether he would get there in time to save her.

Ling sat stunned on the stairs; German stood stunned a few feet away. Both women looked like boxers getting slowly and unsteadily up off the canvas after having been knocked out cold.

Ben stood in front of Danielle's door and tried turning the knob, but it was locked. He knocked on the door but there was no answer. He banged on it but only silence followed. Stepping back, he brought both hands to his face. A moment later he took them away.

"All right." He stepped back to the door and this time put his hands on the knob. He twisted one to the left, the other to the right. With both arms he pushed straight forward. The door swung open. He walked in.

To a garden: a restaurant in a garden. There were tables spread across a wide area. Colorful paper lanterns hung in the trees. Diners were sitting here and there; waiters in crisp white shirts and black trousers walked by carrying large metal trays stacked with food.

"You would like a table?" a smiling Oriental man came up and asked. Ben assumed he was the boss, because he was the only one with sleeves rolled up to his elbows.

"Actually, I'm looking for someone here. Do you mind if I try to find my friend?"

"Yes, okay," the manager said and walked away. It was a busy night in the Lotus Garden and he had much to do.

Ben saw her after looking only a short time. She was one of those people whose face doesn't change much as they grow older. And Danielle was only, what, twenty-nine years old now? Danielle at eighteen did not look so different. He walked over to their table. Both kids looked up. She smiled but the boy didn't. Danielle knew who he was the second she saw him.

"Hi, Ben."

"Hey, Danielle."

"Dexter, this is my friend Ben Gould."

"Nice to meetcha." The two men shook hands. Dexter's handshake was ten times too strong. The boy was intent on demonstrating to whoever he met that he was all guy.

"How'd you find me?" Her voice was calm and quiet. She did not appear the least surprised to see him in her world.

Ben said only "I figured it out."

She knew they could skip this conversation forward a few chapters. "I'm going to stay here, Ben. I've decided."

"You can't."

"I can. You know I can. That's part of this deal, right? People like us can go anyplace we want in our lives and stay there. It's our decision."

"Danielle, you can't. There's too much at stake. You have to come back."

She tightened her mouth and looked away. He was right, but her mind was made up. "I don't want it, Ben. I don't want that life anymore. I live alone in a pathetic little apartment and work at a loser job. I wake up every morning hoping it's Saturday. You know why? Not because I have anything special or great planned on the weekend, but so I can *sleep* longer. That says a lot about my life, huh? I don't want it anymore.

"This"—she waved an open hand at their surroundings— "this life is my bird in the hand. Do you understand what I'm saying? When I look back, Dexter here probably *was* the love of my life. So, now that I realize it, I can appreciate him much more than I did back then."

The thin boy across the table loved hearing he was the love of her life and sat back in his chair a happy man. He had no clue to what was going on with Danielle and this older guy, but her last two sentences were enough to make him proud and hold his peace for a while.

Frustrated, Ben raised his voice. "But you've got it reversed. You're supposed to take what you've experienced in life and use it to try and improve yourself today and tomorrow."

Danielle shook her head. "Nope, not anymore. I've had enough todays and tomorrows to know one's basically going to be like the next. And way too many of them are worse.

"I'm only being honest, Ben. I know I'd be content with medium-level happiness: a five on a scale of ten. I want to be loved. That's all. That's it. But I wasn't happy or loved yesterday. I wasn't today, and chances are pretty slim that I will be tomorrow.

"So I'll just be realistic and choose my bird in the hand: I'll go back to where I *know* I was happy and really loved and just stay there. I'll settle; I accept that. Plus, I'll go back knowing it never got any better than that night, which means I can appreciate it ten times more than I did."

She was absolutely right, but that didn't make her right. He needed something now to convince Danielle to return to the present and not remain in her past. He needed something to bring Pilot back from whatever ominous otherworld he was in. He needed something to help himself recognize what he was supposed to do now with all this new knowledge and insight coming to him at impossible speeds. How can you learn what to do when you're given no time?

His father once said life was deeply unfair. At birth you're given a very complicated board game but no instructions on how to play it. You must try to work out all the rules yourself. At the same time, you must play the game. Once. If you lose, doom. No, oops, I'm just a beginner, can I try that wrong move again? No, you cannot. No second chances. Figure out the rules now from nothing while simultaneously playing the game of life. How could a person *not* fail?

And yet—

"Danielle, do you remember when you died? Do you remember the moment or anything else about it?"

"No. Only when I woke up from the operation."

"Me too. The last thing I remember was hitting my head and how much it hurt. Nothing else till I woke up in the hospital."

"What's he talking about, Danielle? What's this about dying?" Dexter Lewis was now getting frustrated. He wanted to know what was going on and when this older guy was going to get out of there and leave them alone.

She put a hand over her boyfriend's and said, "Ben's a friend of my father's from church. He came over to our house the other night and we got into a big discussion about deep things. You know, life and death and what's it all about. We were talking about it for a long time and we're kind of finishing up now. Just give me a minute, Dex."

Ben waited till she finished calming the boy before continuing. "Maybe we're not *supposed* to remember everything, because it's not relevant. We don't remember night dreams the next morning because they're not relevant now—"

Danielle interrupted him. "Ben, how did you get *here*? How did you know where to find me?"

"I—I walked through your door. I opened the door to your apartment, walked in, and here I was."

She looked at him, considering what he had said. Then she shook her head. "Impossible."

"What do you mean? What are you saying?"

"There's no way you could have found me here. Eighteen-year-old me at the Lotus Garden with Dexter Lewis? No way. How could you know about this night? No one knows how important this memory is but me. No one."

"Danielle, I'm telling you what happened: I opened the door to your apartment, walked in, and here I was."

"I heard you but it's not possible. Choosing from my whole life, twenty-nine years of it, how could you know I would be exactly here? Huh? How did you know that this night amongst all the others was the happiest I ever had? How did you know that? How *could* you?"

A small bewildered voice almost not his own asked, "Because I became you again?" All those times without warning that he had suddenly been inside Danielle's mind and body, inside her apartment watching dental procedure videotapes on her television, the taste of her Dr Pepper in his mouth. All those times he was both of them simultaneously. How frightening that had been when it happened. But what if this time his will had chosen to do it? What if he had opened the door to Danielle's apartment and purposely chosen to slip into her head to find out where she was? When he knew, he joined her here at the Lotus Garden.

They looked at each other. Ben also saw scrawny Dexter Lewis. The boy was angrily wondering, How old is this guy? Does she have the hots for him or something?

Dexter stood up. He had had enough. After shooting both of them long, dirty looks, he went off to find the toilet. He hoped his killer glares would make them feel bad about ignoring him. But neither paid attention to his leaving.

A waiter passed. By tilting his mind slightly in his direction, Ben knew the man was wondering if the woman at table six had just given him the eye while her husband paid the bill. Ben looked up at the waiter and saw him smiling. A woman nearby got up and walked toward the toilet. He knew she was hurrying to get there because she was sure from the feel of it that her period had just begun. Embarrassed and feeling like a voyeur, Ben turned his attention back to Danielle.

He asked her, "Can you do that too? Can you go into people's minds and know what they're thinking?"

Unsurprised by the question, she shook her head. "No, but I can travel around anywhere in my own life that I want, backward and forward through time. Like being here at the restaurant with Dexter. Can you do that?"

"No. Not like you do." He thought about Ling taking him back to Crane's View.

"Maybe it'll never happen to you, Ben. Maybe each of us has special things only we can do."

He hadn't considered that possibility but it made sense. "Are you really going to stay here? You're not going back? Even if we need you?"

She crossed her arms over her chest. Bad body language. "Who's this 'we' that needs me?"

"The other survivors like us. There have to be others, Danielle. Let's say you're right: What if each one of us *can* do different special things? That's even more reason why we need to stay together now." The idea sounded ridiculous and the words dried in his throat as he tried to convince her. He could only think of the comic books he'd read as a kid in which superheroes always banded their various superpowers together to defeat whatever villains were threatening mankind in that month's exciting adventure.

Something new dawned on Ben and he straightened. His whole demeanor changed. "But who *is* it that's against us?"

"What do you mean?"

"Who doesn't want us around? Who keeps trying to stop us, Danielle? You met the man in the orange shirt—the bum. Who was *he*? Who sent him?"

"I don't know, Ben. He came for you, remember?"

"Yeah, but then, who was the little boy who came after you in my kitchen?"

She was surprised. "You know about that?"

"Of course. I've been in your mind, remember?"

"Well, then, you already know: it was you. *You* were the little boy."

Ben shook his finger. "No. He only used that disguise to get past German into my apartment, and it worked. He came for you, Danielle, not me. He told you to go to the radio and search for that special song. You would have found it pretty soon and thought it was just a coincidence. But when you played it, he would have gotten you. That's what he said to the verz, remember? He was there to get you, not me."

She asked, "Then who sent the verz that saved us in the kitchen?"

Ben pointed at her face. "*You* did. Something in you sensed trouble as soon as that kid entered my apartment. That's when you called the verz for help."

"I did not."

"Yes, you did. Or some part of you did."

Not believing this, she pointed to her elbow. "Which part?" She pointed to her knee and then her nose. "This part, or this one? How do you know?"

"Who is the enemy here? Who wants to stop us?"

"You already asked that before, Ben."

"And I'm asking it again. Know why? Because we're the good guys of this story. There are even parts of ourselves we don't know about that are working to protect us. So I want to know who the enemy is. Who doesn't want us to live and decide our own destinies?

"Look at the facts: we didn't die when we were supposed to. When both of us got out of the hospital, strange things began happening, and they just got stranger. A bad guy in an orange shirt and a little boy came after us; ghosts and verzes showed up to protect us from them.

"You're able to visit your past like it was a personal Disneyland. I can go in and out of your mind like I have my own entrance to it. And I can talk to dogs and understand when they talk to me."

"Dogs?"

He scratched his head. "Yeah, well, *my* dog, at least. By the way, have you seen the pink fog yet?"

"What pink fog?"

He considered explaining but decided it would only complicate things. "Never mind, it's not important now."

She accepted that and went on thinking things through in her head as she spoke. "You believe because we didn't die when we were scheduled to that we now have special powers?"

"Absolutely. Look around you. Look where we are. How else could we be here if we didn't have powers?"

"And you want to know who's trying to stop us?"

He nodded.

Danielle said matter-of-factly, "I can answer *that*."

"You can? Who?"

"It's one of the reasons why I'm staying here and not going back, Ben."

"Who is it? Tell me!"

On the table was a small black beaded silk purse. The very feminine, impractical kind so small that it's only big enough to hold a pen, some paper money, and a pack of cigarettes. Danielle reached over and picked up this purse. It was her teenage self's idea of chic. Tonight's date with Dexter was the first time she'd used it since buying the bag at a secondhand store. Opening it, she took out a white plastic compact. Opening that, she turned to one side and gently blew powder off the small mirror inside. Then she offered the compact across the table to Ben. "Right in here. Have a look."

Puzzled by her gesture, he reached for it. As he was about to touch the compact, everything around them went black. The pitch black behind your eyes after you close them for the night in the dark. Cave black. Basement black.

"Danielle?"

She did not answer.

"Danielle?" He sat still, not moving an inch, waiting for the lights of the world to come back on. At the same time he knew this was not just a power failure or blown fuse. The black was too absolute and unnatural. A moment before, they were in a large outside garden. There are many lights outside at night: street lamps, lights from windows, auto headlights. But now there was nothing. The blackness was complete. If he had held his hand an inch from his eyes, he would not have seen it.

"Danielle?"

. . .

Pilot landed flat on his back, the wind knocked out of him. Pain coursed through his body. The dog lay gasping and disoriented. In a small corner of his mind he was outraged at what had just happened. Enough was enough!

Why was everyone and everything beating up on the poor dog when he was only a bit player here? Pilot knew that was his role in life and he accepted it. But since when did bit players get treated so outrageously? How much torment did the universe have planned for him?

Once he could breathe normally again, Pilot twisted onto his side and carefully got up. Somewhere along the way something bad had happened to his right front paw. When he stood and put pressure on it, the paw almost buckled from pain. Perfect. Just perfect. All he needed now was to walk with a limp.

Looking down the hall, he saw the two women. Both of their backs were to him. Nearby, the door to Danielle Voyles's apartment stood open. He limped over to it and walked in.

The next thing he noticed was the strong smell of Chinese food in there. Pilot loved Chinese food. When he was living rough on the street, one of the first things he did every day was to forage in the garbage cans outside two separate Chinese restaurants. Give him dim sum and he was a happy dog. Danielle's apartment smelled strongly of chop suey and hot monosodium glutamate. It smelled of vegetables boiled too long and steamed rice. Otherwise it was a normal empty apartment. He walked into every room and peered closely in corners but discovered nothing out of the ordinary there besides that inappropriate smell.

"Danielle?"

The dog froze. He recognized Ben's voice instantly. But Pilot was certain after having just visited every room in the apartment that no one was there.

"Ben?"

"Pilot? Pilot, is that you, boy? Where are you? Are you okay?"

"Yes, I'm okay. Where are *you*?"

"Here, Pilot, I'm right here. But since it's so black, maybe that's why you can't see me."

Pilot rubbed a paw across his nose. "What do you mean, 'black'?"

"Everything. It's totally black here. What, you don't think so? Hey, can dogs see in the dark?"

"No! But it's not black where I am. It's not even dark."

There was a pause, as if Ben were thinking over this new piece of information. Eventually he asked in a very different tone of voice, "Just where are you?"

Pilot said, "In Danielle's apartment. Where are you?"

Ben said curiously, "Me too. I mean, sort of."

"What do you mean, 'sort of'? I hear your voice, so you must be here."

Ben's voice became softer. "Where are the women? Where's German?"

"Outside in the hall. Down the hall with Ling."

"Can you go get them, please?"

Pilot kept looking around the apartment, sure that any moment he would see Ben Gould . . . somewhere.

"Pilot, are you still here?"

"Yes."

"Could you do that for me? Could you go get the women?"

"Okay."

"Thank you very much. I'll be right here waiting."

The dog remembered something. Tipping back his head, he looked at the ceiling. Perhaps Ben was up there, like the little boy on the kitchen ceiling. But this time there was nothing on the ceiling of Danielle's apartment.

"Pilot?"

"Yes?"

"It's really not dark where you are? Not at all?"

"Uh, no. It's normal. I can see everything." While speaking, Pilot looked around the room. "No—no dark here."

"Okay. That's all. I just wanted to make sure."

Pilot left the apartment to go get German and Ling. In the darkness, Ben lowered his head and waited.

Twelve

The compact fell off Danielle's fingertips and dropped on the table. Ben was supposed to take it from her but he'd suddenly disappeared. Looking around, she did not see him anywhere. There was a spring roll on her plate. She picked it up and bit into the half-crunchy, half-soggy food while staring at her open compact lying upside down on the table. Where did he go? How had he disappeared in the seconds it took to hand some-one a small object? And more than that, *why* had he gone? She was about to tell him her big discovery when he vanished. "Ben?" She didn't expect an answer but felt she had to say his name anyway just to be sure. Where was he?

"Where's your friend the old guy? Did he finally get the hint?" Dexter pulled out his chair and sat back down. "Who was that, anyway? He was a friend? How come you never told me about him before?"

Dropping the egg roll onto her plate, Danielle lifted her head. "Did you hear that?"

"Hear what?"

"My name. Someone just said my name. You didn't hear it?"

"No." Dexter lifted and dropped one shoulder in a half-hearted shrug. He'd had enough of other people saying Danielle's name tonight. This was supposed to have been their big special night together. But now it seemed like his girlfriend was suddenly the most popular person in the restaurant. How about making some time for him?

She held her head at a strange angle, as if waiting to hear something else. Dexter kept quiet because he was considerate and a coward and didn't want to make her angry, especially not tonight.

"Ben? Is that you, Ben?" She turned back to Dexter. "Did you hear *that*? Didn't you hear someone say my name again?"

"No. Sorry."

"You're sure?"

"Yes." Dexter made two fists under the table.

"Well, I did. I know I did. And I know it was him too."

"Who?"

"Ben. The guy I was just talking to."

In spite of himself, Dexter looked around to see if he could locate this Ben. "Where did he go?"

"I don't know."

"But, Dani, how could he be calling you if he already left?"

"I don't know, but I'm sure it was him."

"Okay. If you say so." He looked away. He looked at the ground. He looked anywhere but at Danielle.

"Dexter?"

"Yeah?" The expression on his face was that of a little boy who just wanted to be hugged.

"Everything's okay. Everything is going to be fine, don't worry. Just hold on for a few minutes."

• • •

Pilot could not wait any longer. Always the gentleman, he had stood a long time at a respectful distance while waiting for one of the women to turn around and see him. As soon as they did, he would relay Ben's request. But neither of them moved. Neither woman appeared to be doing anything but standing with her back to him.

"Excuse me?"

No response.

Pilot said it louder *"Excuse me?"*

Ling looked over her shoulder and saw him but did not react. Something was very wrong with her. Pilot could see that even from a distance. She looked sick and not "all there." Silently, the dog asked if she was okay. The ghost did not respond. Pilot had the feeling she had not heard his question so he asked it again. She remained silent.

He walked over to them and nudged German in the butt with his head. The tall woman touched her eyes before turning, as if trying to clear her vision. "Pilot! Hey there, are you all right?"

"I'm fine. What's the matter with Ling?"

They looked at the ghost but she didn't look back. She didn't look at anything. Her eyes were vacant.

German had not seen Ben touch Ling earlier and take out of her what he needed. Nor had she seen the array of expressions on Ling's face while it happened: the electric twitch the moment she was touched; the furious resistance; the eyes screaming *No!* before drooping a moment later into acquiescence.

German thought Ling's strange passivity now was due to her being confused by everything going on. "She's okay. We're both just rattled . . ." She didn't know what else to say. The perfect winter morning in bed with Ben that she'd just been reexperiencing so completely was fading, although it still had a powerful hold on her. Now she felt the same kind of strong sweet sadness and longing that comes after good sex with someone you care about a great deal.

Pilot said, "Ben wants to see you two. He wants you both to come into Danielle's apartment."

"All right."

Pilot considered telling her about Ben not really being in that apartment, but decided not to. Let German see and make up her own mind about what to do next.

"Ling?" German touched the other woman on the elbow but there was no reaction. Ling just stood slumped, as though all the power inside her had been switched off. In time she looked at German, looked away, then walked down the hall and straight into Danielle's apartment.

Upon entering, she didn't react to the darkness. Closing the door behind her and locking it, she moved a few feet into the living room and stopped. "Ben? I'm here."

"Ling? Great. Where's German?"

"She's coming. She's down the hall. I thought you'd want to talk to me first, though." Her voice was a monotone, like a recording. It could have come from a cheap answering machine.

"Yes, you're right, I do want to talk to you."

"I know what you want, so it's not necessary to mince your words." Her dead tone was unsettling, especially in light of what she knew was about to happen to her.

He did not know how to respond. What could he say?

"It's not fair, Ben. There's nothing I can do to stop you, but I think it's totally unfair."

"Okay. I hear you."

Her voice roared back to life. "You *hear* me? That's not an answer. That's all you're going to say about this—'*I hear you*'?"

"What do you want me to say, Ling?"

"How about 'I'm sorry'? How about you know what you're about to do is really, totally wrong and you're sorry to be doing it? How about saying *that*, Ben?"

But there was no sorry in his voice when he answered. "I have to do it. There's no other way. I have to get out of this darkness and I don't know how. But you do."

"You're right—I do. I knew as soon as you touched me before out in the hall that you were going to end up doing this. I *knew* it would happen. But what about me, Ben? What about what *I* want?"

"I thought it was going to be different, Ling. I swear to you. Before, I honestly believed I could just take part of you and leave the rest. But I can't. I know that now after seeing Danielle: I can't do what I need to do with only part of you. I need everything."

"You need everything." She tried to repeat his statement with both scorn and resentment, but her words came out sounding only wretched. Hers was the out-of-control, pathetic voice of a rejected lover or an employee who has just been fired.

• • •

German reached for the doorknob to Danielle's apartment but discovered it would not turn. She tried again. Nothing. It wouldn't budge. "It's locked."

Standing behind her, Pilot asked, "What? What do you mean?"

"I mean it's *locked*. It won't open." She tried it again so the dog could see for himself.

"That makes no sense. It was just open. It had to be—I came out of there."

"Well, it's not anymore. One of them must have locked it from the inside."

"Why would they do that? Ben asked me to come out here and get you."

"Maybe Ling locked it."

"Makes no sense."

"You already said that."

They looked at each other. Then German thought, I'm having this conversation with a *dog*.

From the other side of the door, someone started singing.

"That's Ben."

Another voice joined in, a voice that sounded exactly like Ben's, but there was no question two voices were singing in Danielle's apartment now and not just one. Having lived with Ben, both German and Pilot knew how much he loved to sing. As a boy, his Russian grandfather had entertained him for years with beloved stories about his childhood in the countryside near Omsk. How in those mortally cold Siberian winters, people had little to amuse themselves with when the January wind was monstrous and the temperature outside was forty below zero. Traditionally, families and visitors gathered around the kitchen table because it was in the warmest room in the house. There they sang Russian folk songs. The custom of transcendent a cappella singing grew out of that and came to be known worldwide as Russian table music.

When Ben was eleven, his grandfather took him to the Bushnell in Hartford, Connecticut, to hear the famous Russian choir Peresvet sing a medley of these songs. The thing he remembered most about that night was how almost everyone in the audience seemed to know each song by heart. Many people, including his grandfather, hummed or sang along with the performers. The applause after each song was thunderous.

Once when little Ben was sick in bed a long time with a serious case of chicken pox and bored out of his mind, his grandfather visited on several consecutive afternoons and sang/taught
him some of these songs. The boy's favorite was called "The
Young Man Has Flown Like a Bird," because in that dreary time
he always pictured himself as the young man flying up from this
sickbed and out the window into a healthy world. Years later,
when Ben encountered the paintings of Marc Chagall for the
first time, they reminded him of those days in bed, slowly learning the long Russian words to that song.

And now he was singing it again. It's what Ling had requested
they do before it happened. That's what she wanted to be doing
while it happened. To her, there was no more perfect way to
leave.

She said to him, "Do you remember 'The Young Man Has
Flown Like a Bird'?"

"Yes, I do." In the dark two feet away from her, he closed
his eyes and called up the memory of the song and of his grandfather teaching it to him.

"Can we sing that song now, Ben? Can we sing it while—"

"Yes, Ling, absolutely."

"Thank you. That'll make it easier for me. I'm over here,
Ben. In case you can't find me in this dark, I'm right here. I'll
keep talking until you find me."

Moments later she felt fingers touch her and then once again
he took hold of her shoulders. Ling wasn't frightened by what
was about to happen to her, only sad. She must give him everything now. Then she would be gone forever and the unexpectedly
large number of things she had grown to like about being human
would be taken away from her.

The saddest thing of all was losing German. You obviously
can't miss someone if you no longer exist. But Ling was con-

vinced that somehow, somewhere, wherever her atoms went after Ben was finished, they would still miss German Landis. The ghost had known from the beginning that nothing could ever develop between them. Yet, now that everything was about to end for her, Ling indulged one last time in the fanciful idea that perhaps some kind of new magic would surface one day that would have made it happen.

"Just so you know, Ben, I'm in love with German."

He chuckled and said, "You have good taste."

"No, I mean I really *love* her. If it were possible I would have taken her away from you. That sounds ludicrous but it's true."

"Okay." Someday he would tell German that a lesbian ghost had once been in love with her.

"Do you think it's funny?"

"No, Ling, I think it's wonderful. German is the most lovable person in the world. I meant it when I said you have good taste."

She said, "I always wondered if I loved her because I'm you or because I'm me."

Ben asked quietly, "Aren't they the same thing?"

Ling ran a hand through her hair. "Yes, I guess they are. That's one of the things I hated most about this: I'm only part of you. There's no real separate me *in* me. Everything I am is only some Benjamin Gould leftover. A part you never used in your lifetime, recycled into a ghost named Ling. Wouldn't it shock the world to know that's all that ghosts are: leftovers?

"Enough of this. I'm ready now, Ben. Can we sing?"

Outside in the hall, Pilot asked, "What are they singing?"

"A Russian song. Ben sang it once for me."

"What's Russian?"

German kept forgetting she was talking to a dog. "It's a language."

"Humans have more than one language?"

"Uh, yes, Pilot."

"Interesting. Because dogs only have one."

"But you're speaking to me now in human language."

Pilot looked up at her. "No I'm not. I'm speaking dog."

German wasn't having it. "Right now you're speaking dog to me?"

"Yes."

"But I'm speaking English, uh, *human*, to you."

"No you're not. You're speaking dog."

"No I'm not, Pilot. I'm speaking English."

"What's English?"

Before their conversation deteriorated further, the singing stopped on the other side of the door. That sudden silence stopped their bickering. German leaned forward, thinking she might hear better if she was closer. She put a hand on the doorknob to steady herself and this time it turned with no resistance. "The door's open."

"Go in."

She wasn't so sure. "You think that's a good idea?"

"Why stay out here?" Pilot moved around her and walked in. German followed. Ben was sitting on the yellow couch.

She saw him and asked, "Where are Ling and Danielle?"

Ben said, "Ling is gone. She won't be back. Danielle's——" He lifted his hand off the armrest as if about to illustrate something. Instead he made a sour face and left the hand dangling in the air.

"What's happening, Ben? Will you please explain all this now?"

He nodded. "You need to meet someone first.

"In my life there have only been two people I genuinely hated, because both of them traumatized me for different reasons. One was a boss I had named Parrish. The other was an old girlfriend named—"

"Alayne," German interrupted.

"Alayne Stewart, that's right. You remembered."

"I remember everything, Ben. Both good and bad."

He smiled, remembering how good her memory was. "That's right—you do. The odd thing is I'd forgotten Parrish's last name over the years because I only remembered him as the Jerk: Carl the Jerk. Carl Parrish, the jerk. Alayne Stewart and Carl Parrish. Stewart—Parrish. Do you remember *that* name, German?"

"No."

"But you remember *him*."

The bum in the orange shirt walked out of Danielle's kitchen eating a peanut butter sandwich and holding a can of Dr Pepper. He sat down on the couch next to Ben as if it were no big deal and continued eating.

Both German and Pilot moved back, the dog growling. They looked at Ben as though he were nuts to remain sitting next to that madman.

"Don't worry, he's harmless now, right?" Ben looked at Parrish for confirmation and slapped the man on the arm. The bum nodded and took another big bite of the peanut butter sandwich on white bread with the crusts cut off.

"You don't have to worry about Stewart anymore. He's been declawed."

"Please, Ben, please—tell me what's going on. What *is* all this?"

He nodded understanding at her confusion. "I created Stewart Parrish, right down to that orange shirt he's wearing. I'll tell you how: My unconscious tossed many things that have scared me my whole life into a big bowl." His hands described a large circle in front of him. "It stirred them around till all that poison was mixed together. Then it slid the mix into the oven, which is my *head*"—Ben touched his forehead—"and baked it at a low temperature for years. Then recently it took Stewart Parrish out of this oven and he was ready to go and scare everyone."

Of course, German didn't understand. How could she from this bizarre explanation? Her face pleaded to know *What are you talking about?*—which made sense, because Ben hadn't understood, either, until only a little earlier. It was obviously time for him to show her and not tell.

From out in the hall a white verz walked into the apartment. The animal went unhurriedly over to Stewart Parrish. The man in the colorful shirt bent down and offered the verz what was left of his sandwich. The animal stretched forward and opened its mouth. It ate the sandwich, then Parrish's arm, and then the rest of the man. This happened rapidly, silently, and fluidly. The verz appeared to inhale the man as if in one long breath. It did not chew and it did not swallow. When Parrish was gone, the white animal walked over to Ben and into his right leg. It simply entered his leg and disappeared.

Even Pilot was impressed. The dog had seen verzes all his life but thought they originated in some remote verz place, helped humans in trouble, and then returned to wherever again until the next time they were needed. Sort of like fire trucks returning to the firehouse. Pilot never once imagined *humans* created verzes. Sensational! In hindsight, though, the idea made sense, because the only time the white creatures appeared was when people were in a fix and needed help.

German stood stiffly holding her right elbow in her left hand, her right hand flat across her nose and mouth. Incredulous. Her eyes skittered from Ben to Pilot to the space on the couch where Stewart Parrish had sat eating peanut butter moments before.

"German, are you listening? Can you hear me?" Ben tried to make his voice like a hand shaking her gently awake. *"German?"*

Her panicky eyes still jumped back and forth, but for a few seconds they stopped on Ben and stayed.

He licked his lips and spoke slowly. "Remember when I fell down in the snow last winter and hit my head? Well, I *died* when that happened. Or I was *supposed* to die, but I didn't."

Hand still pressed against her face, German said through the fingers, "I know. Ling told me that."

"Okay. And you already know about some of the strange things that have been happening to me since then. Danielle said the same sort of stuff has been happening to her since her accident."

"I know that too, Ben."

He wanted to touch her now, to hold her hand tightly while he told her the most important thing. "Ling was me. Stewart Parrish was me. The verzes are me. Everything, all the craziness that's been happening, has come from me. A part of me, or because of me . . . all of it—I am to blame."

"Why?" German asked.

The simplicity of her question took him off guard. That one word struck him like a punch in the chest. He could feel his mind stumbling backward, reaching out for anything to grab onto and regain its balance.

Why? Did she mean why him? Or why this insane turn of events? He did not know the answer to either. He knew only a few things now. He knew he was alive when he should have been dead. He knew he loved German Landis more than ever before. He knew all of the impossible things that had happened recently stemmed from his having miraculously survived the fall in the snow.

"I don't know why, German. I'm trying to figure it all out

as fast as I can, but it's hard. I could lie to you but I won't, not anymore. You don't deserve lies."

She pointed to his leg. He knew what she meant: How did a verz walk into your leg and disappear—after eating Stewart Parrish?

"What about that, Ben? Do you know what *that* just was?" Before he could answer, she asked another question. "And do you know why we're suddenly able to understand our dog when he talks to us? Or a ghost materializes, or—"

"Yes, I do."

"You do?"

Pilot asked, "You *do?*"

"Yes, I do."

Thirteen

Even though she knew very well what she saw, German had to ask. "What is that?"

Ben smiled at her. "You know better than anyone what it is. You've been talking about them for as long as I've known you."

"It's a Ferrari. It's a Formula One Ferrari!" She bent forward to get a closer look at the gleaming machine. "I've never seen one in person."

"Would you like me to introduce you?"

"I don't believe it. It's real. It's a real one."

A red-and-yellow Ferrari Formula One racing car was parked on the street in front of Ben's apartment building. Multi-colored sponsor advertisements were stuck all over the body. It looked like some kind of enormous spotted water bug.

Ben said, "It goes from zero to a hundred miles an hour in three seconds. But what I think is even more impressive is that it decelerates from a hundred eighty miles an hour to zero in four seconds."

"*Four* seconds? I didn't know that." Nevertheless German knew a great deal about Formula One racing because her father and brother back in Minnesota had always been big fans of the sport. She'd spent many satisfying childhood Sundays watching these metal monsters on TV as they whizzed around racetracks in exotic places worldwide: Monte Carlo. Kuala Lumpur. Melbourne. Zero to one hundred miles an hour in three seconds. One-two-three.

Like a mirage, this striking machine was parked on the street. It looked absurdly out of place there, especially because it was parked between a small Hyundai and a pea green Toyota Camry. An old man walked by, saw the red racer, and did an exaggerated double take. Ben, German, and Pilot stood together at the top of the same stairs where Stewart Parrish had recently sat.

"Why is it here, Ben? Did you bring it? Why are we even out here looking at it?"

"Because I need it to show you something." He walked down the steps and over to the Ferrari. "You know a lot about these cars, right, German?"

Back at the top of the stairs, she crossed her arms and shrugged noncommittally. "I know some things, yes."

"You do; you used to talk about them all the time. You love racing. Okay, so do me a favor: Get in this one and start it."

"*Start* it?"

"Yes, and if you're able to figure out how to do that, then please drive it around the block a few times."

German said nothing but looked at her ex-boyfriend as if he were being silly. "I don't know how to start a Formula One car! How would I know? And you don't drive a thing like that around the block, Ben. It's not a scooter. It has a thousand horsepower. Zero to a hundred in three seconds, remember?"

"Pilot?"

"What?"

"Do you want to try?"

"Try what?"

"Driving this car."

"What does 'driving' mean?"

Both humans realized dogs only know how to ride in cars, not drive them. The word isn't even in their vocabulary.

"Never mind." Ben walked around the gleaming machine, touching it here and there, kicking a tire, squatting down low to see what it would be like to sit in there. "How do you even get into the thing? The cockpit is so small and narrow."

German said, "They take out the steering wheel first. The driver gets in and he reattaches it. The seat is custom made to his body. It has to be a perfect fit because of the g-forces exerted on him when he goes around curves during the race."

"Really? Every driver has a custom-made seat?"

"Ben, why are we here? What's going on?"

Standing up, he put a hand on the thick silver roll bar. "This is the fastest and most technologically advanced car in the world. It goes three hundred miles an hour. It's the best, right, German?"

"Yes. For what it is, it's the best."

"But neither of us knows how to even turn on the ignition, though we've both been driving for years and you're a big fan of racing. Even if we did know how to *start* it, chances are we'd get into an accident in five minutes driving it because we couldn't handle the power."

"Especially not on a city street," she added. "It's not meant to be driven anywhere else but on a racetrack. They're useless as regular cars. It's *not* a regular car. It's like the difference between a propeller plane and the space shuttle."

"The space shuttle—I like that. Still, it's ironic, isn't it? The greatest car in the world, the automotive ne plus ultra, can't be used as a car. They're only good for one specific purpose that, like, only a hundred people on earth know how to do."

"So?" Where was he going with this? What did this have to do with their situation? She was getting impatient.

Ben patted the roll bar again. "So—imagine one day you went out to get your car. But instead of your three-year-old Ford, somehow overnight it had turned into *this*: the greatest, fastest, meanest, most powerful car in the world. But you have no idea of how to even start it, much less drive the thing.

"Still, there's this incredibly important place you must drive to right now that's a hundred miles away from here and there's no other way of getting there but with this.

"But you can't even get into the car because you didn't know the steering wheel has to be taken out first. But somehow you work that part out and climb in. Next you have to figure out how to turn the motor on. *Then* you have to drive it those hundred miles without killing yourself. Zero to a hundred in three seconds, German. How do you even give it gas without crashing into a tree?"

"You *don't*—you call a cab. Or you rent a car. I don't know, Ben. What is your point?"

The Ferrari's engine suddenly started by itself. The sound was huge, brutal, and high at first as the perfectly tuned machine revved fast. Then it dropped down into a sexy, popping, throaty, uneven *vroom-vroom*. It idled that way for half a minute and then turned off without warning. The silence that followed was thick and almost tangible.

Ben put his hands behind his back. "Cool trick, huh? Makes you think I know how it works, but I don't. I don't have a clue. I don't know anything about this car other than what you told me. I can turn on the engine but that's all. How did I do it? *I—*

don't—know." He looked at the Ferrari for a long time. Instinctively, German knew to keep quiet until he spoke again.

"This is exactly what happened to me: One day I went to get my Ford but this Ferrari was in the garage instead. One day I fell down and hit my head. I was supposed to die but I didn't. Instead, I woke up and became . . . like a racing car.

"Do you understand, German?" He touched his mouth. He wanted to speak clearly. He wanted to tell her everything exactly as it was.

"I think so. I don't know, Ben. Tell me more."

"You understand Pilot now because I made it possible. Pilot understands us because I made that happen too. Me. I did it, German. Some part of me, some*where* in me, knows how to do things like that now. It knows how to go into Danielle's head and look around in her life as if it were a furniture showroom. It knows how to make a ghost appear. My own ghost, even when I'm not dead. It knows how to bring Ling here. And how do I do all that amazing stuff? *I do not know.* That's the trouble: I don't know." Incongruously his face broke out in a smile. He tossed a hand in the air in total frustration. "It's like a part of me turned into this thousand-horsepower Ferrari. But I don't know how it works. The rest of me doesn't even know how to turn it on, much less drive it without crashing. I know this much." He held up two fingers half an inch apart. "I know how to start it and turn it off."

"When was the first time these strange things happened to you, Ben?"

"The night we saw that guy stabbed. In the bar we went to afterwards. That was the first time I went into Danielle's head."

"And you really believe you created this Stewart Parrish too?"

"I don't *believe* it, German—I know it. You saw what just

happened." He patted his leg to remind her. "Stewart Parrish, the verzes, Ling—all of it was my doing. But I have only the vaguest idea how I did it or why."

"Where did this car come from?"

Ben pointed to his chest.

"Then make it go away now. Show me."

He shook his head. "I tried. I can't."

"Why not?"

"I just told you: because I don't know how most of this *works*. I don't know how I work anymore, German. I made the car appear"—he pointed to the Ferrari—"but I don't know how I did it or how to make it go away now. I just kind of think in a certain way and then sometimes what I'm thinking happens, but most of the time it doesn't. It's completely out of control. *I'm* out of my own control."

"It's like Ling said when she was cooking," Pilot said.

Ben and German turned to the dog. Pilot described how Ling would stretch out her hand when she needed something while cooking and the object would appear there. He also told them about asking the ghost if she were to envision an elephant in her hand, would it materialize, too, and she had said yes.

"How did she do it?" Ben asked.

Pilot shifted his feet and closed his eyes to recall her exact words. "She said, 'When a person dies, then they're taught the real structure of things. Not only how they look or feel but the essence of what they really *are*. Once you have that understanding, it's easy to make things."

"It sounds like you're repeating her."

"I was. I have a good memory."

"You remembered word for word what Ling said?"

"Yes. If I want to remember something, I do."

"That's amazing, Pilot."

"It's normal. All dogs have faultless memories. Haven't you ever noticed?"

"Uh, no, not really."

Hearing that, Pilot realized again how obtuse human beings were to the really important things in life.

Ben started to speak but stopped halfway when an idea blossomed in his mind. "You remember everything?" Walking around the Ferrari, he started back up the stairs toward where the other two stood.

Pilot said, "If I want to, yes. Well, not everything, because that would be boasting, but—"

"Do you remember the day I fell down and hit my head? The day I got you from the animal shelter?"

"Yes."

"Do you remember everything that happened when I fell down?"

"Probably. I'd have to think about it first. Gather my thoughts."

When Ben was halfway to them, Pilot said, "On the day you fell, you were wearing purple socks."

"I don't own purple socks, Pilot."

Undaunted, the dog insisted, "You were wearing purple socks. I saw them on you when you were lying in the street."

Ben stopped to think that over. Did he own purple socks? Oh, yes, he did: his mother had sent him a pair of thick wool ones that he'd forgotten about because he almost never wore them, they were so loud. He kept them only because on her periodic visits, Mom inevitably asked about the clothes she'd sent. Did he like them? Did they fit? If he didn't wear some of them at least once during her visits, she pouted. The rest of the year her gifts hibernated in the back of his closet or dresser drawer. The day he bought Pilot was very cold and it was snowing hard. Of course he had worn heavy wool socks that morning. He'd just forgotten until now which ones.

"You're right, Pilot. But can you remember if I said anything when I fell? Or when I was down? Maybe something strange happened to me when I was on the ground."

Pilot smelled something. He smelled sex/youth/freedom/ sex/food/running/playing/sex—all together. In other words, he smelled a female dog in heat close by. Despite being smart, eloquent, and able to communicate handily with human beings now, Pilot was still a male dog. He ran off after that ambrosial smell without another thought.

"Pilot! Stop!"

The female dog was near. Near enough to transform every quick breath of air he inhaled into desire. The more Pilot breathed her scent, the more he wanted her. The more he wanted her, the more the rest of the world—humans included—faded away. Pilot dashed toward the only thing that mattered at that moment.

Helpless to stop him, Ben watched the dog run away. However, with his newly gained knowledge, he understood immediately why it had happened. Pilot's memories of the day he hit his head might provide answers to important questions. But a commanding part of Benjamin Gould did not *want* him to know those answers. It had created Stewart Parrish from old fears. It had killed the verz that lay under the tree. It had prevented Ben from talking to Danielle in the Lotus Garden when she was about to divulge who was to blame for their difficulties. Part of Ben Gould had deliberately blocked or hampered him ever since he survived what should have been that fatal injury.

He was the bad guy: Benjamin Gould was his own enemy.

After watching Pilot disappear down the block after the phantom female, Ben told German everything he knew about what was happening. He kept the account as honest and short as possible.

Seconds after he'd finished, a car pulled to the curb directly opposite them on the other side of the street. The driver looked vaguely familiar, like a stranger you once sat next to on a long bus trip. As the hours passed, you two had a long chat. By the end of the trip, your good-byes were heartfelt. I know that face, don't I?

"Hello!" the driver called out to them. His car was navy blue, nondescript. The man was too. His face was so plain that it was as if they had seen it a hundred times before on a hundred different men.

He got out of the car and, after checking both ways for oncoming traffic, crossed the street and walked right over. Both of them watched him while thinking, What now? He was dressed in a brown shirt with the sleeves rolled up to his elbows, gray corduroy slacks, and black jodhpurs. Forty-something, he was tall and paunchy, and most of his hair was gone.

He came toward them smiling and it was a nice smile, not fake or professional. This man looked genuinely glad to see them. German turned to Ben and raised one eyebrow.

On reaching the stairs, the man bounded up them like a game-show host at the beginning of the program. "Remember me? No, you probably don't." He was all energy and good cheer. His whole demeanor said it was really okay if they didn't remember him.

Speaking for both of them, German said a shy no.

"That night in the pizza place? I was the guy who got stabbed."

•   •   •

He had a bottle of very good wine and three glasses in his car. After they had talked about that horrendous night, silence gradually fell between them. That's when he went to get the wine. For quite a while afterward they just drank his Bordeaux in a now much more companionable silence. He seemed to be a great guy. When German asked his name, he said they should call him Stanley.

"*Stanley?* Is that your real name?"

"No. My real name is the Angel of Death, but that's quite a mouthful. Stanley is easier. Stan, if you prefer."

"You're really the Angel of Death?"

"I am." A big fat annoying fly had been buzzing around them for some time. Stanley pointed a finger at it and the insect instantly dropped out of the air as though it had been shot. He smiled and said, "Special effects."

Ben repeated the words slowly because he wanted to try them out on his tongue. "The Angel of Death."

"That's me."

"You were with a woman that night in the pizza place."

"Ling. I was there with Ling."

"Why are you here now?"

"I don't know, Ben. Why *am* I here?"

"Who sent you?"

"I'm here because you just summoned me."

"I did?"

"Yes. And them too." Stanley pointed over to his car. Inside, it was full of people. Ben and German gawked because they were certain no one else had been in there before.

"We're all here because you called for us, Ben." Stanley nodded toward the car as the doors opened.

The passengers got out. Ben did not recognize any of them. They stayed together on the other side of the street, watching and waiting.

"Who are they?" he asked.

German answered, "I know who they are," and went down the stairs to the street. She was smiling. Ben tried to catch her eye but she only looked toward the blue car.

Puzzled, he watched her go. She crossed the street and walked over to Stanley's car. Five people greeted her enthusiastically and with great affection. German hugged one woman and then a thin man in a green shirt. Someone said something and they all laughed. German kept reaching over and touching arms and elbows: sign after sign that she knew each one of these people well and was delighted to see them. Ben caught snatches of lively conversations but not enough to discern what was going on. Frustrated, he turned to Stanley and asked again, "Who *are* they?" But he wasn't really asking the other man so much as the universe at large.

"Figure it out for yourself," the Angel of Death said and poured more wine into both their glasses.

"How does German know those people? How come I don't?"

"Figure it out for yourself."

Someone bent down into the car and a moment later music started playing. A piano began slowly, a few lonesome notes that little by little opened up into a waltz. Ben immediately recognized the tune because it was one of his favorite pieces of music: Scott Joplin's melancholic waltz "Bethena."

The man in the green shirt opened his arms and German moved into them. The two of them began waltzing right there in the middle of the street. The other passengers stepped back and watched, smiling. A little while later the woman German had embraced earlier cut in and the two women waltzed together.

Ben looked at Stanley. The angel shook his head no: I am not going to tell you anything.

What else was there to do but go over and find out who these people were? Maybe they were all minor angels of death—Stanley's assistants. Or Angel of Death roadies who set up the equipment for Stanley's different productions. But how could German know them? These thoughts churned around in Ben's head as he walked in the direction of the crowd. Before he had a chance to reach them, another woman from the group stepped forward and asked him to dance. He looked at her but saw only a stranger.

"Do I know you?"

"Come dance with me."

"But do I *know* you?"

Saying nothing, she took his hand and led him over to the others. Looking at Ben, German waved and grinned. It was the first time she had smiled at him in so long. The two couples glided in the waltz's formal circles around and around that tree-lined street. It was such an odd but amusing thing to do in this wrong place. German had taught Ben to waltz when they lived together, so he had no problem doing it. His partner was a nimble dancer but remained silent and only smiled with her eyes closed as they whirled in and out of light and shadow. Halfway through the piece Ben began to smile too. Weird as it was, waltzing on a city street with this stranger in the middle of the day was a memory he knew would live in him a long time.

When the tune ended Ben thought, Okay *now*. But immediately another song came on—something entirely different. Zouk music: "Bay Chabon" by Kassav'. The festive Caribbean music Dominique Bertaux loved so much and introduced him to when they were together. Its mood was the exact opposite of the solemn "Bethena." Zouk music made anyone jump up and dance all out. You had to—it was that infectious. Caribbean, African, and South American beats swirled together in one frantic jumping sound. The first time Dominique played it for him, Ben was so impressed that he listened to her Kassav' tape three times in a row. German had the same reaction: She loved zouk music from the first.

Now every one of the passengers from Stanley's car started dancing, whether they had partners or not. They walked out into the street and started moving, gyrating, twisting, dipping. It didn't matter what you did: hearing zouk filled you with the best kind of life energy and a need to dance it out however your body felt like moving. Some people waved their arms or hopped from one foot to the other. A man high-stepped in a big circle as if he were in a marching band. Another did the twist too fast and lost his balance. Everyone dropped their guards, opened their doors, and danced as though no one else were there—danced like it was the last thing they'd ever do. They danced their joy.

Ben's partner threw both arms straight up in the air, tipped her head back and whooped at the top of her lungs. The whole moving scene was nuts and loonier by the moment, but it was happy-nuts, so let's just dance and forget the rest for the moment.

Stretching both arms out to his sides, Ben began spinning around like a Sufi dervish doing a Sema. The spin was too slow for the music but that's what his body felt like doing, so he went with it.

Before closing his eyes to drop deeper into the music and the whirl, Ben glimpsed Stanley at the top of the stairs watching everything with a big grin on his face. He held the wine bottle in one hand and a glass in the other, and both were empty. He was sort of penduluming from side to side in time to the music. The Stanley dance. The Angel of Death dancing, ladies and gentlemen.

Ben shut his eyes and spun. And quickly bumped into

someone. The breath. Before he had a chance to open his eyes, Ben smelled this other person's breath and it was so intimately familiar, so reminiscent of something memorable but illusive, that he kept his eyes closed to concentrate on the smell to work out what it was.

When the recognition struck, spontaneously he said, "It's *ful*!" *Ful medames*, the fava bean dish people eat for breakfast in the Middle East because it's tasty, filling, and very cheap: fava beans, garlic, olive oil, parsley, and onion. Simple to prepare and often delicious. Whoever was standing near him now, their breath smelled exactly like *ful*. Before opening his eyes to see who it was, Ben remembered the last time he had prepared the dish.

It was his first date with German Landis. He had invited her over to his apartment so he could cook dinner for her. They had met several nights before in a public library. She was sitting by herself on a couch in the reading room surrounded by books on Egypt. Among them was a large cookbook of Middle Eastern cuisine. She was preparing a unit on Egyptian art and culture for her seventh-grade students. Watching from afar, Ben was attracted both by her looks and the fact that this handsome woman read Middle Eastern cookbooks.

Mustering his courage, he walked over and asked if she liked *ful*. She looked him straight in the eye and asked, "Do I like *full*? What are you talking about?" He pointed to the cookbook and said no, *ful*, assuming she'd understand the connection. Anyone interested in Middle Eastern cuisine would have to know about *ful*. It was one of the most ubiquitous national dishes in that region, like hot dogs in America or Wiener schnitzel in Austria.

When German's facial expression moved from I'm listening to guarded, Ben managed to keep the conversation alive by describing exactly what *ful* was and the first time he ever tasted it, on a backstreet in Alexandria, Egypt. She asked why he'd gone there. Ben said because he loved *The Alexandria Quartet* by Lawrence Durrell. After finishing it in a reading frenzy, he knew he had to go see the city and experience it for himself. Particularly the famous new library there that looked like a giant flying saucer. By coincidence, German had just been reading about that library and poring over pictures of it. In due course she invited him to sit down on the couch.

So the first time he cooked for her, Ben decided to prepare *ful* as an hors d'oeuvre. He taste tested it three times before she arrived just to make sure it was perfect.

Touched by his thoughtfulness, German took a taste of the stuff. Revulsion flashed across her face. Seeing this, Ben panicked and told her to spit it out, spit it out. But there was nowhere to spit except into her hand. German had good manners and managed to swallow the warmish library paste without regurgitating it as she had done on occasion in the past when she accidentally ate something awful.

Ben was so shaken and embarrassed by her reaction that he ruined the rest of the meal. He'd planned everything so carefully, but in the end it would have been better if he had called out for a pizza because everything he served after the *ful* was overcooked or undercooked or simply tasted *off*. The meal was a total disaster and both of them knew it. When it was over and neither had taken more than a few bites of the chocolate *Palatschinken*, which tasted of far too much espresso (his secret ingredient in the recipe), they put their spoons down, careful to avoid looking at each other. Since he had begun cooking seriously years before, Ben had never made such a thoroughly rotten meal.

German stood up. He thought she was going to the toilet. Then for a worrying few seconds he thought, No, she's leaving! How can I stop her? What can I do?

Instead, the tall woman walked around the table until she was standing directly behind him. She put both of her hands on top of his head. Leaning down, she kissed one of them loudly. She did it that way because she didn't have enough nerve to kiss him directly. She said, "Thank you for making all this," and walked out of the room.

Ben picked up the dessert spoon and wiggled it upanddownandupanddown between his now galvanized fingers. That fromout-of-nowhere kiss and then her thank-you knocked him flat. How was he going to keep her here? What could he do after this fiasco to make her stay and see that he wasn't a total loser?

He needn't have worried. In his bathroom German stood in front of the mirror, hands pressed tightly to her sides, staring at her reflection while on the verge of tears. That's why she had walked away from the table after the kiss. She was overcome and didn't want him to see her cry if it came to that. No man had ever made this kind of effort for her before. And even better, on a first date, when they didn't know each other. How beautiful just the salad alone was. Or the unmistakable care he'd taken in arranging everything from the flowers to the way each course looked on the plate.

Who *was* this guy? A man who went to Egypt because he read a description of a city in a novel and was captivated enough to actually go there? German didn't know anyone who did such gutsy, impulsive things, male or female. He'd made that badtasting *ful* just because he wanted her to see and taste it. The tender hesitant look on his face when he brought it out and told her what it was. How could you top that on a first date? His actions were as kind as his eyes. What was she going to do now? How could she tell him that he'd already won her heart three times before they'd even tasted that bitter dessert?

She managed. Later that night, after they went to bed for

the first time, a strange but pleasant thing happened to her. After they were both exhausted and in that idyllic state of drifting in and out of sleep together, German remembered Mr. Spilke. It made her smile because she hadn't thought about the man in years. Why did he come to mind *now*?

Her seventh-grade earth science teacher, Mr. Spilke with his never-ending array of green shirts and passion for inspiring young people. He loved science, teaching, and his students. Eventually most of them grew to love him, too, because he was such a good guy and his gusto for his subject was contagious.

In bed, German turned to her brand-new lover. Touching her fingertips to his warm cheek, she mumbled, "You remind me of Mr. Spilke." Ben smiled but was too tired to ask who she was talking about. How peculiar that here in bed—sated, raw, and content—she would think about her seventh-grade science teacher, but that's what happened. Before falling asleep on Ben's outstretched arm, German realized why: although she didn't know this Benjamin Gould very well yet, he exuded the same kind of bigheartedness and generous enthusiasm as Mr. Spilke. Which was a very good sign, because that teacher was one of the few who had genuinely affected German Landis's life and helped to make her the woman she was. Part of the reason she became a teacher was because of the way Spilke had made learning an exhilarating adventure, even when his subject did not interest her at all.

In life there are only a small number of people whom we choose to keep in our hearts. Over the years a lot come in and go out: lovers, family, and friends. Some hang around for a while, and some want to stay even after we have ordered them to leave. But only a handful, no more than two handfuls if you're very lucky, are welcome forever. Mr. Spilke was one of these people for German.

And that's exactly who Ben saw when he opened his eyes on the street in front of Danielle Voyles's apartment building: Mr. Spilke, the man in the green shirt, whose breath now smelled like *ful*.

The two men looked at each other but said nothing. Fantastic music surrounded them. Dancers surrounded them. Ben looked at the man and, although he had never seen him before today, was certain he knew something about him—but what? Long ago German had described her favorite teacher, but it was one of a thousand conversations the lovers had. How was Ben supposed to remember everything she said? German loved to talk and he loved that about her. However, sometimes he listened more closely to her than at others, and maybe Mr. Spilke was one of those other times. Still, he was sure he knew something important about this man in the green shirt.

He looked at Stanley, still standing up on the steps, and remembered the Angel of Death saying Ben himself had summoned all of the people in the car. He looked at the woman dancing with German. He looked at the other dancers.

Mr. Spilke looked at the small watch on his wrist. "You'd better hurry. They're coming soon."

Glad the other man had spoken first, Ben asked, "I'm sorry, but do we know each other?"

"We do. I'm you." Spilke pointed to each of the other passengers. "And he's you and she's you and, well, all of us are you."

"You're *me*?"

"We are. We're the parts of Ben Gould that German loves. You're just seeing us today through her perception rather than your own. It's as if instead of using a mirror, you closed your eyes and asked German to describe what you look like. How she sees you is different from the way you see yourself."

"So basically I'm talking to myself here?"

Spilke said, "Basically, yes. Look, you were spinning your wheels before when you tried explaining all of this to German with that Ferrari analogy. She didn't understand it and you saw that. So you did a smart thing, whether it was conscious or not: you told your ego to be quiet and brought us here to explain it to her because she knows us."

"And who are *you*?"

"I said it before: we're parts of Benjamin Gould that German Landis loves. The difference is that today you're seeing them from her perspective rather than your own.

"Why do people love us, Ben? We're always trying to figure that out, but only by using our own point of view. That's so limited. Sometimes they love us for things we don't even know about ourselves. For example, they love our hands. My hands? Why would anyone love my *hands*? But they've got their reasons. You must accept that and realize the Ben they know is different from the Ben you know.

"You don't remember it, but German once called you Mr. Spilke. That's me; I was her teacher in school. The reason she called you by my name was that something about you reminded her of me. Something special about me that she loved and saw in you too. That's true about every one of us in the car: all of us were in German's life at one time or another. There was something unique about each of us that she loved. She saw those same qualities in you too."

"That's why she recognized you before but I didn't?"

"Yes." Spilke looked at his watch again and tapped it once for emphasis.

Ben wasn't satisfied with the teacher's answer. "How could I call you to come here if I never knew you?"

"*You* didn't—German did. She knows us. She's trying to understand what's happening to you, but your explanation wasn't making sense to her. You saw that, so you let her choose the parts of Ben Gould that *could* explain it better to her. And she did."

Both watched German and her dancing partner. They were standing close. The woman was talking fast and using her hands for constant emphasis. German kept nodding nodding nodding, as if trying to keep up with all the things she was hearing.

"That woman is me? But I've never seen her before!"

Spilke extended two flat palms and then slowly brought them together. "She's *not* you; she's someone German knew who has a certain quality that you do, too, Ben. Maybe it's generosity or compassion, maybe insight into a specific thing. You might not even be aware of possessing it, but German believes you have it and that's part of why she loves you. That woman can explain these things to German so that she understands it."

Heatedly, Ben counted off on his fingers, "You, Ling, Stewart Parrish, the verzes, these people here—all of them are me?"

"In one form or another. Yes." A new voice said this. Ben turned to his left and there was Stanley the angel. "We knew this would happen one day, but not when or how. Mankind would finally say, *I want to make my own decisions.* I want to control my own destiny. How I live, when I die, what I do with my life. No outside control or influence, no coaching from the sidelines, no deus ex machina interference, nothing.

"At last: mankind grows up and moves out of the parents' house. Frankly, after all these millennia, we didn't know if it would ever happen. But now it has and you're one of the first to do it, Ben.

"It began a decade ago in Peru with a baby, oddly enough. It was supposed to die at birth but didn't. Then there was a teenager in Albania who was washed out to sea and was there for three days during a winter storm but didn't drown. They were both scheduled to die, but they didn't. Since then, the number has been growing exponentially. All over, human beings are reclaiming their lives, their fates, and their deaths. I say hallelujah, it's about time."

"You lied to me!" Ben said, but it was Ling speaking from somewhere inside him, and for the moment Ben had no control over the voice. He felt like a ventriloquist's dummy.

The angel looked embarrassed. "I'm sorry, Ling, but it was necessary. I couldn't tell you the truth before because it wasn't the right time. Ben had to discover certain things on his own first. You can understand why."

"No, I cannot! You said it was all because of a computer glitch. You said if I came back here and helped him—"

Stanley held up a hand to silence her. "I know what I told you, Ling, but the fib was necessary. Ben is the sum of his parts, like all human beings. He's more important than you because you are only one of his parts."

Ling wasn't having it. "And you lied about that too! You said I was a ghost—"

"Damn it, Ling, you *are* a ghost. But that's only a fraction of Ben. Until recently, ghosts were there to clean up someone's unfinished business after they died. But if people choose not to die now until they finish that business themselves, there's no more need of ghosts."

"Then you should at least have the guts or grace to admit you're a liar and that you used me."

Stanley's eyes turned into giant fiery pinwheels again, just like the night in the movie theater when Ling rejected his popcorn offer. "Be careful what you say, ghost. Don't forget who I am."

"I'm very well aware of who you are. But you don't scare me anymore. You're a liar and a fake, Stanley—a liar and a fake."

Helplessly caught in the middle of their crossfire, Ben held up both hands as if to say, Those are not my words, so don't blame me. Seeing Stanley's burning orange eyes the size of yo-yos proved pretty conclusively that the man was who he said he was. As a result, Ben Gould did *not* want to be on his bad side.

He punched Stanley in the head—a perfect shot, right in the middle of the temple, with enough force and fury behind it to send the angel staggering, staggering to the side; only at the last moment did he regain his balance. It was exactly like the punch Mr. Kyte had thrown at Stewart Parrish when he tried to get into the Kyte house.

Ben was horror-struck, because he had nothing to do with it. He had nothing to do with any of this. It was all Ling's fault. The ghost was using his body and its rage ruled. "Hey, I didn't—"

Stanley sprang at him. When the angel's hands touched his shoulders, Ben was flung backward like a golf ball driven off a tee and landed on his butt on the stone sidewalk. Pain knocked the wind out of him. But before he could even say Ow! he sprang to his feet and went right after the angel again.

Stanley tensed for the attack, but Ben/Ling went down low this time and bit him on the leg. The angel yowled and tried to push him off. But Ling wasn't finished and ghosts bite hard. Somewhere in his hijacked body, Ben was shouting No no no! but he could not stop the angry ghost inside from attacking the lying angel.

If he had been able to look around, Ben would have seen something incredible: the other people did not stop dancing. They saw the two men fighting frantically but not for an instant did they stop what they were doing. They danced and watched. Or they danced and ignored the fighters. Of course German saw the wrestlers, too, but her partner touched her side and said, "Don't worry about them," so she didn't.

Stanley grabbed Ben around the midsection and tried to lift him up but was unable to because he had the wrong leverage. In fact, now that they were fighting, Stanley didn't feel strong enough to even lift the other man at all. Stanley was an angel—the Angel of Death, no less—but all of a sudden he didn't know if he could pick this mortal up even if he had the right angle. So they wrestled around, straining and huffing, grunting and slipping, neither of them good at it but both determined to fight it out. The dancers fought gravity in the street to the zouk music while the wrestlers fumbled and scuffled up on the sidewalk.

Someone living in one of the surrounding houses looked out the window, saw what was going on, and called the cops. But the police didn't come, because something fundamental was happening here and the world was ordered to stay away until it was concluded.

"What . . . do . . . you . . . want . . . Ling?" Stanley gasped from somewhere deep inside Benjamin Gould's left armpit, where he was held in a sort of accidental reverse headlock.

"Say you're a liar. Admit you used me."

"What's the point? It's over now. You don't even exist anymore."

Infuriated by the callousness of the angel and the fact that it was true, Ben/Ling lifted Stanley off the pavement and held him up in the air, rump high and dangling. "Say it! Say you're a liar!"

"Let him down, Ben. They're coming now; they're very close. And you'll need him when they get here," Spilke said from a safe distance.

"Who's coming?" Ben asked, but Ling didn't care and planned on fighting Stanley a lot longer.

"Gandersby, Tweekrat, 1900 Silver, and a bunch of others. You know them all. You know the ones I'm talking about."

On hearing those familiar names, Ben immediately tried to release the angel but Ling wouldn't budge. After trying again, Ben bellowed at the ghost inside his body, "Let go, damn it! Let him go!" His voice was so enraged that Ling did as she was told. Stanley lurched away, coughing and rubbing his neck.

Looking as though he'd just learned he had cancer, Ben walked over to Mr. Spilke and asked him to repeat those names.

"Gandersby, Tweekrat, 1900 Silver, and there are others. A lot of others—a whole lifetime's worth."

"I don't have a chance against them all." Ben's shoulder sagged. He continued to stare at Spilke but the other man said nothing else.

The dancers stopped. One walked over and turned off the music in the car. German asked her partner what was going on. The woman said to ask the men.

"What are those names, Ben? Are they people?"

Ben nodded. "Me. All of them are me too. Or they came from me. Dominique once said her favorite novel was *The Great Gandersby* . . ."

"*Gandersby*? You mean *The Great Gatsby*?"

"Yes, but Dominique hadn't read the book. She was only trying to impress me. That's how she mispronounced the title. That goofy little slip became my weapon: if I ever wanted to make her feel bad or stupid, I'd say something about Gandersby. It worked every time."

"Why would you do that, Ben? Why would you want to make her feel bad?"

"Because I'm cruel sometimes, you know that. Or because I was insecure. Sometimes I was angry for good reason and wanted to get back at her. We always have our reasons.

"Why do any of us do mean things to each other, German? Because the other person hurt us and we want to hurt them back. No one knows how to do that better than lovers because you know each other's weak spots and their Achilles' heel. The more intimate you are, the more you trust each other. The more you trust each other, the more vulnerable you are.

"When you're really close, a stupid thing like *Gandersby* is no longer a word but a dart right into your lover's bull's-eye."

German hated hearing these things but knew they were true. Sometimes you *do* want to hurt the other person. "What about those other names he said? Who were they?"

"They're all me. Just different names for Ben Gould at his worst."

"They're coming." Mr. Spilke said, pointing.

Far down the street a substantial crowd of people was walking toward them.

"There are a lot of them."

"A lot more than I expected," Spilke said.

German squinted to see the group better. "You know them, Ben? You know them all? How can you tell at this distance?"

"Don't give up, Ben. You're doing good. It took me a lot longer than you to recognize who they were."

They had their backs turned and were so absorbed in what was going on down the street that none of them had noticed Danielle Voyles walking their way.

"Danielle, you're here! I thought you said—"

"Only for a little while, Ben. Then I'm going back in. I came to give you a hand if you need it."

"You can help?" He gestured at the crowd. "How can you help me against *them*?"

"I can't, but I can tell you what I learned before when the same kind of thing happened to me. It just happened a different way—in a drugstore parking lot."

Mr. Spilke took German by the elbow and started pulling

her toward the car. She resisted, not understanding. She did not want to go. Spilke wanted to say it nicely but there was no time to be nice. "You can't hear what they say to each other, German. They're different from you. What happened to them makes them different from everyone else."

"Because they didn't die?"

"Yes."

The passengers standing by the blue car moved over to make room for them. Spilke continued, "Those people down the street are different versions of Ben, too, like us. But they're Ben at his worst. Like he told you before about Gandersby—"

"And Tweekrat?"

"Yes, all of them."

"Why are they coming? Why are they here?"

"To get him," her dancing partner said.

"To stop him," another said.

"To pay him back," a third added.

German shook her head. She wasn't getting this. "Pay him back for *what*? What did he do?"

"Promises he made to himself that he broke."

"Being a coward when he didn't need to be."

"Deluding himself. Lies he made up and believed to get him through."

This chorus would have continued if Spilke hadn't gestured to silence them. "Most people don't like themselves for a variety of reasons. It just happens that, in Ben's case, his reasons are actually coming to get him. Every one of the people in that group is a different reason why Ben doesn't like himself."

German remembered Ben saying before that he was the bad guy in all of this; *he* was the villain.

"We constantly disappoint ourselves," Spilke went on. "Over the years that stuff builds up and becomes a big part of who we are: the disappointed me. The bitter me, the failed me, the angry me—"

German pointed. "And that's who those people down there are? Bitter Bens?"

"Bitter Bens, bitter at Ben. Yes."

"What's he going to do about them?"

Spilke shook his head. "I don't know, but we have to try and help no matter what he does. Thank you for bringing us here, German. Thank you for loving us. Thank you for loving *him*."

The other passengers nodded, waved, and smiled their thanks at German. She didn't know what to say. She watched as they prepared to join Ben Gould, to protect him, to defend him. Seeing this remarkable event take place, she kept thinking, Those are my Bens. Those are the Bens I love going back to help him.

Neither Danielle nor Ben saw any of this. Neither of them appeared worried about the approaching crowd, although they were watching it closely. They talked, their heads dipping occasionally toward each other at different times, almost as if they were punctuating their sentences. From a distance German could hear little more than the stray word or sentence out of context. She was tremendously curious to know what the two of them were talking about, especially as the crowd got closer.

And then it was there.

"Hey!" a surly voice called out from the middle of the pack.

Ben and Danielle ignored it.

"Hey!"

Ben lifted his head but his face was impassive. From the months of living with him, German knew when he was calm and when he was upset. All signs now indicated that he was still calm.

He said, "Yes? What do you want?"

"Yo mama!" someone shouted out. Chuckles rilled across the crowd.

"Come on, what do you want? I've got other things to do." Impatience and irritation rose in his voice. It impressed German that in this mind-boggling situation he could pull that tone off. If she were in his shoes now, she would have been scared stiff.

"Oooh, he's got other things to dooooooo. He's a big important man. A very busy guy."

"Stop wasting time—what do you want?" Ben's voice sounded exactly the same: no nervousness in it, impatient but firm.

"One thing's certain, Ben boy: We don't want what you want."

"That's right!"

"Yeah!"

"Uh-huh . . ." Clearly the crowd was of one mind on that issue.

Ben spoke to Danielle, who was still standing beside him. She said something back and he nodded.

"Fine, then, what *do* you want?"

Many different voices called out at once but none was distinct. It was as if the whole group were thinking out loud and speaking its scattered thoughts.

"I can't hear you."

A chubby nondescript man stepped forward. "Do you remember me?"

Ben said only "Broomcorn."

"Excellent! That's right, Broomcorn. And I still hate your guts, in case you were wondering. Do you realize yet how much better your life would be now if you'd done what I told you to do when you were twenty?

"And just so you know, Ben, I was the one who came up

with the idea of Stewart Parrish, in case you were wondering about him."

Unlike when she'd faced her own past selves in the parking lot, Danielle was fascinated to see that most of the people in this crowd didn't look anything like Ben Gould. Yes, there were a few versions of him here and there. But the majority was not: unfamiliar men, women, children, baldheads, people with ponytails, black people, Asians, and old people of every age—as wide an assortment as possible. Danielle knew, though, that they were all Ben both because he had told her and because she could smell them. Every one of these people smelled exactly the same. What she did not know, because Ben hadn't admitted it to her, was they were only the worst aspects or versions of him down through his years, made flesh.

"And now I'll ask a third time: *What do you want from me?*"

Broomcorn turned back to the people behind him and conferred. It took a while, because the crowd was unruly and many of them wanted to be heard. In time he faced Ben again and spoke.

"It's not what we want—it's what we *don't* want. We don't want you to be happy, or whole, or at peace. Because we're the parts of Ben Gould that *like* being unhappy and scared and worried. So long as you live, we'll do everything we can to make you miserable. And there are many of us in you, so that won't be hard. It never has been till now," Broomcorn sneered. He was on a roll, because he knew everything he'd said was the truth. "Whether you admit it or not, people want drama in their lives. They hope for it every single day. But there's no drama in happiness."

"That's wrong!" Ben objected. "I don't *like* being miserable or scared—"

"Yes you do!" Broomcorn thundered and then laughed, as did many of the people in the crowd. Several wore the smile of the vain victor after the race is finished and he's won. All of them had been expecting Ben to say something like that.

Broomcorn continued in a patronizing voice, "Face it, Ben, worry and fear make you feel truly alive. Just popping all over like popcorn. You're really awake only then: no screen saver, low volume, or cruise control, which is what your mind runs on most of the time.

"Being satisfied puts people to sleep. Life's nasty little secret is that contentment is boring. But a broken heart or scary results from a blood test get that old adrenaline and awareness pumping. *Boom boom boom*—feel your heart *hammering*! Great stuff! And then comes that charge of delicious electricity that runs down through you and feels so good inside! What's better than feeling one hundred percent in the moment? Only when you fall in love or fall down on the sidewalk do you feel truly alive."

After a pause Broomcorn said in a quieter voice, "Stanley, *there* you are. Welcome to our quorum."

The Angel of Death walked over but made sure to stay far away from Ben in case Ling decided to ambush him again. The angel no longer had any power over Benjamin Gould. That change had taken place the night in the pizzeria when Stewart Parrish stabbed him in the neck. Stanley understood now that it wasn't Parrish who did it but some part of Ben Gould. That was a revelation. People stabbing angels: the old rules and hierarchies were definitely gone. All of this was new territory for mortals, ghosts, and angels.

German watched the three men and Danielle talk together. But what really interested her was the large crowd nearby. If those people were different parts of Ben's psyche, then she was keen to talk to them. Maybe they'd tell her things that could help him now. Or at least help her to understand Ben better. Maybe they'd even tell her secrets about him that he had never revealed when they were living together.

From the car she walked over to the crowd and said hello to the first person she bumped into. It was a teenage boy who was all shrugs and eyes that didn't move from her breasts. After asking a few questions that got only sullen shrugs and monosyllables from him, she said good-bye and moved on.

Sometimes she glanced at Ben and the others, but nothing over there had changed. The four were caught up in an intense conversation. Every one of them looked either upset or grim. She knew they were discussing epic, destiny-changing matters, but from afar it only looked like a bunch of sourpusses putting in their two cents about something dreary and mundane like local politics. Anyway, she wasn't permitted to hear what they were saying, so she continued her Ben Gould research among the crowd of Bens.

She spoke with anyone she could engage. None of them was friendly but a few were more talkative than others. German heard some things and learned some things. But what came across again and again was a wide variety of anxiety and bitterness: anxiety about the future, bitterness about the past. Happiness didn't live here. Everything good came at a price. Bad always had a return ticket. Contentment, peace of mind—*any* kind of peace—wasn't part of these peoples' vocabulary or experience.

A few minutes later she heard someone nearby say, "I loved you so much."

German stopped talking at once and turned. The speaker was a woman in her thirties, nicely dressed and made up, arms crossed over her chest. She was tapping one foot rapidly on the ground. German had to remind herself again that this woman was only another part of Ben made flesh. Otherwise such a provocative sentence coming from this complete stranger would have been disturbing.

And then the woman said it again: "I loved you so much, but you still left me."

German shot right back. "I left because *you* were impossible to live with. You're blaming me for your own batty behavior? Have you ever tried living with a madman?"

"*Madman*? Nice word. Thanks for caring, German. Thanks for being so sensitive and understanding when I needed you most. I was scared to death! I was sure that I was going nuts and didn't want to drag you down with me. That's why I cut you off. But I shouldn't have worried, because right in the middle of that nightmare you left anyway."

"Don't be ridiculous, Ben. We talked about every bit of this before and settled it."

The woman made a bad-smell face and shook her head. "Speak for yourself. You just walked away. Showed your true colors."

German crossed her arms and went right back at it. "I resent that! I went through fire with you—fire and lunacy. I stayed around much longer than most people would, especially after the crazy way you behaved at the end."

"Say it however you want, you cut and ran."

"Not true." Irate, German glanced over again at the four people talking, hoping Ben would be looking at her. No luck: they were still talking and saw nothing else. When she turned back, the other woman slapped her face.

German was so amazed that her mind went fuzzy. When it came back into focus, she realized that two other people were standing next to the woman now—an old man and a young Asian woman. German recognized the old man as the one who had wandered into Ben's apartment with Pilot and told her he had Alzheimer's disease.

The Asian woman threw a fist in the air and said in a tough voice, "Slap her again, girl. 'Cause if you don't, I will, and that's for *damn* sure."

The old man said nothing but appeared to be enjoying the other's hostility.

The young woman cupped a hand to the side of her mouth and called out to someone in the crowd, "Hey, come on over here. Look who just came to visit us."

A midtwenties Ben Gould walked over, stopped next to the old man, and said formally to German, "Miss Landis, you have real courage coming here." He looked at the old man. "The lamb visiting the lions, eh?"

"What do you all want from me?"

None of the four spoke, but more people separated from the main crowd and drifted over to see what was going on here.

The Asian woman struck a tough-guy pose and snarled, "I'll tell you what we want: We want our life back. We want all the hours we wasted sitting in the kitchen staring at a *spoon* after you left. We want those spoon days back. And the other days we lost feeling gutted, walking like zombies down streets because we missed you so badly.

"We want back the self-respect that you took when you left. Bye-bye, self-respect. Bye-bye, those special days when I liked where I was in my life.

"Just that alone, German—give me that back: the I-like-where-I-am-in-my-life feeling. Can I have it back, please?"

German spat, "No, because it's not true! Feeling good about yourself? Nobody can take that away from you. Nobody but yourself. Don't blame me." She pointed to her chest with two fingers and shook her head. "Not guilty."

The Asian woman made an angry downward slash with her hand that demonstrated everything German had said was nonsense. "Whatever you took when you left, it didn't only belong to you. We made it together—not two hands but four. You had no right taking it." The woman looked as though she wanted to say more but held back a beat, two, and then added, "I wanted to smack you so hard when you left . . ."

German's voice went soft and slow with dismay. "You wanted to *hit* me? Is that true? You hated me that much?"

As if in answer to her question, something hard hit her on the leg. German gasped, grabbed her knee, and looked down to see what it was. A jagged piece of rose quartz the size of an ink bottle lay on the ground next to her foot. Someone in the crowd had thrown a rock at her.

She looked at the Asian woman again but got only a cold stare in return. Out of the corner of her eye, German saw a child fling something else at her. Quickly raising an arm, she blocked a fat clod of earth.

"Ben! Help!"

He glanced over, grasped immediately what was happening and came running. Another stone flew near but missed her. Ben stopped in front of German and shielded her with his body. He shouted at the crowd, "What the hell are you doing? Huh? What the *hell* are you doing?"

"Exactly what you wanted to do to her when she left," the Asian woman said.

Ben's body went rigid. "Never! I never wanted to hurt German. Never!"

"Liar!" a bald man howled at him.

"Don't lie!" yelled the kid who'd thrown the dirt bomb.

"We're you, Ben; we know exactly what you wanted. Don't try to lie to us about it."

German touched his back. "Is it true? Did you really want to hit me?"

"No, never! It's not true."

"Liar!"

"Why are you lying to her? We know everything: we're you!"

Good God, was it true? *Had* Ben really wanted to hit German after she left him? He'd never hit anyone in his life, not even when he was a kid. But hearing this now rattled him because, digging down deep into his memory, he had to admit that, well, yes, possibly for a few poisonous, self-absorbed moments or an hour or maybe even a whole day it might have been true: he might have wanted to physically lash out at his great love for abandoning him. At that time he *was* distraught and confused. Perhaps yes, some despicable part of him slithered out from its dark psychic well and wanted to punish her for leaving when he needed her most. Was that true? Was that part really a strand of Ben Gould's genetic code?

"Get out of the way," the Asian woman commanded.

"What?"

"Get out of the way. Stop blocking her."

Ben felt German move closer to his back.

"No. Get out of here—all of you. If you *are* some part of me, then I'm ordering you to get out."

They didn't move. The bald man said, "She deserves it for what she did. Let us give her what she deserves."

"She doesn't 'deserve' anything," Ben protested. "I drove her away by how I behaved. It was *my* fault: I was crazy. You know that. I don't want anything bad happening to German. Nothing. Never. I love her."

"Yeah, you say that now. But back then part of you wanted to—"

"Don't *touch* her. Put down those rocks and leave."

Ignoring Ben, they moved closer. He could not stop them. He could not stop himself. More people from the larger crowd were coming over—more and more.

"I don't want you here. If you *are* me, then I'm telling all of you to get away."

The Asian woman said, "You can't *order* us because you already set us loose. You can't take back your anger. Once it's out, it's out there forever. We're all here: anger, self-hatred, fear; you can't stop it after its loose. It's the same with everyone."

Frustrated and feeling fear in his belly, Ben wailed, "It's *my* life! I own it!"

"You do absolutely; you're in charge of everything," she agreed. "You decided to open the box and let us out. But once it happened, you lost control over us. Every person has an ugly Pandora's box, Ben. It's always their choice whether or not to open it.

"What's in the box? You at your worst. Bad Ben, weak Ben, the jealous, the scared, the vengeful, the petty, the self-pitying Ben . . . You know every one of us.

"The difference now is this new you is going to have to deal with all of us at the same time till you die. All the Ben Goulds, all here, right now. Before, you were able to separate and ignore us, but not anymore.

"That's where your new powers come from: Everyone's home now at the Gould house. Everyone turned on their lights at the same time. It's ten times brighter in here than it used to be, but that's not necessarily a good thing."

Something nearby made a deep slow growl. Pilot came into

view a few feet away. Growling and staring at the crowd, he stopped next to Ben.

"Pilot—hey, you're back."

"Oh, Pilot," German said, so glad to see him. But when she bent down to touch him, the dog moved away.

Pilot lifted his head and sniffed. "I smell them. They all smell like you, Ben."

"I know."

"I smell their hatred."

Ben looked at the dog. "What do you mean? They hate me?"

"Of course we hate you," the Asian woman answered. "We hate that you get to live now, while we're only little pieces of your past. We hate that you won't make the same mistakes we did because you've learned what to avoid. We especially hate that you know things we didn't—things that would have made life so much easier for us back in our day. And the pain we experienced would have been ten times less crippling."

As she spoke, everything she said made perfect sense. Listening to her was hearing from an unknown part of himself that had never opened its mouth before. It had so much to say. Many of the remarks stunned or touched Ben so deeply that after a while he tuned out her voice, because his circuits overloaded. For a short time he withdrew into the deepest recesses of his mind to recoup and reevaluate. When he came back to the moment he heard her say, "And that's why we sent Stewart Parrish to stop you. That's why we'll never let you succeed no matter how long you live."

He was incredulous. "Why not?"

"Because we hate you, Ben. We do not wish you well."

The large group standing behind her really liked that line. Many of them applauded.

"How can you say that? How can you want to do that? You *are* me!"

"Past tense. You get to live tomorrow, but we don't. We were yesterday."

Ben spoke slowly, as if talking to a retarded child. "But *you—are—me*. If I live tomorrow, you live tomorrow."

Broomcorn, who had joined the group, wiggled his index finger no and said, "When it was our turn to live, we were you one hundred percent. But now we're just memories and past actions, some forgotten Wednesday when you were twenty-six. Most memories are only a few leftover cells in your body: nothing special or important. Who wants to be that? We used to be the whole Gould—the whole angry Gould. The whole scared and scarred Ben. We want that again, but since it's impossible, then we'll make life impossible for whichever you *is* living right this minute. That's a guarantee."

Before Broomcorn could say another word, Pilot ran forward and bit him.

• • •

Pilot was no longer a young dog but he was still a sexy one. Earlier, when he had smelled the electric perfume of a female poodle in high heat, he took off after her like a puppy in pursuit of the miraculous. But a dog's sense of smell is so acute that it took only a mile for him to realize that what had traveled the air to beckon him was no poodle but a skillful fake. Sniffing carefully, he discerned that this ersatz odor was missing both the correct top and bottom notes, and that fact made him stop running. He gave it another chance, though, just to be sure. Standing stock-still on the sidewalk, Pilot closed his eyes and inhaled deeply. Nope—that was not a real female-in-heat smell.

By then he was almost a mile and a half from Danielle's

building. Not thinking there was a need to hurry back, he turned around and trotted in that direction. In his whole life he had never smelled a false female. He wondered how such a thing was possible. The more he thought about it, the less he liked the co-incidence that this irresistible aroma had appeared just when all that other stuff at Danielle's place was happening. He didn't think it was a coincidence and, apprehensive now, he quickened his pace.

A tortoise-colored Manx cat appeared on the other side of the street. It gave Pilot one of those sly, supercilious looks of cool superiority and quick dismissal that the dog detested. Who did cats think they were? But chasing them brought him no pleasure. Cats were barely clever enough to dupe gullible fools into thinking they were mysterious. Fat chance. Any an-imal that played contentedly with a dangling piece of string for half an hour was neither mysterious nor worth the effort of chasing and killing.

A few minutes later, on encountering a still-warm, drip-ping, juicy steak bone lying on the sidewalk directly in front of him, Pilot recognized these seductive diversions one right after the other as part of a plan. Someone was trying to waylay him, divert his pilgrim's progress, and keep him from rejoining Ben and German. Pilot hated tricks. He also hated being tricked. Beginning to trot, he was positive someone had tricked him big-time into taking off after that hot fake poodle.

But getting back to his owners was not easy. As if it knew that Pilot had figured out what was going on, whatever was try-ing to stop him had a teenager on a silver Razor scooter whiz by and kick him hard enough in the neck so that Pilot yelped and almost fell down. But that didn't stop him. A short time later a car roared out of a driveway and narrowly missed running him over. Next a gigantic crow dive-bombed the dog's head, aiming for his eyes as Pilot passed under the oak tree where the bird was perched.

Pilot could have tried speaking to the black bird to ask who'd sent it. But right now was not the time to interrogate an alien species known for its mendacity. And besides, the worst was coming right at him.

Or rather, the unsuspecting dog was moving *toward* its Waterloo. Waiting for him in the next block was a surprise attack, plain and simple. When Pilot was halfway down the sidewalk, a teenager angry at her parents threw open her bedroom window, turned her stereo speakers toward the street, and blasted Neil Young's awful song "Heart of Gold" out into the unprepared ears of the world. Even worse, precisely the part of the song where the harmonica solo comes in.

Pilot stopped dead in his tracks despite the importance of his mission. The dog did not like Neil Young's thin, strangled voice, but he really detested harmonica music. Some human beings dissolve at the sound of a dentist's drill, fingernails on a blackboard, or a knife scratching across a dinner plate. Many dogs have an identical reaction to the sound of a harmonica. Pilot not only loathed it; just the sound of the instrument playing usually paralyzed him. It had been that way since the first time he heard it years before when his then owner played this very same Neil Young song.

Any creature's first orgasm introduces it to a new level of joy. Neil Young's harmonica solo that day had exactly the opposite effect on Pilot the poor puppy. Fast asleep, on hearing the first notes for the first time, he sprang up as if the floor beneath his belly had suddenly caught fire. Instinctively the petrified young dog threw back his head and howled his full horror against the noise assaulting his poor innocent ears.

For the rest of his life, harmonica music always had that same frenzied effect on Pilot: the moment he heard it he would freeze, close his eyes, and wail at the gods to please make it stop.

Whoever came up with this strategy today was especially sadistic because, instead of letting the song continue after the harmonica solo finished, the villain had fiendishly looped it so that the solo played over and over again. Like a death ray in a corny science fiction movie, the unrelenting harmonica zapped the dog into dementia and he began to howl, sounding like a cross between a rooster at dawn and an Arkansas pig auctioneer.

Thank God for sex. Almost as soon as the harmonica began its third hellish repetition, even through his wail Pilot once again smelled sex. Squinting his glazed eyes and shaking his head many times, he managed to break the fiendish grip of the music and stumble drunkenly away down the sidewalk. The smell of sex managed to shove the music aside. The aroma of a female dog in heat triumphed again and made him move his body toward it even though the harmonica assassin continued its assault. The music even got louder the farther away he moved, as if it were chasing after Pilot, but still he managed to escape. A distance that would have normally taken him five minutes to cover took fifteen, but finally the harmonica was only background noise, whereas the scent of the female was all-consuming.

Pilot was walking almost normally when he saw the white animal at the end of the next block. Halfway to it he was clearheaded enough to recognize that it was a verz.

The white animal with dark squiggles on its body spoke to Pilot in a breathless rush. "It took you long enough! Come on, let's go."

"Wait a minute. What's going on? What just happened back there?"

"You should know the answer to that. They were trying to

stop you from getting back to Ben and German. They almost succeeded."

Pilot then noticed that the smell that had pulled him there, effectively saving him, had disappeared. "It's gone—the smell."

The verz started to move. "It was never there. You only created it in your head to get you out of there."

Pilot was dumbfounded. "I made that smell? There was no girl?"

The verz said, "Only in your imagination. Come on, we have to hurry."

"But how'd I do that?" Normally a cool customer who rarely raised his voice about anything, Pilot now sounded like an eager child who's just seen a magic trick performed.

"Ask Ben when you see him. He gave you the power to do it."

"*Ben* gave me the power?"

The verz stepped up its pace. They were running now. "Yes. He's invested you and his girlfriend with the same powers he has. He just doesn't know that yet. But you're going to tell him."

Fourteen

Danielle sent her verz to find Pilot as soon as she'd heard enough blab from the three men, whose conversation was now going in useless circles. Spilke and Stanley clearly had their own agendas that they were pushing. Meanwhile, befuddled Ben just stood there spellbound, listening to them. He did not have a clue what to do next and would probably take any reasonable advice they offered, which was a bad idea. Because of what she had learned at her picnic, Danielle knew that if Ben Gould did not make his own decisions now he would fail, and that failure would ripple out and powerfully affect others as well.

These were the sorts of things that had made her decide she didn't want to be there anymore. Too often life was cruel, unjust, or impossible to understand. All the reading she'd done in the Bible since her accident brought Danielle neither solace nor understanding. Plus, her head ached nonstop from the operation, which was her constant reminder that terrible things could and did happen at any moment. The good times were too few and the bad too many to count. Having mulled over the stories about her past that she heard at the picnic in the parking lot, she realized that no matter what kind of new powers or possibilities for the future she possessed now, she didn't want them or what they could do to change her mediocre life.

Danielle Voyles wanted only to be happy—only that. She knew there was absolutely no guarantee of happiness in anyone's future. But as a teenager in the Lotus Garden restaurant with Dexter Lewis, she had been happier than at any other time in her twenty-nine years. So, very sensibly, she had decided to go back to that time as a teenager and stay forever. Because it was both familiar and fixed, she would return to that happiness in her past and live there for her remaining forty or fifty years rather than hope for some more to come in a future that was as unreliable as the weather and offered no guarantee of anything except eventual death.

Having made the decision, she then chose to come back first and help Ben Gould. She knew he wanted to remain in the present with his nice girlfriend and old dog. There were things she had learned at the picnic she could tell him that might be of use. However, Danielle did not return because she admired Ben's courage or decision to stay and face the formidable challenges ahead. It was simply his choice, like choosing which style of shoes to buy. Her choice was different, but she did not believe that either of them was right or wrong—those untrustworthy, so often misused words.

The first thing she asked the group on reaching it was "Where's the dog?" Ben said Pilot had run off after a female. Danielle didn't believe that for a minute but kept silent about it. When the time was right she conjured her verz way down on the corner of the block. Telepathically she told it to go find the dog and bring it back pronto. The white animal raced away. Danielle turned her attention back to the conversation, which was still going nowhere.

A short time later she watched German walk over and attempt to engage individuals in the swelling crowd of Ben people. Danielle could not get over the fact that when she met her many selves at the parking lot picnic, every one of them looked like her at a particular time in her life. In contrast, these Bens were a wide variety of shapes, sexes, and ages. From that she logically assumed each person's experience would be different when it came to this part of their adventure, if that was the right term for it.

She watched German talk to the woman who eventually slapped her face. Danielle did not move when she saw it happen. Nor did she move when the kid threw the mud ball at German and she called out to Ben for help. Danielle didn't do anything, either, when he ran over to protect his girlfriend from the looming, menacing crowd.

But the moment Ben was out of earshot, Danielle laid into the other two men standing there. She said exactly what she thought of them and what they were doing. It didn't take long, but when she had finished, even Stanley, the Angel of Death, was hanging his head like a schoolboy just caught cheating: he knew most of what she was saying was correct.

Danielle pointed an accusing finger at Spilke. "*You* are a total idiot and have learned nothing. You still want Ben to do it your way, even though you already know it won't work because it's only one way: *yours*. He has tried his whole life to be one single Ben. But that's not who we are! That's what I've learned: we're made up of so many different people inside. We're never going to sand them all down and glue them together into a single 'me.' Look at Brave Ben over there protecting her. But Scared Ben is inside him too. And Ling Ben, who hates *your* guts for lying to her." She pointed her chin at Stanley.

"What people have to realize first is they're not just one single person who does weird, out-of-character things now and then. We're all made up of many different selves that fight and compete with one another constantly. We've got to somehow get them to agree on just a few basic things. Get them to stop fighting with one another. They all have different needs. One part of us wants safety, but another wants adventure. I want to be loved. I want to be left alone . . . Those aren't contradictions—they're independent selves saying 'I want this'!

"We've got to create some kind of United Nations inside ourselves." She touched her heart. "All the different 'me's' working together to try and reach . . ." She stuck out a hand as if trying to grab the correct word from the air.

"Consensus?" Spilke suggested.

Danielle bowed to him. "*Consensus*—exactly! All those separate 'me's' having their say, making their demands, and then working out a consensus."

Next she pointed at Stanley. "I recognized who you were the minute I saw you. You're worse than Spilke because you're an angel, so you know more than any of us do. But you still want Ben and the rest of humanity to act the same way we've been acting for the last zillion years.

"Yoo-hoo, things have changed. People aren't dying anymore according to your schedule. We took our lives back into our own hands. Or some did and everyone will sooner or later. That's going to happen and you know it. People like us are just the beginning. Your rules don't apply anymore. They *can't*. So why don't you and the others just stop and let us find our own way through this without your meddling?"

Somewhat defensively Stanley asked, "And what about you?"

Danielle answered without hesitation, "I know what I want but it isn't here. Respect that and let me live the rest of my life the way I choose. Most people will want to stay here. The ones who do, you should let find their destiny without your interfering.

"People have a hard enough time getting out of their own way. Look at poor Ben over there having to protect his girlfriend from different parts of himself who *hate* her. Isn't that challenging enough for you? Isn't that enough drama? Ben Gould fighting Ben Gould for the woman some of him loves and some of him wants to *stone*."

She would have continued, but just then Pilot appeared and walked over to the couple. They were now completely surrounded by the milling, jabbering crowd. Danielle, Spilke, and Stanley remained silent, waiting to see what would happen. Ben said something to the dog. German said something to the dog. Then Pilot leapt forward and bit a man in the leg.

It was no little nip or playful love bite, either. Broomcorn screamed in pain and utter surprise. Then he kicked the dog in the ribs a glancing blow to get it off.

"Don't kick him!" Ben bellowed.

But the man had already drawn his leg back to boot the dog again. A woman standing nearby holding a purple umbrella ran forward. Handle extended, she caught his foot as he was about to kick. Her move caught Broomcorn both off guard and off balance. He hopped, stumbled, and fell down, banging an elbow on the ground.

Enraged, Broomcorn jumped up and kicked the umbrella woman in the shin. She whacked him over the head with her umbrella. Someone else shouted, "Don't kick a woman!" and gave Broomcorn a shove. He hit the shover, the shover hit back, and away they went.

In seconds fists were flying. Fights broke out all across the crowd of the various bad sides of Benjamin Gould. Those that weren't fighting naturally took sides and voiced their support or scorn for the combatants. Which led to more fights when these people started jostling and shoving one another, demanding to know where X got off supporting Y when it was plain that X was to blame. The answers were more punches in the nose. And because all of these people were Ben Gould, they had exactly the same temper and knew one another's weak points and hot spots. Boom.

As the verz had predicted when they were hurrying over there, after the bites came the fights. German Landis snatched up her old dog. She wanted to get him away from there. No luck. Before she'd moved ten feet, the man named Tweekrat grabbed one of Pilot's dangling back paws and told her to let the damned thing go because it needed a pounding.

Ben grabbed the guy hard by the shoulder and told him to let go. Tweekrat smiled and, raising his chin in a challenge, said, "I don't think I will. How's your stomach, Ben? Isn't it feeling a little jumpy right now?" It was a cruel question but an effective one. Tweekrat was Benjamin Gould when he was excited or furious or scared: Ben when his heart was racing because life was challenging him and making demands. *That* Ben unfortunately had a treacherous stomach that often betrayed him at the worst times, particularly in moments of stress. He could never stop it from happening and he had never had any control over it. Frequently, when he got angry or nervous or even very happy, his bowels cramped and he'd have to find a toilet fast or else. It had been like that all his life and always shamed him, particularly as a man. He had spent so much time finding ways to either prepare for it or hide this embarrassing weakness from others. To him, it was emblematic of immature, neurotic, or even broken things in his character. He did not like to think that way, but he did: If I were strong, if I were adult, if I were less insecure, then it wouldn't be this way . . .

Until that moment, the bedlam going on around them was so distracting that he had thought of nothing else. But now that his stomach had been mentioned, he felt it lurch dangerously.

The crowd, the chaos, the stomach, the noise, the confusion, the anxiety about everything—besieged on all sides, Ben spoke now without thinking. His words came from someplace inside that he did not really know but could feel now intensely. A right place, a place of clarity and insight that had remained hidden and obscure until that moment. When he spoke, he knew for certain that the words were both wildly out of place and correct. They were the only truthful ones to say in this calamitous situation.

Faced with this nemesis and enemy—Benjamin Gould at his worst: mean-spirited; self-defeating; undependable, particularly to himself; semifulfilled but never enough; semimotivated but never enough; hopeful but helpless too often when crisis arose— Ben said simply to this man and to the crowd as well: "Help me." Looking straight into the others' eyes—straight into the center of his own worst qualities—he then repeated those words more clearly, in case his antagonist had not heard his plea: "Help me. I know you'll never go away. No matter how much I want to get rid of you, I can't. I know that now.

"You're not my friends and never will be. We just happen to live in the same house. You want me confused and scared, or angry and weak. And I accept that, because you're as much me as any other parts.

"But I'm asking you from the deepest part of my heart— our heart—to help me now. Help me handle all this and get through it.

"If you do, we'll figure out later how to live together without destroying each other. We will find a way. We'll negotiate. I swear to God, we'll find a way. I promise not to fight you anymore. I won't hide you or pretend you don't exist. But now, please, help me."

The entire crowd had stopped fighting. Most of them were staring at Ben now, waiting to hear what he would say next, waiting to hear what he wanted from them.

But he had nothing more to say.

No one had expected that silence. Not the throng of people who were Ben, not German or Pilot. No one, not even Stanley the angel. Everything was quiet for a few tense beats, and then from off to the side Broomcorn said, "No. No deal. We won't help you, will we?" He looked around at the crowd but got little reaction. They wanted to hear what else he had to say before deciding if they agreed.

"Just because you didn't die, Ben, doesn't change our feelings towards you. Just because you have new powers doesn't mean *we've* changed. We still hate you. We're going to fight you forever because that's who we are. We're the negative pole of your magnet. No matter who you are now or what you discover about yourself. As long as you live we're going to keep messing you up, and nothing can stop us. Self-hatred is always the last thing to die. How many people do you know who like themselves—ever?"

Many in the crowd nodded. What he said was right: if they helped Ben now, they would no longer be themselves. No, they would not help him.

After Broomcorn spoke, Ben looked at the ground and breathed. Inhale. Exhale. Try to hold it together. The only things that filled his mind were German and Pilot. They were all that mattered. Let them be safe. He just wanted them to escape because he knew there were parts of him in this crowd who wanted to hurt these two beings he loved so much. Let them be safe. That's all I want: Let them be safe.

This gave Ben a little hope. Not much, and certainly not

enough to help win the battle he knew he was going to have to wage against the dark parts of himself for the rest of his life. But he *was* cheered by the fact that at this perilous time he worried only about his two loves.

The crowd began to move in around Ben, German, and Pilot. None of the three knew what they intended to do.

"Give us the dog and we'll leave you alone!" a voice called out.

"For now," another added, which garnered a big laugh.

"Give us *German*," someone else said.

The crowd moved closer. Ben and German faced them standing side by side. She still held Pilot in her arms. The dog did not try to move.

Stanley was so transfixed by what was happening that he did not notice Spilke slip away. The angel knew he was literally watching human evolution unfold before his eyes. He did not want to miss a minute of it, especially because he really didn't know what would transpire next. That was the truth. Since mankind had begun to reclaim its destiny, God and his many minions only watched now like spectators at a football game as events unfolded.

Standing nearby, Danielle Voyles was not so at ease. It looked as though Ben, German, and their dog were about to be devoured by this seething crowd. Danielle turned to Stanley and asked the angel to help them. He shook his head. Frustrating as it was, she understood why he was saying no. She had just told him not to interfere with their lives.

"What if I prayed?"

That got the angel's attention. He looked at her, amused. *"What?"*

"What if I prayed to God to help them?"

Stanley grinned. "You can't have it both ways, Danielle.

It'd be better if you prayed to yourself to think up a good way to get them out of this."

She closed her eyes, joined her hands together, but then didn't know what to do or say next. She kept her eyes shut for as long as she could stand it. Eventually curiosity and concern made her open them again, even if what she was expecting to see was a train wreck about to happen.

Ben had no idea what the milling crowd was going to do to them. He tried to steel himself for anything. Only about twenty feet separated them. The others were just standing there waiting, waiting, but for who knew what? It was maddening.

A smell that was well known and loved drifted through the air. The aroma captured and filled his mind. It was the smell of Pilot right next to him: doggy, earthy, and eternal. It was so familiar and appealing that instinctively Ben reached over and stroked the dog's head with as much love as he held. That gesture and the look on his face made Pilot push his head up into the hand despite the spot they were in. As Ben was petting him, Pilot clenched his whole body and then went slack.

Forty seconds later the first dog appeared. A grubby sort of black setter mix, you see three of them whenever you visit an animal shelter: dogs that, if they were human beings, would have last names like Smith or Jones. This one trotted down the sidewalk toward the crowd. Hardly anyone noticed. But Pilot saw it. He tracked it, and when the black dog sat down on the edge of the crowd, the two of them made brief eye contact. Then the setter started licking its belly to keep up appearances. Pilot looked away and mentally began preparing himself for what was coming.

Next to appear out of a hedge was an ancient beige-and-white basset hound that had definitely seen a lot of mileage and better days. The edge of one ear was chewed up and her muzzle was dappled gray. She went to the other side of the crowd and enthusiastically started sniffing the ground as if searching for food. She looked up once at the same time that Pilot looked her way. They connected.

In the next few minutes fifteen dogs discreetly appeared and made a complete circle around the crowd of people. In due course someone finally noticed them and nudged a neighbor with an elbow to look. Word spread and people started asking one another, "What's with all these dogs?"

Then the woman who'd slapped German made to walk off to the side to smoke a cigarette. But when she started to move away, a taupe pit bull with a head the size of a wastebasket snarled in a fearsomely feral manner while staring her right in the eye. Petrified, the woman stood still, arms extended out to either side so that she looked like a tightrope walker.

The child who'd thrown the rock at German knelt down to pet a corgi but jumped back as the dog lunged at him, snapping like a piranha. This sort of thing happened all around the crowd, and now everyone knew that a large pack of extremely hostile dogs surrounded them.

"Ben?"

It took him a moment to realize that Pilot had said his name. "Yes?"

"Remember a few weeks ago when I got really sick and you took me outside every few hours all night long so that I could go? And the next day I wasn't eating, so you cooked me a piece of meat?"

Ben nodded. "I remember."

Pilot said, "I remember too."

Still gazing at the woman who had been scared out of her wits, the big pit bull said to her, "I remember too."

The corgi hissed Peter Lorre style at the rock-throwing kid, "I remember too."

And so on. Every one of the dogs said that sentence in their own way to different people throughout the crowd. But no matter how it was spoken, it was clearly both a statement and threat to all the various bad Ben Goulds. It said, Do not touch him or German. It said, We are here now and we won't let you harm them.

One bellicose fool said, "Oh, yeah? Well, remember *this*, Fido . . ." and raised an arm to hit a German shepherd. Instantly the shepherd and two other dogs attacked and mauled him. The man fell to the ground screaming and trying to cover his head with his arms so that the dogs wouldn't bite him there, but they did.

Pilot told the dogs to stop, but not before the man had gotten some sizable wounds.

There was such a rush and flurry of things going on that no one noticed that while the dogs were attacking this man, new people had appeared and worked their way into the crowd. Interestingly, the pack of dogs allowed every one of these newcomers to pass.

When things had quieted again and the only noise was from the bitten man weeping on the ground, German said, "I remember too, Ben. Pilot's just faster than me." She pointed out some of the new faces in the crowd. Puzzled, he looked at them and they acknowledged him with nods or warm smiles. He had never seen any of these people.

"I don't understand," he said.

German and Pilot looked at each other. The dog said to the woman, "You tell him."

"All of them are us, Ben. The dogs *and* these new people are the parts of Pilot and me that love you. We brought them here to protect you. You brought the parts of yourself that hate you. We won't let them hurt you."

"We won't let you hurt *yourself*," Pilot corrected her.

That brought an instant uproar. Ben's people were out-raged, particularly because they knew they were in the minority now.

One woman shouted, "We'll do whatever we want to him. You can't stop us!"

That comment was answered by three throaty dog growls and a slap on the head to the small speaker from a burly six-foot-four-inch man with a military crew cut.

"*We're* Ben and you aren't, so butt out!" someone else whined, but then ran away as soon as he said it. No one tried to stop him.

Silence fell again, because no one knew what to do next. That quiet lasted only a short time, though, for a voice started shouting, "He's dead! He's dead!" which set everyone in motion again.

Ben, German, and Pilot got over there as fast as they could. What they saw on the ground was disturbing: a man in a dark brown suit and an Elvis Presley hairdo was lying on his back, staring up at the sky with eyes as glassy and lifeless as an antique doll's. Ben walked forward and squatted down next to the body. He put an open palm in front of the man's mouth and nose to see if he could feel breathing. Nothing. He looked at German and shook his head.

"Do you know who that is, Ben?" she asked.

"Yes. He was the part of me that never really believed you loved me."

"How do you know that?"

"Because, seeing him dead, I recognize him now."

Mr. Spilke had been standing far back with the other pas-sengers from the car. They blended in with the new crowd of German's people who had come to defend Ben. Her old teacher strode forward but stopped to speak to an attractive black woman. After listening for a few moments, she nodded and said something brief back to him. Spilke touched her shoulder in thanks and continued on toward the others standing around the body.

"The woman over there that I just spoke to? She took this man's place as soon as he died. She was standing near me, so I saw her appear."

Ben only needed one glance at the black woman to know it was true. He recognized that she was the new worry that had entered his mind moments after German's wondrous call to arms had proved without a doubt how great her love for him was. Sometimes fears do die or we manage to outgrow them. But new and different ones always replace them: brand-new fears, the latest models.

He thought of his dead uncle's futile, years-long battle against cancer. First, doctors discovered it on his skin and removed it. A few years later it reappeared in his prostate gland. They cut that out but six months later the cancer showed up in his liver and killed him. Toward the end of his life the ashen man had asked, "What was the point of all that worthless treatment and fighting the disease? Just so I could experience a hundred different kinds of suffering?"

Mirroring that sentiment, Ben said now in despair, "We can never get right with ourselves, can we? We'll never be at peace. As soon as one thing goes away or we're able to overcome something bad about ourselves, it's instantly replaced by something else ugly or dangerous."

Mr. Spilke asked, "Is that a question or a statement?"

"A statement," Ben said, and turned to the crowd. "But it's true, isn't it? I'll get over some of my faults and fears but others will always replace them, won't they? There'll always be

more of you." When he said this, he saw the obnoxious Broomcorn, who took credit for having created Stewart Parrish. Ben
asked him, "What are we going to *do* about this? We've got to
live together whether we like it or not."

The other man looked unhappily around at German's people
and Pilot's many dogs surrounding him. Ben Gould's bad points
were now way outnumbered by the things another person—and
pet—loved about him. Much as he hated to admit it, Broomcorn
knew this confrontation was a standoff at best. "You said it before: we have to negotiate."

Out of nowhere, Ben asked, "Are you hungry?"

"*Hungry?* That's a strange question to be asking now. But
yes, sure, I wouldn't mind eating something."

"Can I cook for you? I can't have you all over because my
place isn't big enough. But if you'd choose five or six representa-
tives, we could go back to my apartment. I'll make something to
eat and we can talk." He turned to German. "Your people too.
Have them choose a few and we'll all eat together and talk."

After some hemming and hawing, Broomcorn and the others
in his group agreed. Having waited till they settled the matter,
Pilot coolly asked if Ben planned on leaving the canine con-
tingent out on the street with a few table scraps to keep them
happy. Embarrassed, Ben said no, no, of course the dogs were invited too. Pilot gave his master a long, withering look and then
went off to confer with his delegation.

"Ben, I'm going back to the Lotus Garden now, but I
wanted to tell you something first." Danielle took him by the
sleeve and led him away so she could talk without the others
hearing. She had walked over with Stanley. On the way the angel had tried to no avail to convince her to stay there and see
what life with her new perception and powers would be like,
but Danielle had adamantly refused, saying she only wanted to

talk to Ben a few minutes and then she would leave. Stanley had no power to stop her.

"I couldn't do what you just did, Ben, even if I wanted to," she said when they were out of earshot. "The way you gave your powers to German and the dog. The way you made Pilot understand. I couldn't do that. I wouldn't know how. I know some things now but I don't know how you did that."

"I don't either, Danielle. It just happened, but I don't know *how* it happened."

She nodded. "It's like me with you. I don't know how or why I suddenly started seeing you. It was, like, from one minute to the next, there you were."

Ben offered, "Maybe when you understood what was really going on with people like us, you allowed yourself to see me."

Hearing that, something struck Danielle: an idea, a possibility, a long shot, but why not? "With German and Pilot, maybe *you* didn't do anything, Ben. Maybe *they* did it. Maybe just because you love them as much as you do, they were able to take what you have now and use it. Sometimes you love in other people what they don't even know about themselves.

"You were right: we'll never get rid of all our bad sides and weaknesses, because there'll always be new ones. But sometimes other people can rescue us from ourselves when we can't. Not always, but sometimes. German and Pilot love you. Just by being in their lives, you gave them something fantastic and powerful. They used it now to save you from your demons.

"Sometimes, when we're in love, we give the person things we don't even know we're giving. My father used to say the best thing about my mother was she always made him feel loved. Know what Mom said to that? 'I *do*?' And she meant it: she really didn't know she was doing that.

"You know what else my dad said? The truest sign of a successful life is when you're loved by the people you most respect or admire."

Ben asked delicately, "And what about those people who are alone?"

Danielle paused before answering. "Like me? Well, not everyone can be saved. We both know that. Anyway, it's not always a person that saves us. Some lucky ones find their love in a friendship, or politics, even a sports team . . . I don't know.

"I realized I found mine when I was a teenager with Dexter Lewis. I don't love anyone now. I haven't really loved anyone in years. That's why I couldn't do what you just did with them. And that's why I'm going back to Dexter: I want to live in that amazing zone again where you don't want to miss a single minute. That's what love does: it makes you so excited about whatever is coming.

"It also teaches you things about yourself that you never knew before—both good and bad. What you learn always makes your world bigger. Not always nicer, but definitely bigger." She took hold of his arm again. "I don't know what's going to happen to either of us now, but I'm optimistic about it, Ben, I really am." She leaned over and kissed his cheek. Then she walked off toward her home. He watched her go.

One of Pilot's dogs accompanied Danielle all the way there. Why not? It had nothing else to do. It was hungry but had not been chosen to go to Ben's place for the meal. The dog was hoping this woman would give it something to eat when they were in her place. Little did the black dachshund know that, by accompanying her now, it was about to walk into a Chinese restaurant named the Lotus Garden and never return.

When Danielle was gone, German walked over to Ben and stood face-to-face with him. She put her hands on his shoulders. "I think you won."

He moved up closer to her. They could each feel the other's body heat. He put his hand gently against her cheek. "If I did, it was because of you and Pilot. Alone, I would have been eaten alive. I was a goner."

She took his hand from her cheek and kissed the palm. "I don't know what to do now, Ben. I don't know what to say. All I want is to go home. I want to go home and eat doughnuts with you."

He smiled. "Doughnuts?"

"Yes, in bed with you and Pilot; maybe under the covers. All of us together under the covers eating doughnuts from a peach-colored box. It has to be a peach box."

"Okay."

"Okay." She kissed his hand again. He put his forehead against hers.

Music began playing. This time it was the cartoon-fast, lunatic Romanian Gypsy music of Fanfare Ciocărlia, one of Ben and German's favorite bands. Someone inside the blue car had switched the music on again. The auto bounced around as all the passengers inside did car-seat dancing to the song "Asfalt Tango."

Ben said, "I just realized that I don't have much food at home. I'm going to have to go to the market first and do some shopping." He said it to German and Stanley as they stood a few feet away from the jiggling car. He loved that music. He had purposely not listened to the CD since German moved out. It only reminded him of good times with her. He knew if he heard it when he was alone it would cut him off at the knees.

"We'll go with you to the market. We'll help," Stanley offered, and then quickly looked at German to see if she agreed.

"*You're* coming to my place?"

"Of course I'm coming, if it's all right with you. This is the first time I've ever seen this happen: a person having a summit meeting with himself. I'm witnessing history."

Ben appeared to listen to something. Then he said as tactfully as possible to the angel, "Ling says you're not invited. She says you're a lying skunk and she's not cooking for you."

German asked, "What if I invited him as my guest? Would she let him come then?"

Ben and his ghost were once again touched by German's gentle diplomacy and typical kindness. It only made them love her more. Somewhere inside Ben, Ling rolled her eyes in exasperation and tightened her mouth before muttering, "Oh, *all right*. He can come."

• • •

The town was always pretty quiet at that time of day. So when the police dispatcher received the call about the disturbance in the supermarket, they were able to send a unit right over to investigate. The two veterans in the patrol car weren't expecting anything much. The dispatcher said something about people throwing food at one another inside the market. The two cops assumed that probably meant a bunch of drunken college kids were in there having a food fight. It wouldn't be the first time that had happened.

Arriving in the parking lot, the policemen saw a crowd of people standing outside the market looking into the building. What was odd was the large pack of dogs standing together right in front of the doors, almost as if they were guarding them. Even stranger was that scattered among these dogs were several bright white ones that appeared to have no ears.

One of the cops pointed at them. "Look at that, willya? What kind of dog is that?"

His partner said, "That's a verz. You've never seen one before?"

"Hell no. The damned thing doesn't have any *ears*, Bob. This is the first time in my life I have ever seen a dog without ears."

His partner, Bob, who had saved his life two years ago in a deadly gun battle and been shot in the chest doing it, recognized in an instant what was going on there. Fighting off a smile, he just had to keep cool now and handle this situation as though it were no big thing, no matter what was happening inside the market. More than anything Bob was excited because seeing the verzes meant that there would now be someone else to compare notes with. Their group was growing all the time, and that was awesome.

"*Verzes*, huh? Where do they come from?"

"Norway, one of those little islands in Norway. The breed is very popular now in Hollywood. It's a prestige thing to own one of them out there."

"Really? Well, there must be six over there. Maybe we should catch a few and sell them."

The two cops walked over to the market to check things out. As they approached, they could see people running around inside the building, throwing food at one another, grabbing stuff off the shelves, laughing. Most of the people seemed to be laughing.

The policemen saw Broomcorn, holding plastic-wrapped chickens in each hand, get hit square in the face with what looked like a whipped-cream cake by a very tall woman. They saw a man who one cop recognized as Stanley the angel skid across the slick floor on spilled papaya juice and crash head-on into high shelves full of snack food. Straightaway a cascade of multicolored bags of potato chips, popcorn, tortilla chips, Doritos, Cheetos, Tostitos, Fritos, and other tasty treats rained down over him.

The cops saw Ben Gould get shoved in the chest by a bald man who looked angry as hell. Ben shoved the man right back while laughing in his face. Baldy came at him again and the two fell to the floor wrestling. The police saw other fights and even a dog—how did that get in there?—chasing a kid. People were laughing, shouting, or running full speed down the long market aisles with their hands or arms full of groceries, dropping stuff, dancing—was that music they heard in there too?—and everywhere food was being thrown. There was not a salesperson in sight. They'd probably all gone into hiding.

Watching this pandemonium, the cop who didn't know about verzes suddenly remembered something great from his youth for the first time in decades. When he was a boy, a local TV show for kids had a yearly contest at Christmastime. The contest winner was given ten minutes alone inside the biggest toy store in the city. Whatever the kid could get into a shopping cart in that time he or she could keep.

The boy and his three best buddies had engaged in long, heated discussions about just what they would take if they won. In the days leading up to the contest, it was just about all they talked about. One afternoon his gang even made a special trip together to that toy store to scope it out. They walked slowly through the entire place, discussing the fastest, most effective routes to get from the toys they wanted on aisle one to the rest of their hearts' desires. It took some time, but when they were finished they had drawn an actual map with carefully noted directional arrows to use in the event one of them won those glorious ten minutes. Each boy in the group then made his own copy of the map while they were in the store and kept it for a very long time. After leaving, they went to their favorite hamburger joint and treated themselves to the most delicious cheeseburgers on the planet.

The cop had forgotten all about that day and the meal, but now the memories of both came flooding back to him. In retrospect it was one of the few outstanding days of his youth but, as is typical, over the years he had somehow misplaced it in the mundane clutter of the rest of his life. His chest tightened when he remembered the details and just how perfect that experience had been.

He had had a very rough time when he was a boy. But the day at Tom & Tim's toy store with his best friends, making plans and dreaming and then eating delectable cheeseburgers, was one of the shining exceptions. Wouldn't it be crazy and fine if somewhere in a drawer at home he still had that toy store map stashed away? It wasn't impossible. He would look for it when he got home that night. He would definitely look.

For an instant or a few seconds, maybe even longer, he saw the people racing around inside the supermarket as if they were him if he had been the winner of the toy store contest. Running everywhere as fast as he could go, grabbing everything that he had dreamed of owning, laughing the whole time at his great good luck. Swimming back up to the present, he smiled broadly with a treasured memory held tight in his hands that he had found at the bottom of his sea.

He knew that he must be a police officer now and restore order to this foolishness. But his attitude toward the drunks or nuts or whoever they were throwing food around inside the market changed. He was embarrassed to admit he kind of loved them.

A Note About the Author

Jonathan Carroll's novel *The Wooden Sea* was named a *New York Times* Notable Book of 2001. He is the author of such acclaimed novels as *White Apples*, *The Land of Laughs*, *The Marriage of Sticks*, and *Bones of the Moon*. He lives in Vienna, Austria.